Green   c.2
    The price of victory.

DATE DUE

		JUL 28 1999	

AUG 14 '92

DEMCO

THE PRICE OF VICTORY

THE PRICE OF VICTORY

A Novel

Vincent S. Green

Walker and Company
New York

c ·2

IN MEMORY OF MY MOTHER,
FOR MY FATHER,
AND FOR CHRIS

First published in the United States of America in 1992 by
Walker Publishing Company, Inc.

Published simultaneously in Canada by Thomas Allen & Son
Canada, Limited, Markham, Ontario.

Library of Congress Cataloging-in-Publication Data
Green, Vincent S.
The price of victory : a novel / Vincent S. Green.
p.   cm.
ISBN 0-8027-1200-2
I. Title.
PS3557.R37566P7   1992
813'.54—dc20   91-39870
CIP

Printed in the United States of America

2   4   6   8   10   9   7   5   3   1

BL   BL
AUG 14 '92

Thanks to these creative writing teachers who pushed this book along: Anne Bernays, John Milton, George Garrett, and John Casey. To Fran Collin, my agent, much gratitude for taking me on. And for my editor, Peter Rubie, a tip of the hat for great advice on shaping this book.

It is better that ten guilty persons
escape than one innocent suffer.

—Sir William Blackstone
Commentaries

Trials are not about the truth;
they are about the appearance of truth.

—Irving Younger

PART I

A career soldier is courtmartialed on charges of drug dealing.

ONE

"Listen carefully," Lieutenant Robert McCormick said into the telephone. "This is the Red Army Faction. We have planted a bomb in the Frankfurt MP Station. It goes off in five minutes. The Zionists and their American puppets must pay for their crimes against the peaceful people of Iraq." McCormick hung up and stepped outside the phone booth next to the Officers Club.

MPs began scrambling out of the three-story, dun-colored, brick and stucco building that served as the MP station. A few moments later, lights in the surrounding barracks popped on. Men ran into the company street wearing only their underwear, boots slung over their shoulders, pulling on uniforms as they stumbled down the stairs into the warm September evening. Once outside they clustered in large groups, laughing and talking, not taking the bomb threat seriously.

McCormick was disgusted. What kind of officers and NCOs allowed their men to become easy targets like this? Why hadn't they positioned men at the fence to provide perimeter security? Why wasn't someone checking lines of fire between the buildings? Ever since the division's return from Iraq, the men were too cocky, puffed up from their victory over a third-rate aggressor. If he were really a terrorist, they would be dead. A few well-placed claymores and he could have taken out most of the company.

Earlier that afternoon, the MP security had not been any better. Simply by pretending to renew his license plates, he

[3]

had wandered through the station, looking for a place to hide the bomb. No one questioned what he was doing. Not one MP gave even a second look at the package of C-4 he carried.

He checked his watch, counting down the seconds. At exactly 2230 hours, the MP Station exploded. A flash of white light blinded him momentarily, a huge orange fireball shot out the front door and burst in the air, a roar made his ears ring—then an intense quiet filled the night. Seconds later, plaster and glass and bits of wood rained through the trees, peppering the street. The air was choked with gray dust. Papers were strewn everywhere. The MP Station appeared to have been turned inside out and its files held to the wind. The sidewalk and street glistened with glass shards. Men barked orders, screamed. MPs circled the building, .45s drawn, trying to determine what had happened, what to do next.

McCormick walked out the front gate, returned the unit policeman's salute, and headed for the rendezvous point. A stream of MP cars and jeeps passed him, their flashers strobing the buildings red and blue. The night quickly became a cacophony of different sirens coming from every part of the city, all heading for the bomb site. His plan was working perfectly: he had destroyed the MPs' means of command and control. They were all responding to this incident and wouldn't be available for other emergencies.

Five minutes later, McCormick heard what sounded like the distant thud of artillery. His men had blown the door off the safe of the Finance Center and were collecting the end-of-the-month pay for the Third Armored Division.

McCormick was proud of them. They were basically good men. The Army had ignored that. One mistake these days—a DWI, a short AWOL, a barracks fight—and a soldier's career was finished. He of all people understood that kind of injustice, being declared a security risk and left behind to guard the barracks while the division fought in Desert Storm. His chance to prove his battlefield acumen squandered. All for a minor mishap.

He couldn't have known the Russian colonel and his men were trying to defect when they crossed the East German border into his sector. The division had been on alert. Sure, they carried a white flag but they also had their weapons. It could easily have been a trick. Frankly, they were lucky he'd just had his men fire over their heads instead of killing them. "Nearly set off an international incident," his battalion commander had written in his officer efficiency report. A "zero" in the block for judgment.

It no longer mattered. McCormick could see God's larger plan in this development. It was why the elders had sent him on his mission to Germany before he started at BYU. He had ridden his bicycle over most of Germany, spreading the faith, and as a result, knew the terrain as well as most locals, spoke the language fluently. Soon all his training would be needed. The United States was hurriedly pulling troops out of Europe, thinking the USSR was no longer a threat. Fools. Hadn't they read their history? Wait till the republics had no food on the table, no coal in the stoves. Gorbachev and Yeltsin had staved off one coup, but a winter of hunger and ethnic civil wars would make the people crave a dictator again. The right wing would have its excuse to take back the Baltic republics and the former satellites too. And the U.S. would not be ready to stop them. The Army would need his expertise. They would come to him as France had to Napoleon at Elbe, begging him to save Germany from the surrounding chaos. And even though the Army had mistreated him, he would agree to do it for the good of his country. It was his destiny.

Two

Sergeant First Class Billy T. Frazier had just sold the answers to yet another driving exam when he received a phone call to report to the CO's office. He put the twenty dollars in his wallet and yelled for his clerk.

"What do you need, Sarge?" asked Specialist Fourth Class Thompson. He slouched against the doorjamb, watching Billy put on his raincoat and hat.

"I've got to go see the CO," said Billy. "I should be back in time to grade the test. I want you to stick around until I get back. Understand?"

"Is something up?" asked Thompson.

"I'm probably getting a medal and they just want to surprise me," Billy said.

Thompson snickered. "You're too much, Sergeant Frazier."

Two weeks earlier Thompson had been transferred from the personnel office to the driver-testing center because he wouldn't follow orders. Billy preferred the dopers waiting to be discharged. They didn't do any work, but at least they weren't poking around like Thompson, asking lots of questions.

Billy left his basement office in the converted World War II barracks and started up Panzer Avenue past a row of troop billets. During the war, American and British planes had bombed the rest of Hanau but spared these buildings so the Army could occupy them. The Army's renovation had consisted of neatly chiseling away the swastikas from the wreaths the Nazi eagles held above the doors and painting in the colors of each of the units—blue for infantry, gold for armor, red for artillery. Each barracks was two hundred yards long and looked like a gigantic Monopoly-board hotel. The buildings' white stucco walls and black tile roofs were covered with a film of grit from the Dunlop tire plant a half-mile north of the front gate. On a drizzly day like this, which in central Germany could be expected at least two hundred times a year, acrid fumes from the processed rubber hung in the air, irritating Frazier's eyes. The sensation made him think of the unit's last days in Iraq: the sky black from the oil fires in Kuwait, everyone coughing up dark, greasy phlegm, thinking that maybe years later this is what would do them in.

The five-minute walk gave Billy time to wonder if Thompson might be a snitch. It would be just like the CO to plant someone in his office. Why else had Captain Olson been so eager to give him a trained clerk instead of keeping Thompson for himself? At this point Billy didn't need the extra $200 a week he made from selling the answers to the driving tests. The days were past when he and his family depended on the extra income to live in a decent apartment on the German economy, instead of in Army stairwell housing. He did it now to insure that he had enough to live on when he retired. Everywhere the Army was cutting back. The *Army Times* predicted a fighting force a third of its present size. No one was safe, no matter how many wars you had fought in: NCOs like him with fifteen years of service were barred from reenlistment if they had any blemishes on their records. He had been careful around Thompson, but it probably wasn't worth the risk anymore.

Headquarters Company was the last barracks in the row. A five-by-four-foot sign stood in front of the main entrance and announced:

FIGHT SMART TO STAY ALIVE
HEADQUARTERS COMPANY HANAU MILITARY COMMUNITY
CAPTAIN THOMAS G. OLSON
COMMANDING
CLARENCE R. HAMLIN
FIRST SERGEANT

[7]

Billy hurried into the building and stopped outside the Orderly Room. He took off his raincoat and looked at himself in a full-length mirror. A sign above the mirror told the viewer: LOOK SHARP TO BE SHARP. Billy examined his uniform carefully, knowing that Captain Olson didn't summon NCOs to his office unless he had some complaint about their conduct. The toes of his jump boots were freckled with mud, so he braced one arm against the wall and shined the tips, one at a time, on the backs of his calves until he could see his reflection in them. He had put on freshly pressed camouflage fatigues that morning, so the creases on his shirtsleeves and pant legs were as sharp as a person could make on a new twenty-dollar bill. He slid both hands down his butt to make sure his rear pockets were buttoned. Next he looked for ropes. He checked his left shoulder and found a three-quarter-inch thread hanging below the word SPEARHEAD on his triangular Third Armored Division patch. He pulled out his nail clippers and snipped it off. He turned his right shoulder to the mirror to look at his combat patch. His Special Forces patch, a lightning bolt and bayonet superimposed on an arrowhead, looked fine. He faced straight ahead. Something about the sergeant stripes on his left collar wasn't right, so he took a dime and put it at the tip of his collar. The rocker on the SFC pin was not down far enough. Billy unfastened the pin and moved it until the edge of the stripe touched the dime. He patted down his brown hair and licked his upper lip to smooth his mustache. Finally, he looked at himself one more time in the mirror to steady his nerves.

First Sergeant Hamlin sat behind a large metal desk, positioned so that he could see directly into Captain Olson's office. The Orderly Room served as a waiting area for the CO as well as his office. Plaster was beginning to crumble so badly on the walls that many places would no longer hold a patch. Hamlin tried to hide the holes with reenlistment posters: BE ALL YOU CAN BE—ARMY IT'S A GREAT WAY OF LIFE. The first sergeant was a stumpy man who seemed to have only two expressions—a permanent sneer and a sneer that was occasionally punctuated with bellowing, red-faced anger. Even though he was just a few years older than Billy, his paunch and bald head made him look like a man in his late fifties.

Hamlin glanced up momentarily when Billy walked in, then went back to his paperwork. Billy tried to tell from his expression what might be coming, but Hamlin gave nothing away.

"Hey, Top," Billy said, "got any idea what the CO wants to see me about?"

"Have a seat." Hamlin nodded to the couch opposite his desk. "The Old Man would only tell me it was a discipline problem."

Billy was certain this was a lie. Whatever was going on, Hamlin knew and probably had been a party to the planning. Every NCO in the company knew that Captain Olson couldn't take a crap without consulting Hamlin first.

Most of the men in the company hated the first sergeant, but Billy felt sorry for him. He knew that once Hamlin retired, he would have nothing to show for his time except an old man's body and a pension that was impossible to live on. Billy didn't fault Hamlin for not knowing the score. From the minute a guy came in, he was told that he couldn't make it in civilian life, or at best, that he couldn't provide the same standard of living for his family. Every reenlistment NCO who had ever talked to Billy pitched the benefits the same way: "Where else can a guy without a college education have a secure job that provides his family free health care and housing and allows him to retire after twenty years at half pay?" For thirteen years he'd believed the re-up lie.

Then his father died of a heart attack. He'd had to borrow money from the Red Cross to pay for the flight home to Fort Worth. Once he got there, he discovered that his father, a self-employed carpet layer who had always bragged that he didn't need to support his family by living off the government tit the way his son did, had left Billy's mother with a half-paid mortgage and nothing but Social Security to live on.

After the funeral, Billy caught a cargo hop back out of Dover. He sat huddled in a sling seat among the cases of C-rations and tank parts, with a blanket wrapped around him to

[9]

keep from freezing, and thought about where he was in his own life.

It didn't take long to decide that if he died, his family wouldn't be any better off than his mother. He'd always told himself they didn't own a home because they'd never been stationed anywhere long enough. But the truth was that even if he had wanted a place, he didn't have the savings it took for a down payment. For that matter, he couldn't remember ever having any extra money to save while in the Army. And no matter how much he tried to fool himself, he would have to get a job after retirement to pay the bills. By the time his plane touched down that night in Frankfurt, Billy had resolved to change things for his family.

Captain Olson kept him waiting thirty minutes before buzzing the intercom and telling Hamlin he was ready. Billy knocked and the CO shouted, "Come in and leave the door open."

Ever since the unit returned from Saudi, Captain Olson had acted as if he were Rommel. Artillery camouflage netting covered one wall. Two metal file cabinets on the opposite wall were stacked with his canteens, web gear, sleeping bag, poncho, and helmet. Taped on the side of the first file cabinet was a photocopied picture of Saddam, a bull's-eye over his face, with the caption I'D WALK A MILE TO SMOKE A CAMEL. On each side of the desk stood a polished 155-mm howitzer shell casing used as a flag stand. The American flag was on the right; the company pennant, a white and red flag with a yellow HHC in the middle, was on the left. The desk was cleared except for a stack of legal-sized papers and the CO's name plate. Billy walked to within two feet of the desk and saluted.

"Sergeant First Class Frazier reporting as ordered, sir!"

Captain Olson continued to read the papers in front of him as though Billy weren't present. Billy got a kick out of the intimidation games West Pointers played. He figured they must take classes on it—"The Commander as Asshole 101." Olson's problem was being in Germany fifty years too late. Billy believed Olson would have been much happier goose-stepping in charge of the German engineers who used to live in this barracks. In fact, Olson could have passed for a German with his blond hair, fair complexion, wire-rim aviator glasses, and stick up his ass. Finally, he stopped pretending to read and returned the salute.

The captain picked up an index card and read without looking at Billy. "You do not have to say anything. If you do say anything it can and will be used against you in a trial by court-martial . . ."

He'd been right. It was Thompson. Olson couldn't have any proof. Billy had never given out the test answers; it was all done when he graded the test. If Olson was reading the charges, though, the worst it could be was an Article 15. Olson could take some pay but couldn't reduce him in rank. Billy could live with that kind of punishment. That was the price of doing business.

Olson continued, ". . . A lawyer will be detailed for you free of charge. You may also request a military lawyer of your own choice, and if he is reasonably available, then he can defend you as well. You may also hire a civilian lawyer of your own choice at no expense to the government."

Olson finished the *Miranda* warnings and picked up the charges.

"Conspiracy to sell hashish. Violation of Article 81 of the Uniform Code of Military Justice. Charge I, Specification 1: In that Sergeant First Class William T. Frazier, Headquarters Company, Hanau Military Community, did conspire with Lieutenant Robert M. McCormick, Staff Sergeant James R. Babcock, Sergeant Randal McHenry and Specialist Fourth Class Thomas Johnson on or about 20 February 1990, to transport from Amsterdam, the Netherlands, to Hanau, Germany, for the purpose of selling, five kilograms more or less of marijuana in the hashish form. In furtherance of said conspiracy Sergeant First Class William T. Frazier purchased said hashish in Amsterdam, the Netherlands, and transferred it to Staff Sergeant James R. Babcock . . ."

When Olson said "hashish," a fist of heat surged up Billy's spine and made his cheeks and ears burn. Billy tried to calm himself, taking deep breaths and exhaling through his mouth.

Captain Olson read several more charges before he was able to interrupt.

"Sir," Billy said, his voice quivering with anger, "I want you to know this is all a *goddamn* lie."

"You're at attention, Sergeant. Don't say anything until I'm through," snapped Captain Olson.

Billy glanced down and saw a half-dollar-sized wet spot near the bottom of his fly. Fortunately, Olson didn't seem to notice.

He droned on: "Sale of cocaine, Violation of Article 134, Specification 5: In that Sergeant First Class William T. Frazier . . . did sell an unlawful, habit-forming substance, to wit, cocaine . . ."

Billy realized that he never should have loaned Babcock the money to hire a civilian lawyer. The bastard was probably the one telling Babcock to dime Billy. He and Babcock were friends, but he sure as hell didn't plan to go to jail for the guy.

Billy shivered. All he could think of was a gang of blacks cornering him in his cell in Leavenworth and reaming him in the ass. Still, he could always go AWOL. He had his civilian passport. He could go to Frankfurt, buy a ticket like an American tourist, and be gone. He had retired Special Forces buddies in Honduras and El Salvador that he could live with, who could help establish a new identity.

Captain Olson finished reading the charges, jabbed his aviator glasses up on his nose, and folded his arms across his chest. "Are you willing to discuss these charges, Sergeant Frazier?"

Billy nodded. "Sir, all I can tell you is none of it is true. I don't even know some of those people."

Captain Olson forced a pinched grin. He took his glasses off and cleaned the lenses with his OD-green handkerchief. Billy imagined the first sergeant and Olson rehearsing this scene before he arrived. The first sergeant trying to talk Olson out of it, telling him to let CID handle it. Captain Olson insisting they go through with it, believing he could frighten Billy into confessing. After thirty seconds of this game playing, Captain Olson put his glasses back on.

"I really thought you'd be smarter than this," Captain Olson said, blinking several times to refocus.

"I'm not following you, sir?"

"With these charges you'll end up spending thirty, maybe forty years in jail. That's as good as a life sentence for someone your age. I'd think you'd want to avoid that."

Captain Olson paused and waited for Billy to react. When it became apparent Billy wasn't going to speak, he continued, "I didn't have the MPs arrest you, because I didn't want it broadcast all over Hanau. There's still time to help us get those who are higher up. I don't believe you're smart enough to have planned this entire operation by yourself. If you were to cooperate with us and give us the name of who you've been working for, I think your lawyer could get you a very good deal."

Billy stared straight ahead, answering in the formal tone he used to report during formations. "Sir, I'd like to help you, but like I said before, I don't know anything about this. If I gave you names, it'd be a lie just like the lie that's being told about me."

Captain Olson waited a few moments, then slid the papers across his desk. He shook his head. "All right, Sergeant Frazier, if that's the way you want it. Just keep in mind, once we get closer to trial, you may not get this chance again. Your buddies are already starting to abandon you like rats jumping a sinking ship."

Billy picked up the charge sheets. "Is that all, sir?"

"Think about what I said."

Billy saluted, did an about-face, and left the office.

Hamlin watched Billy come out and shut the door. His eyes went to the urine stain on Billy's trousers, and Billy thought he saw the flicker of a grin at the corner of his mouth. Even though Hamlin had to have heard every word that was said, he acted as if Billy had just had a routine meeting.

"Why didn't you tell me that was coming, Top."

Hamlin laid his pen down and cradled his hands on his stomach. "I tried to warn you time and again to stop your wheelin' and dealin'. Your war record's not gonna' get you out of this one." Hamlin wet his bottom lip with his tongue, catching a fleck of tobacco and spitting it toward the floor. "If you're innocent like you claim, you can count on getting a fair trial."

Sure, thought Billy. There are three things you can always count on: I'll respect you in the morning, I won't come in your mouth, and you can count on getting a fair trial in the Army.

PART II

THREE

Captain Jack Hayes arrived for work at seven-thirty A.M. and found the waiting room at the Butzbach Legal Center overflowing with Article 15 clients. The lucky ones had grabbed spots on the two red Naugahyde couches, while the others either leaned against the candy and soda machines or sat braced against the wall with their legs sprawled out in front of them. Most of the group seemed content to sleep or stare at the ceiling instead of being at work. As Jack stepped over the tangle of legs and walked to his office, the sergeants who had been sent as escorts to make sure their men went to the legal center instead of the snack bar nudged their people to wake up.

He looked very young for a captain. Not a fleck of gray in his brown hair, no lines in his high forehead or below his sharp chin. When he occasionally let down his guard, there was a boyishness to his smile. And although almost six-three, he seemed shorter due to a slumped walk. It was the one telltale sign of insecurity left over from coming up the hard way in Grand Rapids. The only person from his North High School class to become a lawyer instead of needing one; the first to attend college in his family and the only way to pay for it, ROTC. When he worked on the law review at Michigan, the advisor had sensed his anxiety and taken him aside: "Stop being so midwestern about succeeding," he had warned. "You're as smart as anybody on the staff. Your problem is you think you don't deserve to be here. Relax. No one can take it away from you." But the only thing that seemed to reassure

Hayes, to make him believe that he was holding on to his hard-fought advances, was winning cases. The more difficult the better.

He hurried to his office and shut the door. The two defense lawyers and their paralegals occupied the second floor of a Romanesque castle that a Falkenstein nobleman built in 1300 A.D. The outside shell of the castle was all that remained of the Hessian kings' former glory. Inside, the rooms had been gutted and remodeled with drop ceilings and cheap, blue indoor/outdoor carpeting. All the walls were painted an anemic green. Even with his diplomas prominently displayed on one wall and law books neatly shelved behind his desk, Hayes's office felt like an Orderly Room. To distract himself from the surroundings, Jack had bought a yellow and gray cockatiel, named it "Jailbird," and kept it on a bookshelf beside his desk.

He brushed birdseed off his chair and sat down. Jailbird scuttled back and forth on his perch, squawking at him. He tapped on the bird's cage to get his attention. "Jailbird, Jailbird," he coaxed. "What do you think?"

"Bullshit, bullshit."

"Good boy."

His paralegal, Specialist Bortman, had already made a pot of coffee and brought him a cup.

"How many are out there, Frank?"

The nutty taste of the coffee made him realize he was starving. He had begun drinking too much on the nights before Article 15 counseling, thinking it would help him relax and sleep better. It didn't. And now his head was throbbing on top of the fatigue.

"Forty-six. Plus the new client we got from Hanau—Sergeant Frazier—is here and says he has to see you."

"I thought we had him scheduled for Friday."

"We do."

Jack rubbed his neck, trying to make his headache stop.

The other clients would be pissed that he was seeing someone out of turn, but Jack didn't care. He had heard their excuses for missing formations and lipping-off hundreds of times.

Jack fished a couple of dollars from his pocket and gave them to Bortman. "Why don't you get us some doughnuts. I really need a sugar fix this morning. On your way out send Frazier back."

A few minutes later Sergeant Frazier walked up to Jack's desk and saluted smartly. "Sergeant First Class Frazier reports, sir."

Jack didn't return the salute. "You don't have to report to me. Have a seat."

He watched the small, dark-complected man, trying to gauge the impression he would make on a jury. Frazier took off his fatigue jacket and draped it neatly over the adjacent chair, then sat down. His jump boots gleamed like mirrors. There was an easy dignity about Frazier that Jack liked. He had already studied his 201 file and came away impressed: Silver Star for "highest bravery and sacrifice beyond the call of duty" in saving a captain's life in a firefight in Grenada, Bronze Star for valor in taking out a machine-gun nest in Panama City after he had been shot in the leg; Army Commendation Medal for "assisting" the armed forces of El Salvador. Frazier was certainly brave and what some people might think was crazy. What Jack needed to know was whether living on the edge had spilled over into peacetime pursuits.

"What's up, Sergeant Frazier?"

Frazier took out a pack of cigarettes and offered Jack one. Jack shook his head and nodded to go ahead and smoke.

"I'm thinking of hiring a civilian lawyer and wanted to know what you thought, sir."

Old fears. You wear the same green suit as the man trying to put me in jail. He pays your salary. Why should I trust you?

"It's up to you," Jack said.

"Don't mean any offense, sir. I just thought it might help."

"Not in a drug case." Jack shook his head. "A jury sees an NCO with a civilian lawyer, they figure he must be dealing in order to afford the fee. Doesn't matter what the facts are." Jack pointed to the acetate-covered board above Jailbird's cage. "See those twenty-five names? All of them are facing felonies. Some of them I may even be able to keep out of jail if I have enough time. The problem is the other lawyer and I have to see all those people in the waiting room today. Then I do it again on Thursday in Friedberg. This is like the docs in combat, Sergeant Frazier. If you don't want my help, I need to move on to someone who does." He stood up and motioned to the door. "Have whoever you hire give my clerk a call so we can get off the case."

Frazier remained seated and finally grinned. "They told me you were like this, sir. People think maybe you're the best defense lawyer around. I read about you getting off that colonel they found in drag at the Frankfurt *bahnhof*. You're a fighter. I just had to make sure you had what it took to stand up to Uncle Sugar."

Always a test of whether you were good enough, thought Jack. As he sat down a cloud of pain rolled from the back of his brain to his forehead. He opened his middle desk drawer, found a couple of aspirin, and washed them down with coffee.

"I've been doing some things to straighten this out," Frazier said, taking a long drag on his cigarette, then exhaling. The smoke blurred his face momentarily. "I wrote to my senator. Told him I was being framed by Sergeant Babcock. This stuff that crazy lieutenant did, hell, I was just back from Saudi then. I'm telling you, the only thing I get high on is bowling and Budweiser. Senator Bentsen—"

Jack cut him off. "Let's get some things straight. Writing to your senator won't do shit. I used to answer congressional inquiries when I was a prosecutor. All they want to know is whether you've got a lawyer and if the case is going to trial. After that"—Jack grimaced and shrugged—"they could care less what happens to you."

Frazier tried to interrupt, but Jack held up his hand. "Just hold tight a minute and then you can talk. Another thing. If you want any chance of getting off, you better change your attitude, right now. You're your worst enemy."

Frazier appeared stunned. "What do you mean?"

"Saying things like 'I only get high on bowling and Budweiser' may sound funny to the NCOs pounding down a cold one at the club, but to a jury it sounds like a smart-ass remark from someone who's guilty. Don't ever say it again."

"I'm innocent, sir. If you don't believe me—"

Jack immediately shut him off again. "Doesn't matter. What's important is that you look and sound innocent. *Being* innocent and *sounding* innocent aren't the same things. A guy who's innocent is scared shitless. He doesn't have time to be thinking up sarcastic remarks."

He watched a flush of anger narrow Frazier's brow, then suddenly the significance of his words seemed to sink in. "Never say it again."

Jack took a business card from his wallet and gave it to Frazier. "Here's my card. Anyone wants to ask you questions about this case, you don't say anything. You tell them I'm your lawyer and to contact me, okay?"

Frazier studied the card a moment, then put it in his pocket. "Right, sir."

"I've got a few questions," Jack said. He reached in his drawer and took out a thick jacket full of Frazier's military records.

"If it's whether I'm guilty, I'm not. I know Sergeant Babcock, but the others . . ." He held up his hands in exasperation. "I do have an idea of why they're framing me, though."

"Let's just wait," Jack said. "I'd rather hear your side of the story after the Article 32 investigation. That way you and I get to hear the other side's best shot at you."

Frazier nodded in appreciation.

"What I need to know is how come an NCO with the Silver and Bronze Stars suddenly gets out of Special Forces and becomes an admin specialist?" Jack leaned back in his chair and waited for Frazier to answer. There was something in Frazier's past that had derailed a career, even if it wasn't in the file.

"It's really pretty boring," Frazier said.

"Why don't you let me be the judge of that."

Frazier smiled wistfully as he stared at the floor. "It was supposed to save my marriage. My wife, Sherri, said she was sick of my being gone. I was on a Special Forces "A" team out of Bragg. We were spending lots of time in Central America— Honduras, Costa Rica, El Salvador—training the locals. Some of the missions were classified—I couldn't even tell Sherri where I was going. I'd be out in the bush for a month or more at a time. When I'd get back, I'd be all whacked out. Jumping for cover when a car backfired. So weird my two little boys were afraid of me. Anyway, we get the call for Panama, I got shot up, and Sherri gives me the ultimatum 'Do something safe, or I'm taking the kids and leaving.' " Frazier sighed deeply. "So I transfer to admin branch and request Germany, thinking this would be the last place we'd go to war. Nine months later we're packing for Saudi. I bring home my will for Sherri to look over and she just flips." He snapped his fingers. "Gone that week."

Jack's wife's reaction had not been much better. He understood Frazier's frustration. When Jack came home and told Anne that the division was mobilizing and, yes, they were making the lawyers go too, she had thrown a fit. All her resentment about him not using his heart murmur to get out of the Army and take a job at her father's law firm had been thrown in his face.

"I've got a question for you, sir."

"Shoot," Jack said.

"Any way you could get this cleared up in a month? I think if I could get back to the States and see my wife I might be able to talk her out of a divorce."

Jack chuckled loudly. "You're kidding."

Frazier answered in the same deadpan. "No, sir."

"I don't know what somebody else told you, but it will take at least three or four months before this gets to trial. As serious as these charges are, you're lucky they don't have you locked up in pretrial."

"Yeah, but couldn't they decide this is all a bunch of lies and drop the charges. I mean, aren't I innocent until they *prove* me guilty?" His tone seemed to dare Jack to challenge him.

"I'm not going to dance you on this. If they've brought the charges this far, they figure there's enough to nail you and they're not going to drop them. As far as being presumed innocent"—Jack brushed the idea away with his hand—"forget it. Nobody gets off hoping the jury presumes them innocent. Juries figure that if you're in court, you did something. To have any chance, we'll have to show how the facts are consistent with your not being guilty, or at least frighten them into believing they *might* be convicting an innocent man."

Frazier scowled in anger. "Sir, that's not fair!"

"You're right." Jack nodded calmly in agreement. "But that's the way it is. I'm not going to pump you full of false hopes. We've got an uphill battle in front of us."

Frazier lowered his head.

"Don't lose all hope yet," Jack said with as much enthusiasm as his headache would allow. "I don't like losing. If there's a way to get you off, I'll find it. What I'd like to do now is go over what's going to take place during the next few months."

Sergeant Frazier nodded okay while he stared numbly at Jailbird.

"The first step is the Article 32 investigation. It's like a civilian preliminary hearing. We'll get to hear the witnesses the government has against you. I usually don't ask any questions there. It just tips off the prosecution. The investigating officer will make a recommendation on whether there's enough evidence to go forward with the charges."

Frazier perked up momentarily. "So he could say drop this thing?"

"Yeah, but even if he does, the general's not bound by his recommendation. Forget about the government dropping the charges."

The answer seemed to destroy the last of Frazier's illusions. He leaned forward with his arms on his knees: a club fighter not wanting to come out for the last round.

"Everyone in your chain of command makes a recommendation on what level court-martial this should be—special, BCD, or general court-martial."

"I already know what the CO will do. He hates my guts," Frazier said.

There was nothing Jack could say that would help, so he kept going. "The general refers it to trial. We may have some sessions where we argue motions, then we have the trial. I'll need a month or two to investigate. So we're looking at three to four months before it's resolved."

Jack was supposed to be tough and think, *Too bad, Frazier. If you can't do the time, don't do the crime.* Somehow it was easier with the eighteen- and nineteen-year-olds.

"I'll be at a conference—Sergeant Frazier, are you with me?"

"Sorry, I was just thinking, sir."

"I'll be at a conference the end of next week. If an emergency comes up while I'm gone, call my clerk. He knows how to get in touch with me."

Jack stood up and walked Frazier to the door.

Frazier shook Jack's hand hard. "Ironic, isn't it, sir?"

"What's that?"

"I spend all that time in Special Forces duckin' bullets and then get bushwhacked by a friend." He smiled ruefully.

Frazier pulled on his fatigue hat and jacket and through the open door, Jack watched him walk jauntily down the hall and out of the legal center. If only from pride, Jack was certain Frazier didn't want to look defeated when he passed Bortman and the other NCOs in the waiting room.

Jack motioned for Bortman to come in.

"What do you think, Frank?"

Bortman snorted. "Trouble, sir. The kind of client we work our butts off for, then claims ineffective assistance. I read the file yesterday. Guilty."

Jack didn't say anything. A long time ago he stopped believing he could know what really happened in his cases. All anybody—the lawyers, the judge, the jury—knew was fragments of the truth, all colored by the angle from which it was seen. Frazier had said he was framed, innocent. For now, that was all Jack needed to know.

FOUR

Jack saw Major Bob Dresman, Hanau's chief prosecutor, heading toward the bar and purposely walked to the other end to avoid him. Jack didn't feel like going through the motions of being civil—he had already done too much of that tonight, every few minutes forcing himself to be cordial to members of the staff judge advocate's prosecution staff, many of whom acted all week as if he and his clients were the scum of the earth, but now in front of their wives pretended he was one of their best friends. As late as this afternoon he had tried backing out of the Hail and Farewell, but the other defense lawyer, Larry Sanderford, convinced him he had to attend, that being part of the big, happy Army family was the main reason their clients received better deals than the civilian lawyers'.

They had gathered at the *Zum Alder*, a cozy, new *gast-haus* located on a small hill near the outskirts of Frankfurt. The bay windows afforded a wonderful view of the glittering sprawl of city to the north and the barge traffic drifting down the Rhein. The smell of gravy-covered schnitzel and *pomme frites* wafted in from the main dining room and had everyone anticipating dinner.

As Jack waited for the bartender to return with his beers, he felt someone poke him hard in the ribs.

"You weren't trying to avoid me, were you, Slick?" asked Dresman.

Jack paid for his beers and planned to say "No," then

politely excuse himself. But as he turned to leave, Dresman stood blocking his path.

Dresman was tall and broad-shouldered, with bad teeth. What light brown hair he had left was combed over to the right side to hide a large bald spot. He'd served in Vietnam and then gone back to law school after a couple of years in the insurance business. Commanders loved him. During Desert Storm, he had held a court-martial in a GP medium tent five kilometers from the Iraqi-Saudi border a day before the invasion. And though Jack hated to admit it, Dresman was effective. Jurors viewed him as one of them, liked his physical aggressiveness.

"I've got some more good news for you," said Dresman.

"This isn't more crap about not cutting McCormick a deal under the table, is it?"

Dresman clamped his hand on Jack's shoulder and looked at him with feigned concern. "Ja-a-a-ck, I can't believe you'd think we'd do that. Lieutenant McCormick just wants to see justice done." He kept a straight face for a few seconds, then burst out laughing. "I just wanted to let you know that we're bringing Colonel DiMarco up from Stuttgart to try this case."

Another second of this and Jack knew he would say something disrespectful. He peered around Dresman's head, pretending that Anne was signaling for him. "Sorry to cut this short, but Annie wants her beer."

"I'll call you Monday about the Article 32."

Jack edged past Dresman and moved through the crowd, holding the beers high. Over and over he repeated, "Don't get mad, get even," using it as a mantra to calm himself.

Halfway through the crowd, Jack spotted Anne standing across from Larry and Cathy Sanderford, talking with several of the new attorneys' wives. Her tall, freckled good looks were even more striking next to the other women. Seeing her like this always made Jack marvel at how lucky he'd been to convince her to marry him.

Anne listened to something one of the women said, tossed her copper-colored hair off her shoulders, then laughed, her husky voice carrying across the room.

As Jack drew closer, he overheard her say, ". . . trial work is the worst. You'll never see him."

Jack stepped up and handed Anne her beer. She thanked him and smiled, but his return brought the conversation to a momentary lull. He edged closer to Larry Sanderford and they began talking shop.

"What do you know about a Judge DiMarco from Stuttgart?" Jack asked.

Sanderford hummed the first strains of Chopin's "Death March." "Go in and *beg* for a deal right now. If they're bringing in the Whopper, it's all over with. Don't even bother looking at the file."

"What are you talking about?"

"Before you got here, DiMarco used to come up and try some of our cases. He'd give these whopping sentences and he's Italian, so we started calling him the Whopper. Dresman won't even need to prosecute, the Whopper will do it for him."

Jack glanced over to the bar at Dresman, who had been watching Sanderford's short, beefy arms punctuate the air in frustration. He raised his glass in a toast to Jack.

Jack forced a thin smile. "Asshole," he said under his breath.

Now that Sanderford had started, Whopper stories came in a cascade. "I had a case that was based almost entirely on circumstantial evidence. It was really close, maybe even an acquittal, until DiMarco instructed the jury. They were only out fifteen minutes before they came back and nailed my guy. Haven't I ever told you about his instruction using a dog's footprints in the snow?"

"No," Jack said flatly, not really wanting to know any more.

"DiMarco gets down off the bench and reads the instructions from the podium so he can look all the jurors in the eyes. He gives the normal circumstantial evidence instructions but at the end he says, 'I think I have a story that might help clarify matters. If you wake up in the morning and it has snowed the previous night, and there are dog prints in the snow, you can take that as circumstantial evidence that a dog crossed your yard during the night. Of course, you could choose to believe it was a walrus as the defense suggests—' "

"Come on," Jack said. "He didn't say 'walrus.' "

"He didn't say 'walrus,' but that was how he made my client's story sound. He did it all with his voice and expressions. You read the record and it looks fine. It's how he—"

Cathy Sanderford interrupted. "Do you two always have to talk about the law? I'd like to go out just *once* and not have to hear about your clients."

Larry turned and glared at his wife, a small, mousey woman from South Philly whom he'd met on a blind date at the Army-Navy game. "Why don't you just can it, Cathy."

"Can it yourself, buster," she snapped back.

The Sanderfords' bickering always sounded ugly, but Jack and Anne had been around them long enough to realize it was harmless. By the end of the evening they would be cuddling like newlyweds. The other two women didn't know this, of course, and looked as if they wanted to sink into the floor.

"The Whopper makes damn sure the jury knows your client is guilty . . ."

Sanderford railed about another case where the Whopper had beaten the defense lawyer out of an acquittal, not seeming to care that Cathy grew angrier by the minute. Jack listened uneasily, catching Anne's hostile glare. He couldn't have been happier when Colonel Basham tapped his water glass and asked everyone to take their seats.

Jack walked Anne to their assigned seats and pulled out her chair. "I'm sorry. But it's not like Cathy's a brilliant conversationalist or anything. Besides, this is what my life is. It's important." He put his hand on Anne's back and felt her tense. "Are you really mad?"

"I'll get over it."

Long after Jack had undressed and gone to bed, Anne lingered at her vanity table. She sat with her back to him, still in her slip, slowly rubbing in skin cream. The light from her table lamp made the downy red hair on her neck and shoulders appear golden.

On the ride home she had said little. When Jack asked

whether something was wrong, she shrugged and said she was tired. He was beat too, yet he wished that she would come to bed so they could make love—something they seemed to be doing less of in the months after his return from Saudi and always at his instigation.

Anne started to brush her hair, then stopped and faced the bed. "Are you still awake?" she asked.

"Yeah, what is it?"

He turned on the light beside their bed and propped himself up on one elbow.

"They've offered me a job as a supervisor," she said.

"Terrific!"

"It would get me out of the emergency room." She added tentatively, "But it means working four night shifts a week."

"Oh." He made no effort to disguise his lack of enthusiasm.

Anne already spent two hours each day commuting to her job as an emergency-room nurse at the 97th General Hospital in Frankfurt. Most days she left before he was up, and they didn't see one another again until seven-thirty at night.

His reaction did not sit well with her. He watched a shadow of sadness cross her face and settle into disappointment.

"It hardly seems like we see each other as it is," Jack said.

Anne sighed heavily.

"And that's my fault?" Her green eyes grew wide, bright. "I didn't go over and play Boy Scout in the desert for three months. I'm not the one in the office every weekend, getting ready for trial."

The sharpness in her tone took him by surprise. He knew she was still angry over the deployment, but that had been beyond his control. He certainly hadn't volunteered; the division commander said everybody shipped out, including the defense lawyers. Working on weekends was another matter. Obviously he had missed something all those weekends she assured him it was "okay" to go into the office.

"I'm not saying it's anybody's fault. I just can't do this job in a half-assed way. Some people can, I can't."

Anne was silent for a moment, her face drawn and lipless.

She started to say something, stopped herself, then went ahead and spoke. "I don't get it. You don't want to work at my father's firm because of all the hours you would have to put in, but you'll spend every free minute you have on these *thugs.*"

"It's not just the hours." He sat up and leaned against the headboard, thinking of a tactful way to explain why he hated her father. "I can't see myself defending big insurance companies. Plus your father and I don't care for each other's politics." A major understatement. Anne's father thought Reagan a great president; Jack thought he'd crippled the country. Jack's father was a shop steward on the GM parts line in Grand Rapids, where he worked with Jack's two uncles; Anne's father claimed unions had destroyed American industry. Their disagreements seemed endless.

Anne stood up and took her bathrobe off a hook in the clothes cabinet. "I don't want to live like this all our lives," she said, gesturing to their cramped government quarters. "It would be nice if I could quit my job, so we could start a family someday. But you know as well as I do we can't afford it." She shook her head in dismay. "Look, if the job doesn't work out, I'll transfer back to day shift. Maybe we'll be able to save a little."

With that, she walked across the hall to the bathroom. Her trivializing the decision to go for the money sank him into depression. How could he be so good with words in the courtroom, yet not find the right ones for his wife. He heard her brushing her teeth, and at that moment he could think of nothing he wanted more than for her to come to bed so he could hold her. He listened intently, waiting for her to click off the light. The last thing he remembered before falling asleep was the sound of water running for a bath, then steam pouring out from the cracked door.

FIVE

The following day Jack made the two-hour drive to the Confinement Facility at Mannheim to interview Lieutenant McCormick and Sergeant Babcock. Having reread their confessions, he decided that if they were half as believable in person as they were on paper, Frazier was dead meat.

Commanders loved threatening their troops with the Confinement Facility. "If you don't shape up, I'll send your butt to Mannheim" made the place sound as if it were Devil's Island. But after his first visit, Jack realized there wasn't the feeling of angst and brutality that oozed out of the walls of a real prison like Marion or Leavenworth. On the contrary, Mannheim's T-shaped, cinder-block building was painted a pastel yellow that might as easily have housed a day-care center. Though the building and grounds were surrounded by a twelve-foot-high, chain-link fence topped with concertina wire, it seemed as much for show as for preventing escapes. Even the recreation field, which was visible from the parking lot, had a scoreboard dubbing the area "Freedom Field."

For Jack, the fact that such an utterly humorless group as the Military Police Corps allowed this sign to exist was proof of Mannheim's difference. Not that the guards were any kinder or more enlightened than at a civilian prison. It was just that the nature of Mannheim's population allowed for less of the iron fist. Only those soldiers awaiting trial or shipment back to prison in the States were kept here. As a result of this short stay—four to six months at the most—the normal prisoner hierarchy, based on favors, stabbings, and forced sodomy, never had time to develop. Mannheim was still a jail, but one where the guards and not the inmates ran the place.

Jack parked in one of the visitor stalls and put on his fatigue jacket. It was raining and cold again. Before he'd gone to the Gulf, he resented German weather, but after three months of sand lice, no showers, and sweating in his chemical suit, he had grown to appreciate this climate. He cataloged it the way an Eskimo might discuss snow. Today was tin gray. There was also ash gray, dove gray, mouse gray, or gunmetal gray.

He grabbed his briefcase from the backseat and ran to the wooden guard shack outside the front gate. As he came through the doorway, the sergeant sitting behind the desk fumbled to hide the paperback he was reading and jumped to attention.

"Yes, sir!"

He's new, thought Jack; he doesn't know I'm a defense lawyer. Once the guards discovered he wasn't a "real officer," they showed just enough military courtesy to stay above disrespect.

"I'm here to see two of my men who fell asleep on guard duty," Jack said.

The guard exchanged Jack's military ID for a salmon-colored, clip-on visitor's badge, logged his name, then made a cursory inspection of his briefcase—all the while trying to keep his name tag out of view.

At the front gate, Jack could see the guard's hand shaking as he put the oversized skeleton key in the lock.

"Have a nice day, sir!" the guard said, saluting with exaggerated stiffness.

"Stop worrying about the book—I'm a defense counsel. I've got too many clients as it is."

Jack returned the salute and walked briskly to the prison's main entrance. He pressed the intercom button, identified himself, and waited as a small TV camera above the door pivoted and methodically looked him over. A few seconds later, an irritating buzz was followed by the hard thud of the door unlocking. It took both arms to open the thick steel door wide enough to squeeze through. Once inside, Jack leaned back and used his hip and shoulder to nudge it shut.

The door thundered as it closed, sending the echo bouncing off the polished floor of the control court, down the long corridors to the cell blocks.

Jack squinted at the glaring overhead lights, and it was several seconds before he was able to see who was in the control booth. Sergeant Grooves sat in an enclosure that resembled a movie box office, watching five TV monitors. From this location, Grooves electronically controlled all the major doors and gates in the prison. He waved as Jack came over and set his briefcase on the ledge in front of the booth.

"Which guilty bastard—I mean client—are you seeing today, sir?"

Jack took out Frazier's file and flipped to the charge sheet. "You mean which soldier mistakenly accused of a crime, don't you?"

Grooves shook his head in mock exasperation, never seeming to tire of their ritual.

"I need to see Lieutenant McCormick, Robert, M., and Sergeant Babcock, James, R."

Grooves glanced at his clipboard for a moment. "Sir, no problem in getting Babcock up here, but you'll need to see the commandant about Lieutenant McCormick. He's the only one who can authorize it."

In the three years Jack had been coming to Mannheim, he had never once had to have clearance to see anyone, not even his capital murder client. This added bit of red tape seemed ridiculous, especially for an officer inmate.

"What's the deal?" Jack asked.

"Security risk, sir."

"Christ," he said, stuffing the file back in his briefcase. "Is Colonel Hubbard here?"

"Yes, sir," said Grooves, then added apologetically, "I'll make sure they have Babcock up and ready to go by the time you finish with the colonel."

Colonel Hubbard's civilian secretary ushered Jack into Hubbard's office and shut the door. The room was large enough to hold a twelve-man conference table, several overstuffed chairs, Hubbard's executive desk, yet still seem spacious. One could have almost called the surroundings comfortable—the walls painted the same soft yellow as the building, the autographed generals' photos on the east wall thanking Hubbard for his service, the institution's motto stenciled prominently behind Hubbard's desk: OUR MISSION, YOUR FUTURE. Then Jack noticed that all the windows had bars over them. Why anyone, let alone Hubbard, enjoyed working in a prison—where even with all his power and control, the warden was still behind bars ten or more hours a day—baffled Jack.

Colonel Hubbard came around his desk and shook Jack's hand enthusiastically. Even in fatigues, Hubbard had the air of an academic. Rather than the ubiquitous aviator wire rims, Hubbard wore tortoiseshell glasses that made his gaunt face seem even more birdlike. His brown hair was washed with gray to the color of lightly creamed coffee, and though well within regulations, had been neatly trimmed by a hairdresser rather than the hack in the PX. Hubbard was that occasional officer who surprised Jack. He commonly mixed his discussion of prison operations with Dostoevski's thought that a society's worth should be judged by how it treats its prison population. Even though the idea of a "military free spirit" seemed as much an oxymoron as "military intelligence," that was Martin Hubbard.

After motioning Jack to take a seat, Hubbard sat across from him. "How may we help you, Captain Hayes?"

"Sir, I understand I need your clearance to see Lieutenant McCormick."

The moment the name was mentioned, Hubbard sat back in his chair. "Why do you need to see him?"

Jack was stunned by how quickly Hubbard's bonhomie vanished, and felt as if he had stumbled into the middle of an ugly argument and unwittingly taken the wrong side. "He's a witness against a client of mine."

Hubbard closed his eyes and nodded an apology. "I'm sorry for being sharp. We're just trying to be especially careful with this man. He's already attempted to escape."

"Really?"

"It was just luck that we caught him. He was working a carpentry detail in the east wing. Somehow he managed to overpower a guard and get his weapon. Normally that wouldn't have done him much good, but McCormick made the guard change into his prison browns, then knocked him unconscious. He took the guard's uniform and ID badge and calmly walked out of here." Colonel Hubbard grinned slightly. "It seems this guard was new on his shift. When he came to, he had trouble convincing anyone that he was a guard and not an inmate. By the time we sorted things out, McCormick had managed to find the guard's car and was on his way off the *kaserne*. If he hadn't been caught speeding, I'm sure we wouldn't have found him. Most of our inmates never give us any trouble. This man is a . . ." Hubbard held up his hands, searching for the right word. "He's capable of anything."

"Not very trustworthy?" The moment Jack asked the question in such an obvious manner he regretted it. Hubbard knew exactly what he was attempting and smiled.

"Look, Captain Hayes, I make it a policy never to be a character witness for or against inmates. All I know is McCormick is dangerous. For your own protection, I'd like to have a guard in the room with you."

"I really need to be alone with the guy to get any useful . . ."

Hubbard had pursed his lips and was shaking his head before Jack even finished.

"Sir, I can tell you a court will rule that I have the right to speak to him alone."

Jack was uncertain whether a judge would agree, especially the Whopper, but he sounded convincing. He was counting on the one thing he'd discovered in his dealings with administrators: free spirits or not, they were terrified of lawyers and courts.

Hubbard pulled at the skin under his chin. He seemed genuinely concerned—whether for Jack's safety or for his own career, was another question.

"I think we can reach a compromise," Hubbard said finally. "I'd like to keep McCormick in shackles, and I'll just post the guards outside the door."

Shackles. Jack had never seen his clients in anything more than handcuffs. The whole idea seemed like something from a Southern chain-gang movie. He was ready to use his line about how the prisoners saw him as one of the "good guys," then hesitated, sensing that Hubbard had gone as far as he would go.

"All right, sir, I'll give it a try."

Jack stood in the narrow corridor outside Colonel Hubbard's office, waiting for the guards to bring Lieutenant McCormick. He had decided that Babcock, who was sitting on a bench up the corridor, could wait. Getting any useful information out of McCormick would be tough enough without forcing him to sit in shackles for an hour. Besides, he wanted to see the man.

On the drive from Butzbach, Jack had tried envisioning the kind of mind it took to organize a platoon of men to run drugs from Amsterdam, blow up an MP station as a diversionary tactic, and then rob a Finance Center. Nothing came together. What prevented a clear picture was McCormick's statement at his own trial: "I waited all my life to fight a war. Then I was unfairly denied my chance. I needed to approximate the experience so I would be ready to fight the Soviets." Not, "I needed the money to pay off debts," or "I needed it for drugs," but this, the Army's black secret; the drug that made men want to stay in the Army, and for those who had fought in a war, the reason those years were still their strongest memories. McCormick had broken the code of silence and admitted that there was no greater high than the risk of killing or being killed.

Of course, no officer and gentleman would ever acknowledge enjoying combat and, if asked, would say he hated war like everyone else and hoped that a strong defense would prevent further conflicts. But Jack believed these statements about as much as he believed cops when they said their dream was to wipe out crime. McCormick had been brutally honest about the Army's appeal, and a jury had given him ninety-nine years to repress the same thought they had every day. McCormick had to be a fool or see himself as completely above judgment to throw that kind of reasoning into other officers' faces.

Jack could hear McCormick's name spoken over a walkie-talkie before he actually saw him. Belches of static and amplified voices grew louder until finally five men rounded the corner, stopped, then waited for the barred door to roll back along its track. There were guards in front and back and one on either side of him. The group moved at a pallbearer's pace. McCormick's legs were cuffed in leg irons, so he could take only six-inch steps. His hands were pinched together at the waist in a pair of handcuffs. A black box, the size of a deck of cards, fit over the chain between the cuffs and prevented his hands from moving forward. Finally, at the bottom of the box, a thick chain ran through a metal eyelet, wrapped around his waist and then clipped on one of the links of chain behind his back. These restraints—shackling was indeed the right word— kept a prisoner in a continual position of Oriental greeting. Jack wondered how Hubbard reconciled this treatment with Dostoevski's admonitions.

As McCormick came completely into view, all the precautions—guards, belly chain, black box, handcuffs, leg irons—seemed even more shocking.

McCormick was a runt.

If Jack had been forced beforehand to predict what McCormick would look like, he would have guessed a burly football player, a psychotic John Wayne—not this small, almost too ordinary-looking fellow. Why did the mind always want the worst criminals to look different? Meaner, grotesquely deformed: anything to help one recognize them. McCormick's face betrayed none of that. His hair was light brown and neatly parted on the left side. His oval face had just a hint of whiskers on the lip and chin. If one were to see any abnormality in him, it was more in how he carried himself. Part of the hidden agenda behind shackling had to be humiliation; a man was restrained as though he were some sort of vicious, uncontrollable beast. McCormick, however, showed absolutely no self-consciousness. If anything, he seemed to revel in all these precautions. It was as if they demonstrated to the world his superiority.

The guard who had been trailing the procession came around and unlocked the final gate. Jack was curious about whether Babcock would say anything. As the group passed, Babcock continued studying the floor as if the answers to his fate were scuffed into the green linoleum. McCormick glanced at him and acted as if he might spit on him.

"Sir, which room do you want him in?" the guard asked.

"Number three," Jack said, pointing to a room off to his left.

The interview rooms, which had been solitary confinement cells at one point in Mannheim's history, were just large enough to hold a collapsible field table and two folding chairs.

McCormick shuffled into the room first. With the help of two guards, one on each elbow, he was seated in the chair closest to the door.

"Sir, if he gives you any problems whatsoever, we'll be right outside," said the sergeant in charge of the detail.

"Thanks, I'll be fine."

Jack sat down and took out his legal pad. McCormick was studying him with a smirk that made Jack feel as if all the precautions were a joke on him.

"I'm Jack Hayes, Billy Frazier's defense lawyer. I'd shake your hand but that doesn't seem very practical."

McCormick said nothing. He continued staring at Jack with a quizzical expression.

So much for jail-house humor.

"I need to ask you about the drug operation," Jack said.

"What'd Billy tell you?"

In court he would have put McCormick in his place by telling him who asked the questions. For now, though, it made sense to allow McCormick to push him around a little.

"He says it's all a lie dreamed up by Babcock, that he's being framed."

McCormick rolled his eyes. "And you believe that?"

"I get paid to believe him."

"I wish I'd come up with something like that for my lawyer." McCormick's voice was high-pitched, adolescent. He stared morosely at the table. "My mistake was being honest.

If I'd just kept quiet, they couldn't have proved most of the charges."

"What do you mean?"

McCormick stopped, seeming to weigh his own sense of warning with the need to talk to anyone after a month in an isolation cell. Finally, he relaxed his shoulders, apparently realizing that the damage had already been done.

Once he began, the words came in a flood: "The night of the Finance Center mission last July, the *kriminalpolizei* had a roadblock set up at Maintal, just outside of Hanau. My men and I had executed everything brilliantly before that point. I had eliminated the MP Station, so law enforcement had no command and control. It was very simple for my men to enter the Finance Center and blow open the vault. In hindsight, my one error in planning was the bomb threat. I said we were Red Army Faction, so the *polizei* shut off all roads leaving Frankfurt. When they stopped us, I was ready to kill them. Unfortunately, one of my men panicked and got out of the car. Before I could do anything, a KRIPO agent had a nine millimeter at my temple . . ."

Hubbard was right. McCormick talked about killing people the way ordinary people discussed buying a new set of tires.

"Anyway," McCormick continued, "they took us to the KRIPO station in Hanau and tried to kill me. They had this animal who must have weighed three hundred pounds come in and sit on my chest so I couldn't breathe. I would pass out and they'd bring me to with smelling salts, then do it again." McCormick's eyes filled with such venom that Jack checked to make sure the guard was available. "The swine broke two of my ribs."

"Didn't your lawyer bring any of this out?"

"Captain Hansen?" McCormick laughed derisively. "Yeah, he tried. The *polizei* lied through their teeth. They claimed I resisted while they were taking me down a flight of stairs."

"I'm confused," Jack said. "I thought you made your statement to the Criminal Investigation Division."

"That was later. Two CID agents, Maxfield and Black,

showed up and were supposed to take us back to *Pioneer Kaserne*. They came to the room where Jumbo was working on me and watched. They said maybe they should leave me overnight, that I was getting what a cop killer deserved. Maxfield said I was facing the death penalty. He was lying, of course. The MP just had his legs blown off, and that would *never* have happened if he'd left the station when I phoned in the bomb threat . . ."

Jack nodded sympathetically, acting as if it were entirely the MP's fault for being tardy in leaving.

McCormick went on, "Maxfield said that if I'd go ahead and make a statement, he'd help me out and speak up at my trial."

Jack shook his head in disbelief.

"I know it was stupid," said McCormick. "If you'd been there, you wouldn't have wanted to stay with those Germans. They enjoyed what they were doing. Besides, when Maxfield lied about the MP dying, I thought I needed to cut my losses. Can he do that?"

"If you really committed the crime, can they lie to get a confession? Yes."

"The law." McCormick spat the words out in disgust. "It's all right for CID to lie, but if I do it, it's a crime. Certainly some system of *justice*."

Objectively, Jack agreed with McCormick's criticism. Somehow, though, it didn't sit well, hearing someone who was ready to kill people complain about lack of fair play. Jack resisted the impulse to point out the contradiction and changed the subject.

"Tell me how you got involved with Frazier."

McCormick turned his head away. He appeared troubled by providing evidence against Frazier, as if it breached some point of honor.

"I didn't meet Billy until the very end," he said wearily. "Babcock handled everything. He'd take the drugs and money back and forth. I knew that someone else actually bought the drugs from a Dutchman, but I didn't know who. In the fall of 1990 we were fairly certain that the division would be sent to the Gulf. Babcock said his connection would probably be sent and wanted to sell the operation."

"So you never saw Frazier on any of the runs?"

"No. One of my men would wait in a car near the train station in Amsterdam and Babcock would bring the drugs in a travel bag, get in the car just long enough to make the drop, and then leave."

"Frazier didn't take part in bringing the drugs back?"

"That was our end of the bargain. When the drug mission was in the planning stages, I took my men to Nijmegen on the Dutch–German border and performed a recon. We found a wooded area where they could cross undetected. I would drop them off about seven klicks from the border, and they'd take the stuff across while I drove the car through customs. Afterward, I'd pick them up on the German side. It was much better training than they ever received from the company."

Jack scanned his notes. In allowing McCormick to talk freely, he had skipped ahead and left some gaps in what happened.

"Maybe it's in your statement, but it doesn't seem clear to me how you teamed up with Babcock," Jack said.

"It's not," McCormick said coyly.

"You want to fill me in?"

"I caught him getting high."

Jack looked up from note taking to make sure he wasn't being put on. McCormick grinned.

"He was on CQ duty and I was officer of the day. I caught him smoking hash in the supply room."

"I guess you didn't turn him in."

"I thought about it. Babcock started begging, saying his wife was pregnant and he couldn't afford a court-martial. He said he'd do *anything* not to go to jail. I'd always known he was a doper. He'd come back from lunch glassy-eyed and giggling. I figured there was no harm in seeing if he knew a supplier."

"What did he do when you asked?"

"His mouth dropped open—then he wanted me to get high." McCormick snorted in disgust. "I almost turned him in for that."

"You don't get high?"

"Absolutely not!" McCormick appeared greatly offended. "I'm Latter-day Saints. I didn't like dealing with drugs. Unfortunately, it was the only means we had available to buy weapons and explosives for the Finance mission."

Jack made a mental note to speak with Bret Carlson in Hanau about how to use this Mormon stuff.

"So did Babcock give you Frazier's name?"

"No. I never even met Billy until the day he introduced us to his supplier in Amsterdam."

"Tell me about that," Jack said.

"Babcock drove his car up that weekend. I met him at the train station and he drove me to the supplier's house."

"Where was Frazier?"

"At the place, waiting. I tried keeping track of where we were going, but I think Babcock purposely took the longest route there. Plus, with the way the streets change names every bend of the canal it's hard to keep track of where you're at. It took about forty minutes before we arrived at this place in a street-market area. Jimmy went upstairs with the fifty-grand payment for the rights to the connection, and then came and got me. Billy and Franz were waiting when I went up."

"Franz was the supplier?"

"Yes."

"Does he have a last name?"

"Cugo, Coogie, something like that."

"Can you describe him?"

"Tall, six-one or two. Thin. Brown hair down over his collar. In his early thirties. He spoke English well, but with what sounded like a German accent."

"What about the place? You have an address?"

"Twenty-something Marney or Marnixstraat."

For the first time, Jack thought he saw a flaw in the story. It was possible someone might not know or care about a last name, thinking it was an alias, but it seemed unlikely that someone would pay $50,000 and not know the correct address.

"What happened at the meeting?"

"Billy introduced me and said I was taking over his business—"

Jack must have unconsciously frowned, because McCormick immediately explained.

"I know it may sound strange, but this man trusted Frazier. Besides, if you double-cross someone up there, you're dead. Franz kept a pistol tucked in his waistband all the time."

So far the story followed McCormick's written statement, except for the lack of specifics on the address and Franz's description. If the CID agents even bothered to ask these questions, Jack was certain they had intentionally left out the answers to prevent McCormick and Babcock from contradicting one another. What was left unexplained was why McCormick had not mentioned Frazier in his original statement. Jack decided to try a different tactic.

"How much are they cutting your sentence to say Frazier's involved?"

"None," McCormick said defensively.

"They haven't promised you something under the table?"

"No! Captain Hansen and I have no deal."

Dresman had promised McCormick something, Jack was certain. There was always a chance Babcock knew, and he could play them off one another to find out.

Jack turned over his notepad and stood up to call the guard.

"That's all you want? You're not going to grill me?" asked McCormick.

"Why should I?" said Jack. "It all sounds believable to me."

As the guards led McCormick out, he turned back his head. "Tell Billy to get a deal like the rest of us. There's still information he could give. It's his only hope."

Jack liked to think that he was Frazier's only hope. But McCormick was probably right. Closer to trial, Jack might try to persuade Frazier to identify who he was working for. By then they'd need a name as a bargaining chip to get any sort of deal.

Jack stepped into the corridor and motioned for Sergeant Babcock.

Lieutenant McCormick sneered at Babcock as he walked by. "Make sure you tell him about how loyal you've been."

Babcock cringed, and edged around the trailing guard. He walked quickly to the interview room with his head down. Jack found it difficult to imagine Babcock doing anything dangerous, let alone acting as a middleman in a drug operation. His face was a jumble of attempt and failure—a wet-looking mustache that was too thin, perfect teeth that were too large for his mouth, fine, angular features that were all wrong because of large ears. He would be easy prey once he arrived at Leavenworth.

"What was that all about?" Jack asked.

Babcock glanced around to see if there was anyone standing close to the door. "I'll never admit this in court, but Billy paid for my lawyer."

"Is that what McCormick meant?"

Babcock blushed. He looked back to the door again and said, "I won't admit to this either, because I don't want Billy to get in any more trouble, but he also offered to support my family while I was in jail if I'd keep his name out of things. I told him I would, but my lawyer, Mr. Zimmerman—you know him?"

Jack nodded.

"Mr. Zimmerman said I was looking at forty or fifty years. Captain Hayes, my wife just had a baby. She threatened to divorce me if I was in jail that long. I didn't have a choice."

Frazier might have offered to do all this. What Jack didn't believe were Babcock's assurances that it wouldn't come out in court. If he'd sold Frazier out once, he'd do it again if he thought the information was worth anything.

"Don't worry," Jack said, "I don't see this case ever going to trial. Maybe I can get a deal for him, like McCormick's lawyer."

"That's sure what I'd do."

Jack pretended to search for a pen in his briefcase and asked casually, "Do you know what McCormick's lawyer got for him? I'd like to be in the same ballpark."

"He told me they've agreed to cut his sentence to fifty years."

Jack tried not to grin.

"Tell me how you met Billy."

Babcock smiled. It reminded Jack of a donkey with a mouth full of briars. "I'm not going to testify to this either, but we met when he sold me the answers to the driving exam."

"Wonderful," Jack mumbled. "How much did he charge?"

"Twenty bucks," Babcock said, then added, "It was worth the money. I was having real problems on the German traffic laws."

"Is that where the drug stuff began?"

"Un-uh. About a month later." Babcock tipped his chair back and watched Jack write. "I saw Billy at the NCO club and bought him a drink. He was having trouble with his wife."

"What kind of trouble?"

"She was pissed off. He'd bailed out of Special Forces because he was always in the field, never home with her and the kids. Our CO was making Billy go to gunnery practice at Graf for a month, even though there was nothing for him to do. He was really down, so I asked him if he wanted to go drive around and smoke a bowl."

"How did you know he would?"

Babcock laced his fingers behind his head. He seemed to enjoy having his opinion thought important.

"I figured if he was selling drivers licenses, he wasn't going to turn me in, you know?"

Babcock's logic made Jack cringe. A court might think Babcock was a little punk, but they'd believe him. Jack could already hear Dresman's argument: *We didn't promise you choirboys for witnesses. What you need to ask yourself is whether his answers make sense, whether they ring true.*

"Weren't you worried about being drug-tested?"

Babcock bobbed his head. "Sort of. But if you had money you could pay one of the NCOs who did the test to switch your bottle."

Other information, McCormick had called it.

"So you go and get high. How did you get involved in the drug business?"

"When we were driving around, Billy pulled out a little vial and a coke spoon and offered me a toot. I'd never done cocaine before." Babcock sighed. "I wish I hadn't."

[45]

"Why's that?"

"I wouldn't be involved in this mess. I liked it too much. I started needing it all the time. Billy would sell it to me cheap. We used to play backgammon at his house and get high, and he'd just give it to me."

"You still haven't told me how you got involved in selling."

Babcock's face narrowed to a disapproving frown. "I never sold anything, Captain Hayes. I only took money and drugs back and forth as a delivery man. I'm not a drug pusher."

"Billy didn't pay you?"

"A little, but what I made all went up my nose. But I wasn't selling. I want to make that clear."

"Okay, fine," Jack said, motioning with his hand that he was sorry. "How did you get involved as a *delivery man*?"

The distinction seemed to appease Babcock. Jack figured Babcock had come up with this rationalization to save face with his family.

"Billy had been using a mule. He'd buy the drugs, then this kid would carry the drugs back on the train. The way Billy explained it to me, the mule would hide the drugs in a ceiling compartment in the bathroom. He finally got caught. I don't know all the details, other than he was booted out on an administrative discharge. After that, Billy needed someone to act as a runner. He said he'd pay me, plus give me free coke."

"Were you bringing back the stuff the same way?"

"For a while, until we almost got caught."

"Tell me about that."

"Billy and I were coming back from Amsterdam on a Sunday night. We had one of those sleeping compartments where the beds pull out of the wall. We were asleep when the train stopped at the Dutch border and didn't see the customs police—" Babcock looked at the ceiling and chuckled.

"What is it?"

"I was just thinking about Billy. He's a great actor. When the customs police wanted to search, Billy got out of the compartment and showed them his civilian passport. He told them he was a minister and that it was against his religion to do drugs. He was great. He starts ranting and raving like one of those TV evangelists, telling them God's vengeance will be visited on them for slandering a man of the cloth. It gave me time to hide the stuff. By the end, Billy had them apologizing, and they just stuck their heads in and looked around. I thought it was all over with. After that, I told him he had to find someone else to transport the stuff."

"So how'd he get the drugs back?"

Babcock shrugged. "There was only a couple of weeks' lapse before he paired up with McCormick."

Jack had been waiting for an opportunity to see whether he'd read the incident in the hall correctly. "You mean before McCormick blackmailed you?"

Babcock's lips pulled back over his teeth.

"Is that what he called it?"

"No, that's just how it seemed to me," Jack said innocently.

"Well that's what the asshole should've called it. He knew my wife was pregnant."

"He said he just asked if you knew where he could get a supply of drugs, and you said you'd be glad to help."

Babcock threw his head back. "You know what he told me? He said I had one week to come up with a source for drugs, or he'd turn me in. I told him I didn't know anyone, but he said he didn't care. He said that he was sure I'd find one."

"So you gave him Billy's name?"

"No." He seemed hurt by the suggestion. "Billy didn't want that. His idea was to let as few people as possible know he was financing things. That way if someone got caught, they couldn't turn him in to keep from going to jail."

"I guess that didn't work."

"No," said Babcock guiltily.

"So how did the operation work with McCormick?"

"Billy would change his money to guilders in Amsterdam, buy the drugs, then I'd make a drop at the train station. Later, after McCormick's men sold the hash or coke, I'd take the money back to Billy."

"What about the source, did you deal with him?"

"Franz."

"Is that his name?"

"Franz Koonag, something like that. Yeah, I met him a couple of times. He looked like a kid, but Billy told me he'd seen him kill a Turk who'd shorted him on a kilo of hash."

"Can you describe him?"

"Five-ten, about a hundred and thirty-five pounds, oily light brown hair."

"Did he speak English?"

"Sort of. I had real trouble understanding him."

Jack perked up at this inconsistency in Babcock's and McCormick's stories. But he also knew that a jury would never acquit on a difference in description if the rest of the story made sense, and so far it did.

"What about where he lived?"

"It was on Marnixstraat. I don't know the address, just what the building looked like. It was on the third floor of an apartment house. I always had trouble finding the place."

Or maybe you've never been there, Jack thought. He and Anne had been to Amsterdam to see the tulips the previous spring, and all the buildings looked so much alike they had trouble finding something as well known as the Anne Frank house.

Jack had heard all he needed for today. He had been searching for weakness in character more than inconsistencies in their stories. As he started to put his pen away, Babcock spoke up. "Sir, can I ask you a question?"

"Ask, but I can't guarantee I'll be able to answer."

"What did Billy tell you about this?"

"That you made all this up."

Babcock nodded as if he had expected as much.

"Captain Hayes, I don't like doing this to Billy, believe me. I have nothing but respect for the man. I also know he's stubborn. There are a couple of names Billy could give up right now and get the same deal I've got. If he keeps denying all this, ask him about Cindy."

Jack uncapped his pen and jotted down the name on the margin of his legal pad. "Last name?"

"Just ask him about Cindy going to his apartment. That's all I'm gonna say."

SIX

"Look at this," Jack said. He handed the Criminal Investigation Division report on Frazier's banking records across his desk to Larry Sanderford. "The guy's broke."

To Jack's surprise, Frazier had been willing to provide CID with a power of attorney to search his bank records.

Sanderford stopped leafing through Jack's *Rolling Stone* and took the report. During the two years they had been the defense lawyers in Butzbach, Jack and Sanderford had become best friends. People who knew them both thought this bizarre. Sanderford, the former West Point company commander, friends with Hayes, the ACLU'er? But constantly fighting the same enemy—commanders, NCOs, MPs, CID, and prosecutors—all of whom wanted to see their clients thrown in jail for as long as possible and viewed defense lawyers as the last annoying obstacle, had given them a purpose that made their personal differences irrelevant. Sanderford glanced at the figures and then tossed the report back on Jack's desk. "Jailbird," he whistled at the bird, "Jailbird. What do you think?"

"Bullshit."

"There you have it." Sanderford tipped his chair back and rested his hands on top of his head. He still possessed the stocky strength of a wrestler, but was putting on weight quickly around the middle and neck. A dark-haired English bulldog was what always came to Jack's mind. Sanderford handled the stress of this job with schnitzel and German beer; Jack withdrew into himself, became hard to reach. He wasn't sure which of their vices was worse.

"Hilarious," Jack said.

"Just because they didn't find the money doesn't mean he didn't hide it somewhere. For all you know he stashed it in a safety deposit box in Switzerland."

"I know," Jack said slowly, shaking his head in agreement. "It's just that usually these guys aren't that smart. There's no money trail. I can't believe he wouldn't have put any of it in a bank."

"What about the former wife?"

"She's not real happy with the Big Green Machine right now. Thinks it destroyed their marriage. She told Dresman they would have to get a warrant if they wanted to look at her accounts. She says Frazier's innocent."

Sanderford scoffed. "She's worried about her child support drying up when her ex goes to jail. You really don't think this guy is innocent, do you?"

"I don't know what to think anymore," Jack said. "You know he consented to a search of his apartment, and they didn't find anything. And where's his civilian lawyer if he's got all this money?"

"How does he explain the trips to Amsterdam?" Sanderford asked.

"He was buying a used Mercedes." Jack held up his hand to stop Sanderford's next comment. "I know what you're thinking. He gave me copies of the sales receipt and registration papers. It checks out. The wife got it when they split. She's already sold it."

"So he bought a car while he was buying dope. Nothing to stop him from doing that, is there? And the fact that they didn't find anything in the apartment doesn't mean diddly. He's had plenty of time to clean up his act."

"You're right," Jack said.

A week earlier, when Jack decided this would be a contested case, he'd started his normal process of schizophrenic thinking—one side of his mind knew that all the problems Sanderford raised were valid, that Frazier was probably guilty; the other side of his mind, the side he was working on to present to a jury, *believed* that Frazier was completely innocent, that he'd been framed.

"This kills me," said Sanderford. "You believe him."

"I didn't say that. There's still a couple of things that bother me. When I interviewed the co-accused they were both telling me other people were involved. Babcock gave me some cryptic shit about a woman named Cindy going to his apartment."

Sanderford ran his tongue over his teeth. "You better lean on him. That stuff will come back to bite you in the butt."

"I know, I know."

Jack picked up a paper clip and unfolded it into a wavy straight line. "The other thing is, I feel bad wanting him to cop a deal when I haven't gone to Amsterdam to check things out."

"Go to Amsterdam," Sanderford said calmly.

Jack hesitated. "It's not that easy. I'd need the government to pay Frazier's and my way. I'd need a Dutch interpreter. And from what Babcock and McCormick say about the area of town, I'd want a cop along for protection."

Sanderford brought the front legs of his chair down hard on the floor. "Here's what you do . . ."

Jack hated these lectures. He always felt as if he were a subordinate being counseled for bad debts.

". . . There's an Air Force base right outside the city in New Amsterdam. See if you can get the Air Police to go out and investigate. Take my word for it, none of these dirtballs are worth getting killed for."

Sanderford's suggestion had some appeal, but Jack knew it wasn't what he needed to do to win this trial. If Sanderford had a weakness as a trial lawyer, it was investigating cases from behind his desk. Wallowing with the riffraff, as he put it, did not extend beyond the office.

Jack, on the other hand, loved this part of his job. It provided him the chance to be a voyeur, to mingle in the seamy side of life yet not have to become part of the life-style. Being a defense lawyer gave him the courage to go into places he never would have thought about entering otherwise. And to his credit, he had won several difficult cases on his ability to find witnesses in GI hangouts and persuade them to reveal things they wouldn't say in his office. What caused him to hesitate now and seriously consider Sanderford's advice was knowing that Amsterdam would be different. Men like Franz Koonag wouldn't care about his being an officer, or that he came to the interview in a GUNS N' ROSES T-shirt.

Sanderford picked up the *Rolling Stone* again and started looking at the photos. His tolerance for the game of a client's guilt or innocence wasn't very high.

"What do you think DiMarco would do with a motion to send Frazier and me to Amsterdam?"

Sanderford laid the magazine aside. "The Whopper might grant it. He's funny. If it meant letting him off, no. If all it's doing is costing the government money, he really doesn't care. He'd rather have the government shell out some bucks now than have a case busted on appeal."

Jack bit his thumbnail to the quick and spat the sliver on his desk blotter. His thumb started throbbing. He looked and saw blood seeping out of the cuticle. It would be sore for a week. Good, he thought, a reminder of how stupid I'm being.

"Ah, what the hell," Jack muttered, then pressed his intercom.

"Yes, sir?"

"Frank, call Judge DiMarco's clerk and see when we can get on the docket to argue a motion in the Frazier case."

A week later Jack was at the offices of the division staff judge advocate. He parked in the lot north of the building and used the entrance closest to the courtroom. Frazier was standing outside the courtroom door, smoking, constantly glancing at the legal staff going by. He made a good impression dressed in his Class-A uniform. Shoes spit-shined, brass sparkling, his "fruit salad"—the four rows of multicolored ribbons, Combat Infantryman's Badge, Jump Wings, and Scuba Badge above his right breast pocket—evidence that despite being an administrative specialist now, he'd been a real soldier who'd seen combat.

Billy finally noticed Jack and crushed out his cigarette in a standing ashtray.

"How does it look, sir?" he asked, shaking Jack's hand too firmly.

"Calm down," Jack said. "All we're doing today is seeing whether the judge will send us to Amsterdam. It will be a little while." Jack extended his arm, motioning for Billy to go into an empty room. "I need to ask you about a few things."

Even though efforts had been made to disguise the fact, it was still apparent that the division courthouse had been a barn when built in 1939. Metal feed troughs, now planters, were bolted to the wall behind the long conference table. Soldiers on their way to Leavenworth found this the perfect source for latrine graffiti: COURT IN SESSION, HORSESHIT GETS DEEP; BEHIND EVERY HORSE'S ASS IS A JAGC. Jack set his briefcase on the table and motioned for Frazier to have a seat.

"Sergeant Frazier, I need some straight answers from you today."

"That's what I've been trying to do," he said testily.

"The last time we talked you said that Babcock went with you on your trips to buy the car because his wife was pregnant and he wanted to get laid."

Frazier chuckled. "I couldn't control him. We'd go by the red-light district and these women would be grinding their snatches against the windows. Jimmy was like a dog in heat. You wouldn't believe—"

Jack slammed his hand down hard on the table. "This isn't a goddamn joke. That's the same crap I got from you during our first meeting. There's more to it than that. This guy's buying drugs up there and you don't have a clue?" He caught Frazier with a glare that would have peeled paint. "You either stop feeding me this line of bullshit or get a new lawyer."

Frazier looked away and began turning a pencil around on the legal pad in front of him as if it were a spinner on a game board.

The resulting silence rang in Jack's ears. He wasn't saying another word, though, until Frazier decided to tell him the truth. He heard the throaty cough of a diesel engine nearby and tried to distract himself by deciding whether it was an armored personnel carrier or a deuce-and-a-half.

After several full minutes passed, Frazier looked up, his

face drawn, sallow. "Sir, I know sometimes I sound like a smartass." He raised his eyebrows as a sort of apology. "It's just my way of dealing with the stress. You don't need to tell me I'm in some deep shit. I know I'm fighting for my life again." Frazier breathed deeply, "All right—the truth. About a year and a half ago Jimmy came to me and said he'd been caught smokin' dope on duty. Margaret was pregnant, and he was scared to death about going to jail. He said an officer in his company, Lieutenant McCormick, had caught him and was turning him in unless he found a major supplier for hash and cocaine. He wanted to help, but I told him no way. A couple of months later he asked me if he could tag along when I was buying the car. I should have known better, but I let him come with me two or three times. I worked on the papers for the car, and Jimmy went off and did his own thing. I didn't know what he was doing, and I didn't want to know."

"Did you go on the train?"

"Yeah, but all that crap he said about the customs agent is made up. Captain Hayes, do you really think drug police would be fooled by me acting like that?"

Jack was unsure what to say. He found the best lies always sounded like this: just enough truth woven in to make the story sound plausible.

"And the answers to the driving test?"

Frazier glanced up at the ceiling, seeming to weigh what he was about say. "Let's just say hypothetically that was true. That an NCO needed a little extra money so his family could make it overseas. I'm not saying it's true, but let's just say it was." He stared hard at Jack. "Don't take from that, that I'm the kind of person who sells drugs, because I'm not. I know if I was in your shoes I might be saying, 'He's dirty on one thing, he must be into other things.' It doesn't work that way with me. One other thing you might as well know since we're clearing the air." He closed his eyes and shook his head in frustration. "I loaned Jimmy five thousand dollars to help pay for his civilian lawyer."

"Why?"

"His wife begged me. Look, once he got caught I knew I looked bad going up there with him. I thought, 'Help get him a good lawyer and he won't do any desperate, crazy shit like saying I was involved with him.' It didn't work. What can I say?"

Jack checked his watch. "It's almost time for court. Thanks for being straight with me."

Frazier stood up and stretched. Jack waited until Frazier was almost at the door. "One more thing," Jack said offhandedly. "Why did Cindy go to your apartment?"

Frazier turned back to him and answered without any hesitation. "I don't know what you're talking about."

The great trial lawyers claim that they can tell when someone is lying by watching his eyes. A person supposedly has a slight twitch at the corner of his lid after a deception. If this was true, Billy Frazier's eyes were no help. Looking into them reminded Jack of ice fishing on Reeds Lake back in Grand Rapids. As a kid he would stare into the motionless green water and for an instant think he could see the bottom—only to realize it was an illusion.

"Any idea where Babcock came up with that name?"

"Sir, I swear on my dead father's grave. I don't know any woman named Cindy."

The division courtroom was furnished with items the general's staff no longer wanted: worn carpeting the color of dried blood, two long metal tables that were used as attorneys' tables, a jury box and judge's bench built from cheap pine and stained dark brown in an attempt to look like walnut, and eight rows of church pews that served as a spectator section. What natural light the room received came from four windows near the ceiling on the west wall behind the jury box. They let in just enough dusty light to give one the impression of being in a warehouse. The one element of color in the entire room was a huge American flag that took up the entire north wall behind the judge's bench.

Dresman was already at the left counsel table, laying out his files, when Jack and Billy walked in. Frazier stopped at the gate separating the spectator section from the counsel tables, motioning with his eyes to the back of the courtroom. "Who are those guys?" he whispered to Jack.

Jack glanced back over his shoulder and saw two young privates talking to one another.

"You guys witnesses in another case?" Jack asked.

They both snickered at one another, then the one with curly hair said, "No, sir. First Sergeant sent us to watch. He said we needed to see what was gonna happen to us if we didn't shape up."

Frazier acted as if he hadn't heard the remark and asked if it was all right to sit down. Jack nodded.

"You plan on calling any witnesses for this spurious motion?" Dresman asked, still smirking at the private's answer.

"No. How about yourself?" Jack asked.

"Are you kidding?" He turned his nose up at the suggestion. "This motion is so bogus we'll be out of here in ten minutes."

At exactly nine o'clock, the court reporter yelled, "All rise!" and Colonel DiMarco lumbered into the courtroom. He was a large man, six-six or better, with a barrel chest and thick neck. He had hiked the sleeves of his black robe above his elbows and carried a load of books under each arm; his exposed wrists were so matted with hair that the skin was barely visible. Tufts of hair struggled above the top of his shirt and formed a second collar between his Adam's apple and his razor line. This same thick growth would have continued on his head, but he had the sides whitewalled and the top cut in a quarter-inch flattop. On most men this much body hair would have made them look brutish, but DiMarco's brown eyes prevented this impression. Even behind his black-framed Army glasses, his eyes had the intensity of a predator's. His only sign of physical weakness seemed to be the hearing aid behind his right ear. The defense lawyers in Stuttgart had told Jack that the Whopper had been an artillery officer in Vietnam before he went to law school. "DiMarco's old brown-shoe Army," they said, "spit and polish. But don't ever underestimate how smart he is."

Jack didn't.

He'd read several of DiMarco's articles on evidence in the *Military Law Review* and had come away angry but impressed.

DiMarco could take the most reactionary position and find case law to make his idea sound reasonable. He had been a judge for fifteen years, both in the States and Europe, and according to Sanderford only three of his cases had ever been overturned on appeal.

DiMarco climbed the steps to the bench and put down his books. He surveyed the room, looking over each person, seeming to size them up for defects and weaknesses. He slammed down his gavel and said, "Please be seated."

Dresman moved to the podium and began reading preliminary matters into the record: "This court-martial is convened by general court-martial convening order number seventy-five, Headquarters, Third Armored Division, Frankfurt, Germany. The military judge is Colonel Nicholas G. DiMarco—"

DiMarco interrupted. "Major, my middle initial is P as in Papa. Also, I've circled three typing errors on this order. I want them corrected and clean copy inserted in the record."

"Yes, your Honor," said Dresman.

Frazier smiled at Jack.

Dresman continued, "The trial counsel is Major Robert Dresman. The accused is represented by his military defense counsel, Captain Jack Hayes. The members are absent."

DiMarco had taken off his Army-issue glasses and put on half-lens reading glasses. He picked up the charge sheet and studied it for a few seconds. "Sergeant Frazier, before I ask you how you plead, do you have any motions you'd like raised on your behalf?"

Jack motioned for Frazier to remain seated and rose from his chair. "Yes, your Honor. The defense moves that the government pay Sergeant Frazier's and my way—"

"Hold it," the Whopper said, peering over his glasses. "I don't know if this is your first case, *Captain*, but that's not how you make a motion in *my* courtroom. Is this how they let you practice in this jurisdiction?"

"Yes, your Honor."

The Whopper shook his head in apparent disbelief. "There are two kinds of motions: a motion to dismiss, and a motion for appropriate relief. Now which is it?"

"A motion for appropriate relief," Jack said.

"Fine," said the Whopper. "Then style your motion properly."

Jack cleared his throat and started again. "The defense makes a motion for appropriate relief that the government—"

"Wrong!" DiMarco shouted.

So much for Sanderford's predictions about DiMarco's ruling. Jack bowed his head and wished the Whopper would just go ahead and deny his motion.

After a long pause, DiMarco spoke. "Captain Hayes, the proper way to style a motion of this nature is 'The defense makes a motion for appropriate relief *in the nature of* a request to provide funds for an interpreter, etc.' "

Open sesame.

"State your motion, Captain Hayes."

Jack spoke slowly, making sure he said every magic word. "Your Honor, the defense makes a motion for appropriate relief in the nature of a request that the government pay Sergeant Frazier's and my way to Amsterdam, the Netherlands, so we may interview Mr. Franz Koonag, a material, essential witness. Furthermore, we request that the government provide a Dutch interpreter for the interview."

"Anything else?"

"Yes, your Honor. We would like a CID agent to accompany us for protection," Jack said.

"Anything else?" The Whopper made it sound as if it were a dream list.

"No, your Honor."

DiMarco turned his high-back swivel chair to face Dresman. "What do you have to say, Mr. Prosecutor?"

Dresman moved to the podium and tossed down his legal pad. "Your Honor," he said, his voice full of self-assurance at seeing defense motions routinely denied, "the government opposes this motion on the grounds that Mr. Koonag will not provide useful information to the defense. This is clearly a fishing expedition—"

The Whopper stopped him. "I'll make that decision. Not you or anyone else. Do you understand?"

"Yes, your Honor," said Dresman.

"In the defense brief, there is an attached affidavit from

Sergeant Frazier, stating—" DiMarco stopped and glared at Dresman. "Don't you have a copy there with you?"

"No, your Honor."

"Get it."

Dresman went back to his table and retrieved the document.

"You have a copy now?"

"Yes, your Honor."

"Terrific. In Sergeant Frazier's affidavit, he states that he has never met Mr. Koonag, nor has he ever been to 25 Marnixstraat, in Amsterdam. If that is the case, doesn't that make Koonag a material witness, since he is the person from whom the government claims Sergeant Frazier bought the drugs?"

"Sergeant Babcock and Lieutenant McCormick have testified that is not true," said Dresman.

"Yes, but isn't that a question of fact for a jury, and not the standard applicable to this motion? If we assume what Sergeant Frazier is saying is true, as the law requires us to do, isn't that relevant to a material issue in the trial?"

Dresman was silent.

Jack took back all the terrible things he'd been thinking about Sanderford. Once the judge started extracting admissions from your opponent to bolster your position, you were in the money.

"Isn't that the case?" the Whopper asked again.

"Yes, your Honor," Dresman said softly.

"Captain Hayes."

"Yes, your Honor."

"In your brief you indicate that you have contacted a Professor Heinrich Udo from the University of Marburg to work as an interpreter. What kind of cost are we looking at?"

"One hundred and fifty dollars an hour, your Honor." At the time Jack called Dr. Udo the price had sounded reasonable. Now, under the Whopper's scrutiny, he felt self-conscious asking for this much money.

DiMarco leaned back in his chair, leaving both Jack and Dresman wondering if they should sit down. After what seemed like ten minutes to Jack, the Whopper rocked forward and made two quick notes.

"Major Dresman, I want you to call the JAG shop at the air base at New Amsterdam. I'm certain they'll have an interpreter. Arrange to have this individual made available to the defense. If they give you any static, have Colonel Basham talk to them. We'll take a half-hour recess."

An hour and fifteen minutes later, court reconvened. Jack knew some difficulty had arisen, because Dresman, the chief of justice, and the senior prosecutor had been summoned into Colonel Basham's office for a long conference. Whatever had happened, Dresman refused to talk about it when he came back to court.

DiMarco pounded his gavel three times and began. "What did you find out, Major Dresman?"

"Your Honor, the SJA, Colonel Basham, called the air base at New Amsterdam."

Jack could see that Dresman was reading from a prepared statement.

Dresman went on. "He spoke with the JAG section's interpreter, Mr. von der Horst, and he stated that he would not go into the area of Amsterdam Captain Hayes wishes to enter unless he had a police escort. He further stated that the Dutch police will not go to this section of town in less than groups of five and that he did not believe they would provide assistance in this matter.

"I would like to add, your Honor, that an interpreter is not necessary. Both Lieutenant McCormick and Sergeant Babcock testified at the Article 32 investigation that Mr. Koonag spoke English."

Jack shot to his feet. "Your Honor, that assumes they're telling the truth—"

"Just as much as it assumes your client's not lying," snapped Dresman.

"If they aren't—," Jack started.

The Whopper took off his reading glasses and glared at both of them. "Sit down and be quiet." He calmly put his glasses back on and opened his judge's desk book. Rather than being disturbed by this new development, he seemed to enjoy the challenge. He crossed out several sections written on his legal pad and made new notes, ending the final sentence with a visible punctuation point.

DiMarco rubbed his hand over his flattop several times and then started to read. "I have made the following findings of fact and conclusions of law. First, Mr. Franz Koonag is potentially a material, essential witness to this trial. Second, it is necessary for Captain Hayes and Sergeant Frazier to interview Mr. Koonag to adequately prepare for trial. To insure this, the government will issue travel orders for counsel and defendant to travel to Amsterdam, the Netherlands—"

The Whopper paused and corrected something in the order.

"Third, since two of the government's witnesses indicate that Mr. Koonag speaks English, and my experience from traveling to Amsterdam is that most Dutch speak English, I'm tentatively denying the defense's request for an interpreter. If, Captain Hayes, you attempt to interview Mr. Koonag and he doesn't speak English, I'll gladly reconsider. Fourth, I am tentatively denying your request for a CID escort. No case I've read requires any more than funding a trip to interview witnesses. Any time a defense lawyer personally investigates a crime, there is the possibility of danger. If I were to routinely grant such motions, CID would never have time to investigate real crimes. If, however, you get to Amsterdam and are prevented from interviewing Mr. Koonag, I will be happy to reconsider your motion."

DiMarco had boxed Jack in. To find out whether Koonag spoke English, he would have to risk his own safety. And if he didn't go, the issue would be totally lost on appeal. The order was slimy, but brilliant—DiMarco had granted the motion without giving the defense anything.

"When do you think you can complete your investigation?"

Jack felt whipped, and the case hadn't even begun. "I'm not sure."

"I'll give you two weeks. I'm scheduling jury selection for

the twenty-first of March, 1992, at 0800 hours. If there's nothing further, court stands in recess."

"All rise!" yelled the court reporter.

Frazier leaned over and whispered, "What did all that mean?"

Jack waited until DiMarco was out the door. "We got fucked."

SEVEN

When Jack and Anne arrived at the commissary to do their grocery shopping, the parking lot was full and they were forced to park on a side street. There were never enough spaces on Saturdays, especially now that the new concession-aires—mostly East Germans, Poles, and Czechs—were permitted to sell their wares on half of the lot. Soldiers and their families crowded around the tables, buying velvet paintings of bullfighters, Elvis, "The Last Supper," and beer-drinking Saint Bernards, and ceramic statues of Afro lovers and cobras.

German law dictated that the store only be open from ten until five on weekdays and until two P.M. on Saturdays. The hours were inconvenient, but the real problem was the store itself. One market the size of an average A&P serviced thirty-five thousand soldiers and their families in the Giessen-Butzbach area.

On his initial shopping trip, Jack discovered that items he took for granted back home—iceberg lettuce, taco shells, pumpkin-pie filling—were not stocked or, if they were, had been cleaned off the shelf. Jack mentioned this to his boss and was told, "If you ever see something you want, buy all of it they have. There's no guarantee it will be there the next time you go. If you don't want it, someone else in the office will buy it from you." The only items consistently available were goods that sold well on the German black market—American cigarettes, ice cream, and butter.

At the beginning of his tour, Jack had tried to do something about the commissary. He filed suggestions with the

German manager for evening hours. They were ignored. He went to the Inspector General to find out why another store couldn't be opened, only to be told that German Green Law specially prohibited Americans from building any more facilities. He even tried shopping at a German market, until he discovered that the exchange rate made the items three times as expensive.

After six months of battling, Jack gave up. There were not enough hours in the day to fight the German bureaucracy, run errands, and still try his cases. Not when he stood in line for an hour at the American Express Bank to change dollars into deutsche marks if he wanted to go to dinner; not when he sat for forty-five minutes just to have his hair cut. He had promised himself before he came overseas that he would never turn into one of those people who constantly moans about a different culture. The longer he lived in Germany, however, the more often he heard himself echoing the worst of the "barracks rats"—"I can live *anywhere* for three years, if I have to."

Jack and Anne made their way around the puddles in the parking lot and walked toward the large Quonset hut that housed the commissary. The store was packed. All eight checkouts had waiting lines of twenty-five people. The noise level was as bad as a major airport before Christmas. Shoppers jostled and maneuvered, attempting to get around one another and reach through those standing in line to snatch canned goods off the shelves. He and Anne shopped only for essentials and quickly got into line. Even in the express lane, they were fifteenth in line.

While they waited, Jack thought about Judge DiMarco's order. He had flip-flopped all week about what to do: don't go, it's a waste of time and you won't find anything; go, you're letting Frazier down because you're afraid. He had asked Sanderford for advice on Friday and received an inspired recitation of the West Point Prayer: "Lord, give me the strength to choose the harder right over the easier wrong."

Jack stared at the shelf off to his right. Every bottle of Wesson oil was discolored to a milky yellow. A card below the shelf read:

THIS ITEM HAS BEEN INSPECTED
BY THE HEALTH OFFICER AND IS
FIT FOR HUMAN CONSUMPTION.

Richard P. Gordon
Captain, Veterinary Corps

Only in the Army would people be expected to pay full price for defective merchandise, thought Jack. That's what being here does to a person: it makes him settle for the second rate, beats him down until he doesn't care anymore. Jack heard people talk about their jobs like this all the time: "Good enough for government work." The Whopper was counting on his having the same attitude, of saying, "Why bother? Frazier's guilty anyway." Usually, he thought Sanderford's platitudes were worthless. This time he was on the money.

"I've decided to go up to Amsterdam," Jack said.

Anne looked up from balancing their checkbook, her eyes puffy with fatigue. "Very funny." She went back to subtracting.

"No, I'm serious," he said.

She finished the calculation and jammed the checkbook back into her purse.

"We're not talking about the local *gasthaus* with soldiers and drunk Germans. What if someone pulls a gun?"

The young soldier behind them, his cart full of nothing but cartons of cigarettes, listened intently. Jack glared until he turned away.

"Look," Jack whispered, "I'm not letting any judge push me around. I know how to handle myself. I'll be careful."

"Right," she said. "You'll know how to handle a drug dealer with a gun. I can't even get you to go downstairs and have the neighbors turn down the stereo."

Jack closed his eyes. He felt anger creeping into his voice and couldn't check it. "That has nothing to do with it, and you know it, Anne Marie."

Several people in front of them turned around to see what was going on.

[65]

"I'm not arguing about a client in front of people," Jack said, waving away any further discussion.

Anne muttered what sounded like "idiot" and turned away. During their five years of marriage, they had always argued. In the past it had never worried Jack, because the fights had a pattern: one of them would not speak to the other for a few hours, then they would laugh about the incident and make up. But since Anne had taken the night supervisor position at the hospital, the pattern had changed—they fought and then didn't see each other for days. By the time they talked about the incident, the reasons for the quarrel were forgotten but the resentment lingered.

On the way home, Anne turned up the stereo to full volume and didn't talk. Later, Jack could hear her banging down canned goods while he dialed Frazier's barracks. He had been wrong to cut her off. When this case was over, he'd make things up to her.

The CQ runner had been gone a long time. It would just be his luck that they'd had this fight and then Frazier wasn't even around.

Finally a groggy voice came on the line. "Hello?"

"Sergeant Frazier?"

"Oh, hi," Frazier said, his voice full of sleep. "Sorry, they didn't tell me it was you, sir."

"Look, Sergeant Frazier, I've decided we should go to Amsterdam."

Static.

"You still there?" Jack asked.

"Uh . . . yes, yes, sir . . . You think it's safe? I mean, plus we didn't get the interpreter."

Jack had hoped for more enthusiasm. "If you know something I don't, now's the time to tell me. I sure as hell don't want to get blown away by somebody."

"I can understand that," Frazier said, his voice still non-committal.

"Well, is there something to worry about?"

"No, sir."

Jack was not reassured.

"It's just that you thought we needed police protection

and an interpreter. But if you think it's okay, I'm willing to go."

Frazier wasn't going to make it easy. If they didn't go now, it was all on Jack's shoulders. Whoever handled Frazier's appeal would allege that not going to investigate was ineffective assistance of counsel.

"You told me you speak German, right?"

"A little," Frazier said. "Enough to get in trouble—"

"Call the *bahnhof* in Frankfurt and find out when the earliest train leaves for Amsterdam on Monday, then call me back."

"Yes, sir. I'll get right on it."

Jack hung up and went to the window. He looked out at the field between his building and the next American housing project. A group of small boys were playing soldier, shooting at each other. One of the boys was trying to be the leader, but the others ignored him. Anne was right; what he was about to do was dumb.

Jack and Frazier's train pulled into Amsterdam at two-fifteen on Monday afternoon. The Central Station—a huge glass and steel half-cylinder that resembled an aircraft hanger—was the hub of the old city. It was bound on the north by Het ij Harbor, then spread south onto land in a spider web of canals and streets.

Riding into the station, Jack could see why Frazier liked the city. The tall row houses with gabled, stepped roofs set close to the canal were a welcome change from the monotonous cinder-block and stucco buildings of Germany. Their brick facades, some highly ornamented with elaborate swags and garlands, others painted soft shades of peach, umber, or white, were mirrored by the water.

The sun was beginning its downward swing in the west, causing the buildings to cast long shadows to the east. Being eight hours farther north than Butzbach meant they were going to have much less daylight than Jack had anticipated.

The train shuddered to a stop, and Jack and Frazier were the first people off. Anyone seeing them arrive would most likely have thought Frazier a well-dressed businessman and Jack a college student.

Jack had debated whether or not to wear a coat and tie too, then decided it was better not to look like a lawyer or what some people might think was a cop. He stuck with his GI interview suit: cowboy boots, black jeans, a hooded sweat-shirt, and black motorcycle jacket.

They stood on the cement platform a minute while Jack double-checked the departure schedule, then he and Frazier followed the crowd through the pedestrian tunnel and emerged on the large plaza called Dam Square. The area was relatively deserted, except for a flock of pigeons and a row of men panhandling people on their way to the taxis. It was too early in the year for tourists to see the tulip fields and too cold for the throngs of college travelers who hung out in the summer.

Though Marnixstraat didn't look that far away on the map, and there appeared to be tram lines near the street, Jack had decided they would take a cab. There was an hour, maybe two, of good sunlight left.

They walked briskly across the plaza, and the first of the panhandlers eased close to them.

"Lebanese blonde," he said under his breath.

Prostitute?

"Hashish?" said the next guy.

Jack shook his head no.

A large Asian whose nationality Jack couldn't identify opened one side of his overcoat like a flasher and held up a dark brown ball the size of a softball. "Moroccan, good shit," he said.

They kept walking and Jack leaned over to Frazier. "Why did he have it in a ball, instead of wrapped in grams?"

"If the police chase him, he rolls it along the gutter and into a storm drain. When somebody wants some, he cuts it off for them."

Jack had asked the question out of curiosity, not really meaning to lay a trap. The quickness of Frazier's answer only confirmed Jack's worst fears about what he was doing.

The tourist brochures pictured Amsterdam as a city of

canals, tulips, and diamonds, but Jack knew from his time as a prosecutor that most of the heroin, cocaine, and hash that entered Germany came through this port. People who dealt drugs at this level would not worry about who he was or why he was asking questions. He and Frazier would be little more than a disposable annoyance.

If Jack had been alone, he probably would have gone back on the next train, claiming he went to the address and couldn't find Koonag. With Frazier along, he felt he at least needed to go through the motions. He mentally coaxed himself into the cab with the assurance that if the place looked dangerous, he would refuse to go inside.

Jack gave the cabbie the address and they drove up Damrakstraat. At first they moved slowly through the pedestrian traffic near the hotels, then sped up. Jack was able to keep track of their route as they passed landmarks on his map— the Holshuysen Stoeltie diamond factory, the line of people waiting for the tour outside the three-story copper tanks of the Heineken Brewery. Two right turns later, he was lost.

As they drove parallel to a canal, the buildings began to change. Soot-stained facades gave way to Indonesian and Chinese restaurants and bars; neon storefronts hawked triple-X-rated sex shows, massage parlors, and "modeling." Sailors from different countries and ships in port wandered the street with girls on their arms.

Halfway down the canal street, the driver made a U-turn and stopped. "Down there," he said, pointing to a narrow street a block away. "I don't take my cab. Not safe."

Once the cab drove off, Jack felt a prickly dread creep over him. Why had he ever thought that he could pull this off? The Dutch police wouldn't even go into this place. He should just admit to Frazier that he didn't have the guts to go through with it and turn back. Jack stopped in the middle of the street and stared at Frazier. It was not too late for him to call a halt to this foolhardiness.

"It will be dark in an hour," Frazier said. He opened his topcoat and began flexing his hands. "Let's do our business and get out of here."

Frazier seemed transformed. He had stopped his good-natured chatter during the cab ride. He scanned everything now as if it might be a potential threat. On the train ride, he had told Jack that in a weird way he'd gotten high off the danger in Special Forces. "You hate it," he said, "but at the same time it makes your mind and body go full throttle all the time. Nothing in my life has been that exciting since." Jack was certain Frazier would do fine if there was trouble; he could only hope that Frazier felt some obligation to him if the situation with Koonag turned ugly.

They walked up Marnixstraat toward a blocked-off street that appeared to be some sort of street market. They passed a plate-glass storefront where three women danced nude. Jack stared at one of the dancers, and she moved forward and ground her pubis rhythmically on the window, gesturing for him to come inside. She slid the tip of her tongue languorously around the outer edge of her lips, lolling her head from side to side.

Babcock was like a dog in heat with the women grinding their snatches on the window, Frazier had said.

The dancer ran her tongue up her middle finger, then sucked on it. When it became apparent that Jack wasn't buying, she moved back from the window, her eyes filled with all the desire of a corpse. At that instant Jack saw the reflection of a burly man with long hair tied back in a ponytail and sunglasses who was watching them. Jack turned to see him better, and the man kept walking up the street and disappeared into the market. The guy had just been watching the show, Jack told himself; you're just being paranoid.

The street market went on for two blocks. Vendors sold counterfeit fashion jeans and sunglasses, bootleg tapes and records, along with trashy wooden shoes and plastic windmills. The place was jammed with foreign sailors, scruffy Dutch teenagers, and more Africans and Asians than Jack had ever seen in one place. Unlike the train station, men walked openly through the crowd, shouting out the type of drug they had for sale.

A place in a street-market area, McCormick had said.

He and Frazier snaked through the crowd along the odd-numbered side of the street, looking for 25 Marnixstraat. They passed a doorway where a sailor was slapping a woman, apparently over a difference in price and performance. He yelled in Italian, trying to push her toward his crotch. When she resisted, he slapped her hard in the face. No one seemed concerned. Jack stopped and began to speak, then felt Frazier pull him along.

"Captain, don't even think about it. She has a pimp who'll make him regret he was born."

Frazier was right. People had already been looking at him curiously, muttering things that he couldn't understand but that nonetheless sounded menacing. Jack's GI haircut made him stand out enough as it was; he didn't need to give somebody who was drunk or high a reason to take out their frustration on him.

They walked two more doors down and found 25 Marnixstraat. Jack felt his pulse throbbing in his temple as they approached the building's entrance.

There were three door bells, and beside the middle bell, the name KOOIJ.

They'd all been mispronouncing his name. It wasn't Koonag, but Kooij. Then it started to come back to Jack. McCormick and Babcock pronounced the name something like Cujo or Coogie; it was Frazier who always said Koonag and started Jack saying it that way.

Frazier looked incredulously at the name.

Jack pushed the buzzer several times, but didn't hear a ring. He tried the door. To his surprise, it wasn't locked.

They entered a small dark foyer that had several rusted bicycles chained to the radiator. A set of wooden stairs, barely wide enough for one person and as steep as those going to an attic, led to the upstairs apartments. The stairwell's only light came from a naked bulb on an upper floor. There was loud reggae music coming from one of the apartments.

Jack started up the stairs first. This is how people got killed in combat. Simple momentum.

Four steps up, Jack caught the heel of his boot and stumbled. He cursed himself for not wearing running shoes. He would break his neck trying to get down these stairs if someone was after them.

More steps. Why the hell couldn't he get his breath? And it was so cold.

If he'd called Frazier's bluff, now was the time to stop this stupid game. He gave Frazier one last hard look as they reached the second-floor landing, praying he would say they should go back.

Frazier stuck his hands in his coat pockets and looked stonily ahead.

Jasmine incense, the sweet smell of hash, mildew. *These shouldn't be your last smells.* The music was so loud that it vibrated the floor.

Jack pounded on the door and heard someone stirring. He tried not to think about Babcock's description of Kooij, but it tumbled at him: *He looked like a kid . . . but he killed a Turk for shorting him on a kilo of hash.*

A moment later, the door opened; the odor of hash was overwhelming. Reggae music blasted out of the speakers. A small, round-faced woman with stringy brown hair and a loose-fitting flowered dress barred the way.

"Is Mr. Kooij here?" Jack shouted over the music.

The woman looked malevolently at Jack, then at Frazier. It wasn't clear whether she understood English.

Jack was about to shout again, when the woman nodded and ducked back into the apartment. The music stopped and the woman reappeared at the door.

Jack cleared his throat. Nothing would come out. He tried again, squeaked, "Is Mr. Kooij here?"

"No," she said.

"You speak English?"

"Yes." Her eyes darted back and forth.

"Franz will be back in a half hour," she said suddenly, then shut the door just as quickly.

Jack was momentarily stunned. He had not expected a woman, since Babcock and McCormick had never mentioned a wife or girlfriend. It was impossible to tell whether she thought they'd come to make a buy or that she knew Frazier and hated him because she thought he had double-crossed Kooij. Or worse, she thought they were cops. Whatever the case, Jack did not want to surprise Kooij on this unlit staircase when he returned. He motioned for Frazier to head back down.

Outside, the air was brisk. He breathed it in deeply. The setting sun bruised the western sky crimson, dark purple. A few of the booths were packing up—a development that Jack didn't like. Somehow he felt a bit safer with a large group of people around, though seeing the prostitute beaten had proven how silly that was.

"So what do you think we should do?" Jack asked, secretly praying that Frazier would say they should just blow it off and go back home.

Frazier checked his watch. "Seems that if we came this far, we ought to at least check back once."

Jack looked up the street for someplace where they could get inside and pass the time. There was a bar a block up the street with a large golden apple above the entrance that seemed as good a place as any in this neighborhood.

The Apfel Kafe turned out to be less a bar than a diner-sized room with a bar and one row of stools, where people came to get high. Early R.E.M. played on the tape deck, the music gauzy and mumbled. Most of the patrons, long-haired Dutchmen in their early twenties and their girlfriends, sat openly cleaning pot and smoking joints and hash. The smoke was so thick that it was almost possible to get a contact high. For the first time since law school, Jack wanted to get high, to have his brain fogged so he couldn't think. Frazier had said very little since they had sat down. He had taken hot tea instead of beer and seemed uneasy.

Jack ordered his second beer. He was beginning to relax a little when the burly man with the ponytail came into the bar. He wasn't wearing sunglasses now, but Jack was certain it was the man he'd seen earlier. He seemed not to notice Jack and went to the rear of the bar, where he began talking to two men.

"I think that guy's been following us," Jack whispered to Frazier.

Frazier glanced to the end of the bar. "You're just imagining things."

"No, I'm not. He was behind us at the nude dancers'."

Jack's mind spun through the possibilities: it was Kooij, or maybe it was someone Kooij had sent to take care of both of them. Jack tried not to stare, but at the same time keep an eye on the man.

The long-haired man laughed with his friends and smoked a joint. He seemed totally uninterested in either Jack or Frazier. Maybe Frazier was right, he was imagining things. Even if this was the guy from the street, it didn't mean he was after them.

Frazier ordered a shot of whiskey and set it in front of Jack. "Drink it, sir. You don't want to be jumpy when we go back."

Jack knocked the shot back. It burned his throat, made him gasp for air. He grabbed his beer and chased it.

"So, sir, I bet you're gonna get out of the Army and make some big bucks?"

Inane chitchat. Frazier must have used it to calm his men before missions. Jack was glad for it.

"I doubt it," Jack said. "After my second year of law school, I tried Steptoe and Johnson for a summer. I didn't fit in." He took another long pull on his beer and could feel a buzz coming on.

"That surprises me, sir. I saw all those diplomas on your wall—fancy school. Figured you'd be like that guy defending Ollie North, pulling in three hundred and fifty bucks an hour."

Jack scoffed. "My older brother, Gary, would howl at that. He thinks my whole problem is I got too smart for work I would have enjoyed. 'Ruined by fucking higher education,' he says." Jack drained his glass. "He thinks I'd have been better off working carpentry with him. Happier, anyway. I don't know, maybe he's right. When I was a kid I was always the brain. Where I lived that meant lots of fights. Except I wouldn't do it. Gary thought I was crazy. But I kept thinking— Gotta use my head, be smarter than these guys if I'm ever getting out of here. Then I made it out . . ." He scratched his head, sighed. "I can't stand most lawyers. Doing what I do now seems to be the only place I've ever really fit." He stood up. "Hell, this is liquor talk. I need to pee."

He felt foolish dropping his guard around Frazier. It was bad lawyering. There would be lots of difficult decisions ahead where he didn't want Frazier thinking they were friends.

As he stood at the urinal, Jack heard someone come inside. He finished buttoning the fly of his jeans and heard a click and a sudden metallic hiss. He turned around slowly and found the man with the ponytail holding a switchblade, blocking his way out of the john. At this distance, Jack could see that the man had a knife or razor scar on his right cheek. The man moved closer and put the knife under Jack's chin.

"Money," he said with a thick Dutch accent.

The man jabbed the knife below Jack's Adam's apple. Jack felt the tip of the blade prick his skin. *Piss. I'm gonna die with the smell of piss in my nose.* He reached into his pocket and pulled out some crumpled dollars and guilders. The man snatched the money, then turned the knife so the blade was on his throat.

"Please don't hurt me," Jack said, his voice high and tremulous.

"Wallet, faggot."

The guy had been casing them all along, thinking that Frazier was a high-rolling fag showing his "chicken-lickin' " a good time.

Jack reached for his wallet. Suddenly, a wave of shock passed over the long-haired man's face. Frazier had seemed to materialize from nowhere and was standing behind the man with the barrel of a small handgun pressed to his temple.

"Put the knife down, motherfucker," Frazier said.

The man didn't move. Frazier cocked the hammer of the revolver and repeated the instruction. The man swallowed hard. The switchblade came away from Jack's throat and dropped to the floor. Frazier used his foot to kick the knife back under the stall.

"Captain, I want you to walk out of here calmly, pay the bill, and wait for me outside on the street." Frazier used the barrel of the gun to guide the man so his face was up against the wall and Jack could pass.

"Do you want me to get help?" Jack asked.

Frazier kept all his attention on the man in front of him. "Goddamn it, just do what I say."

Jack walked as casually as he could to the bar. He felt sick to his stomach. He had no idea whether Frazier planned to kill the man or how he would get himself out of the bar. At this point things had gone so wrong he didn't know what else to do but obey. Jack paid the tab and walked outside. The bartender didn't seem to notice him. A few seconds later, Frazier walked backwards out of the rest room, his hand thrust into his pocket. He backed completely out the door and told Jack to run.

They both sprinted down the street and plunged into the crowd at the market. Frazier kept looking back over his shoulder to see whether they were being followed.

"What did you do to him?" Jack asked between breaths.

"Love tap. He'll live," said Frazier.

Jack had already decided this was enough. No one could expect him to do more. They were definitely going back to the train station. "Let's get the hell out of here," he said.

Frazier shook his head grimly as they hurried through the crowd in the direction of Kooij's apartment. "Not smart, sir. He had some friends. I saw one of them hand him the knife as you went in the john. We're better off talking to Kooij awhile. By the time we're done they'll have stopped looking."

"I appreciate what you did back there, but I think we've done enough."

Frazier shot Jack a look of irritation. "Sir, you don't have any idea where you're at or what you're doing. Trust me. I've been through worse than this. Do what I say and I'll get us out of this. We'll be all right at the apartment."

Jack looked back in the direction of the bar. Two men had come out to the street and were looking up and down the sidewalk. They spoke a few moments, then one headed in the direction of the market.

"Shit, one of them is coming," Jack said.

Frazier pushed several people out of the way so they could get to 25 Marnixstraat. Jack found it hard to believe, but he was actually relieved they were going back to Kooij's apartment rather than staying on the street. As they climbed the stairs again toward the second floor, Jack could hear the music pounding out of the apartment. Jack felt himself glide into confusion as his adrenaline pumped overtime. He tried to think about what to do next. Hopeless. He had crossed a point back in the bar where he'd lost control. He was in Frazier's hands for better or worse now. When they got to the second-floor landing, Jack pounded on the door several times. *We'll be all right at the apartment.* He had to believe that. The music immediately stopped. Frazier had his hand thrust in his pocket.

The door opened, the smell of hash overwhelming. A tall, slim male wearing drawstring pajama trousers and an over-sized wool sweater opened the door. His shoulder-length hair was so dirty and full of dandruff that it was difficult to tell whether it was dark blond or brown. He looked questioningly at Frazier for a long time without saying anything.

Frazier stared back without flinching. Two male dogs sniffing each other—fight or a friendly nuzzle. Finally, Kooij looked at the floor and grinned.

Jack immediately started talking as quickly as he could. "Mr. Kooij?"

The man nodded yes.

"I'm a defense lawyer in the Army." Jack spoke as loudly as possible, hoping this would make Kooij understand his English. "I'm representing Sergeant Frazier."

Kooij nodded, then said, "You don't need to shout. I understand English."

"Sergeant Frazier," Jack said, pointing to Frazier before he realized he was still speaking too loudly, "is accused of buying drugs from you. Is that true?"

"Me sell drugs?" said Kooij, forcing a jackass laugh. "That is crazy."

Jack hated the way Kooij answered. It sounded just like Frazier's bullshit. Or maybe Frazier sounded like Kooij's bullshit.

"I'm a student," Kooij continued. "Look at how I live."

He had a point. The place was a dump. Not Jack's idea of

a drug dealer's apartment. He wished the jury could see this place without the hash smell.

Kooij opened his apartment door completely. "Come in and talk."

Jack turned to Frazier for help. Frazier shrugged. In this crazy game of the unsaid—of Jack suspecting that Frazier was guilty but not knowing—Jack wondered whether this shrug meant that it was safe. *We'll be all right at the apartment.*

Kooij had probably said enough already to make him a material witness. Still, it would be better to ask about McCormick and Babcock, get a written statement.

Jack glanced at Frazier one more time and received the same look of indifference.

In the past, Jack had always had an instinct about when it wasn't smart to talk to someone. After the bar, he wasn't very confident about "feelings." Although, at this point talking to Kooij seemed better than going back outside.

"Okay," Jack said, "just a few more questions."

The apartment was a tiny efficiency full of cheap, soiled furniture. Hanging beads separated the small room from the kitchen. The one item of value was an expensive stereo and speakers. It was hard to know whether Kooij even lived here.

Franz took a bong and piece of foil from the table and set it behind a speaker. For the first time during the entire trip, Jack was glad they didn't have a cop along.

Franz motioned for Jack and Frazier to sit in the wooden chairs. He sank down on the couch and let his hand rest between the cushions.

As Jack reached into his rear pocket to take out a business card, he saw Kooij's arm stiffen between the cushions.

"Just a business card," Jack said, holding up his hands.

He took out a card and slowly gave it to Kooij.

Frazier seemed not to be paying attention. For some reason, he was fascinated with the poster on the wall near the kitchen door: Thor the Destroyer, a muscular, futuristic Viking with a half-naked woman curled around his leg.

"All right," Jack said, taking out his pocket notebook. "You don't know Sergeant Frazier."

"Right," said Franz, smiling at his answer.

"Do you know a Sergeant Babcock or Lieutenant McCormick?"

Franz was still grinning. His teeth were bad, with black decay at the edges. Jack tried to judge his age and wasn't sure—definitely not in his teens, but under thirty-five.

"I don't know any American soldiers," said Kooij.

"They say that you sold them large amounts of cocaine and hash."

Kooij burst out in his horse's laugh. "I don't sell drugs. I am art student."

"At the university?"

"Yes, university," Kooij said.

Jack wrote furiously. He was almost home. Just a couple more questions. He asked the next questions out of the habit of keeping an interview flowing.

"You probably like having the Van Gogh Museum so close?"

Franz tilted his head slightly and seemed not to understand.

He must be mispronouncing it. Jack's art history teacher had always used the Dutch pronunciation, "Van H-O-O-GH."

Jack tried in Dutch. "Van H-O-O-GH?"

Kooij still looked puzzled.

" 'Starry Night'? Post-impressionism?"

Franz smiled and said, "Sorry, I don't know them."

Frazier was shaking his head in disbelief as he moved to the edge of his chair. Jack didn't know what to make of this, since Frazier was the one saying they should talk to Kooij awhile.

"Never mind," Jack said, waving the question away with his hand.

"Mr. Kooij, if the Army paid your way would you come to Frankfurt and testify?"

Kooij paused and looked at Frazier fidgeting in his chair. "I don't know. I have studies. How long would it be for?"

"A day, two days at the most," said Jack.

Kooij took both hands and pushed his hair behind his ears. He stared at the spot where his bong had been. "You think it would help this man?"

Jack wasn't sure Kooij would make a good witness at all. What he would give their case was leverage to bargain with. There was no worse pain in the ass for a prosecutor than getting a foreign witness to trial.

"Mr. Kooij, it would help a great deal," Jack said. "It could keep Sergeant Frazier from going to jail."

"Okay," said Franz, nodding his head. "If it means keeping an innocent man from going to jail, I come."

They were going to make it; he wasn't going to be shot.

Frazier stood up and motioned Jack to do the same. "So, I guess the next time we see you will be in court," Jack said.

Frazier nudged Jack in the arm. "How're they gonna call him?" he whispered.

He'd almost blown it. There was no way Dresman would believe any of this, unless he could talk to Kooij.

"Mr. Kooij, do you have a phone number where the government can reach you?"

"I stay with my girlfriend a lot. You can reach me there."

Kooij took Jack's notebook from his hand and jotted down a number while he walked them to the door.

Once the door shut and he and Frazier were going down the stairs, Jack felt giddy. It had been a piece of cake. There hadn't been any reason to worry.

Frazier peered out the door and motioned that it was all right to come outside. All of the booths had shut down, and the street was almost deserted. A few sailors wandered the streets with whores, but there didn't seem to be any sign of the men from the bar. As they hurried to the trolley stop, Jack asked, "Why did you get in such a hurry to leave?"

Frazier raised his eyebrows. "You remember his girlfriend?"

"Shit." Jack hit himself in the head. "I didn't think she was there."

Frazier checked back over his shoulder again. "In the kitchen. She had a pistol aimed at your head the whole time we were in there." He took out a pack of cigarettes and lit up. "You done good today, sir. I saw guys in the bush come apart under a lot less pressure."

Jack looked around the neighborhood, trying to fix it all in his memory—"Mother of all interviews."

EIGHT

The following week, the government's hard line changed. Dresman spoke to Franz Kooij at his girlfriend's apartment and confirmed his story; as Jack had hoped, Kooij had cold feet about coming to trial. "I am an artist," he told Dresman. "My time is important. I cannot miss classes, be away from work to come to Germany."

When Judge DiMarco was informed, he told Dresman that if the prosecution couldn't get Kooij to Frankfurt, he would order everyone onto military buses and they would try the entire case at the air base at New Amsterdam.

The logistical problems involved in transporting McCormick and Babcock, plus their guards, plus the jury, plus court personnel across another country's border, were a prosecutor's nightmare. Dresman called Jack, and in a bizarre moment of humility, hinted that the general would look favorably at a deal for three years, a dishonorable discharge, and total forfeitures, just to be rid of the case.

Jack was ecstatic. With good time and parole, Frazier would be out of jail in a year. Other than the extreme long shot of an acquittal, Jack knew he couldn't do any better for his client.

But when he recommended that they take the deal, Frazier was adamant about going to trial. Something had happened since their return that had changed Frazier. He acted as if he had all the odds covered and nothing to worry about.

Jack leaned on Frazier in every way that he knew. First he

told him that he better get a good chastity belt for his ass, because a little guy like him would be "punked" the first night he got to Leavenworth, and twenty years of being someone's bitch wasn't going to be very pleasant. Then he yelled about how weak their case was—Kooij's bullshit about being an art student, Frazier's conveniently not knowing what Jimmy Babcock did on their trips to Amsterdam. "They have everything they need to prove their case. Drugs, witnesses who say you did it, and you were traveling to and from the place of the crime at the time they say you were. I've seen people convicted on a lot less."

Frazier listened to all the threats and evidence calmly, then said, "Sir, I appreciate what you're saying. But I didn't do it. I know some of the things I did look bad, but how else would they be able to frame me? You may find this hard to believe, but I think our system works. I'll take my chances."

So with that, Jack began his final preparations. He drove to Hanau three days before the trial to interview character witnesses. Frazier's company commander, Captain Olson, was first on the list for the prosecution.

Jack stopped at Headquarters Company's CQ desk and asked the sergeant on duty for directions to the Orderly Room. Soldiers walking past kept doing double takes when they saw the captain's bars on his fatigue hat.

The CQ pointed to the office at the end of the hall on the left. As he walked off, Jack could hear the knot of people who had gathered at the desk whispering that he was Frazier's lawyer, then laughing.

Jack straightened his posture from his normal slump and moved out at attention. He was sure they thought the Army was getting the last laugh on Frazier by giving him a kid for a lawyer.

This floor of the barracks was falling apart but spotless. The brown tile, though badly veined, was so highly buffed that he could see his reflection. To insure that the floor stayed that way, a row of red No. 10-size cans filled with sand were fastened to the wall every thirty feet or so to catch cigarette butts. The walls were painted two shades of blue—swimming-pool-bottom for the wainscoting, robin's egg up to the ceiling. The generals at the Pentagon had figured out long ago that it was cheaper to dump a few million into slick commercials that made operating tanks seem like playing video games than to spend the billions it would take to repair their facilities.

Jack walked into the Orderly Room and was met by a private polishing the floor with an electric buffer.

"Yes, sir," the private said, turning off the machine and coming to attention.

"Are the CO and first sergeant around?"

"Top just stepped out, sir. The CO's in his office," he said, pointing to the door in front of them. "You want me to check if he'll see you?"

"It's okay. He's expecting me." Jack tapped on Captain Olson's door.

Olson shouted, "Come in and leave it open."

The office looked ridiculous. Olson had hung camouflage netting on his wall and ceiling; he looked like he was still hunkered down in Iraq.

"What is it?" Olson said, not bothering to look up.

He walked up to Olson's desk and extended his hand. "Jack Hayes, Sergeant Frazier's lawyer."

Olson ignored his outstretched arm.

"One of the bad guys." Olson put down his pen.

Jack never expected to be liked by commanders. Most, however, did show common courtesy and treat him like a fellow officer. Olson would pay for this on the witness stand.

He waited a moment for Olson to offer a chair. When it became apparent that Olson expected him to stand like a private, Jack sat down without an invitation.

Dresman had given him Olson's name as the government's chief character witness. Jack was still puzzled by this, since Olson had signed two of Frazier's letters of commendation, plus put him in for his fifth award of the Good Conduct Medal.

At the beginning of his career, Jack would have tried changing Olson's mind by pointing out these discrepancies, believing that he was truly interested in providing a fair picture of the accused. It took getting burned a few times to realize that bringing up weaknesses in a hostile witness's testimony only gave him time to come up with hedges and explanations, not the truth.

Jack took out his legal pad. "I understand you're one of the prosecution's character witnesses."

He could hear someone speaking with a thick southern accent in the outer office, then heard a chair groan loudly.

"Top, is that you?" Olson yelled.

A few seconds later, an overweight NCO with a florid face and bald head stood in the doorway. "Yes, sir?"

"First Sergeant, I want you in here as my witness," said Olson. "I don't want my words twisted around."

Hamlin came in and leaned against the wall directly behind Jack. He was standing close enough that Jack could hear his labored breathing.

Olson wasn't just going to be made to pay; Jack planned to make him bleed.

"How long have you been Sergeant Frazier's CO?"

Captain Olson looked over Jack's head at Hamlin. "How long have I been here, Top?"

"Two years and twenty-three days, sir."

From the tone of Hamlin's voice, Jack was certain he knew the exact day Olson was leaving, too.

"And Frazier's duty performance?" Jack glanced up to watch his reaction.

Olson folded his hands on his desk blotter and began twisting his walnut-sized West Point ring back and forth. "I'd say he's been average. Nothing outstanding."

There were ways Olson could have been truthful. The prosecutors in Giessen always had their commanders prepped to say, "His duty performance was great, but that made his misconduct worse, because the men saw it was all just a front, a big lie so he could get away with what he was doing." Olson was circling the wagons. Everything in Frazier's personnel file said he was an outstanding soldier: max efficiency ratings, two of which had been signed off by Olson.

"How about truthfulness?" Jack asked.

Olson took off his glasses and rubbed the bridge of his nose. Without them, he looked even more like a kid trying to play soldier. "I'd say completely dishonest."

"Any examples?"

"Certainly," said Olson, feigning a smile.

Jack made a coaxing motion with his hand.

"Well, of course, there's all this drug dealing, and then his conduct during Desert Storm."

Something wasn't right. Jack knew that Frazier had a letter of commendation from Olson for this time period.

"What went on during Desert Storm?"

"A couple of our jeeps weren't running, so I announced to the men that we needed to make an extra effort to have them good to go." Olson put his glasses back on and blinked several times to focus. "The night before we loaded at the dock in Bremerhaven to ship out, Frazier came up with the parts. I checked later and there were no requisition forms for them. I'm sure they were stolen. Some other unit went into battle missing parts. Who knows if that cost someone their life?"

Battle? The only real battle the division had seen was Iraqis hurrying to get to American lines so they could surrender.

"Anything else?" Jack asked.

Olson pursed his lips and thought a moment. "I'm sure there have been more, but that's all I can think of now."

Jack flipped his notepad shut. He stood up and didn't bother to shake hands.

"You mind if I ask you something?" Olson asked.

Jack shrugged.

"Doesn't it bother you to defend these guilty people?"

When people asked this question Jack usually gave "The Speech": "Our system presumes people to be innocent. There are hundreds of instances of innocent people who were convicted . . ." He wasn't going to waste his time on Olson.

"The guiltier they are, the better I like it," Jack said, then walked out, not giving Olson time for a rebuttal.

First Sergeant Hamlin followed and shut the door. He plopped down behind his desk and took out a cigarette.

There was more to this jeep parts incident than Olson let on.

"Can I ask you a few questions, First Sergeant?"

"It all counts towards twenty, sir." Hamlin took a long drag and blew the smoke out through his nose.

"If those parts were stolen, why did you take them?"

Hamlin looked at the private buffing the floor. "Reynolds, go take your break."

After the private had been gone awhile and Hamlin still hadn't answered the question, Jack decided to prod him.

"Didn't the CO give Frazier a letter of commendation for that inspection?"

Hamlin seemed momentarily surprised. "Everybody got 'em," he said.

"Yeah, but everybody didn't steal parts, right?"

Hamlin looked nervously toward Olson's office. "Look, sir, that other lawyer, Major Dresman, was asking me these same kinds of questions. I'll tell you the same thing I told him. The old man said to get those parts any way we could. I went to Frazier because I knew he would come up with the stuff. He's a wheeler-dealer. There were plenty of spare parts around—you just had to know somebody in quartermaster."

Dresman was stretching on this one. He'd pumped Olson for examples and then twisted what had happened. Now he understood why Hamlin wasn't one of the government's witnesses.

"So nobody died because of missing parts?"

"I can't say if they did or if they didn't." Hamlin flicked an ash in the trash can. "Frazier ain't got no room to complain. I made sure he got a max efficiency report for what he done. That should tell you what I think."

Jack nodded casually, as if the information was of no importance.

"Thanks for your time, Top," Jack said.

He thought he could hear Hamlin mutter "asshole" as he was leaving.

Frazier had given Jack a long list of character witnesses, most of them NCOs he bowled with twice a week. When they found out they would have to testify and be connected with an accused drug dealer, they all claimed not to know Frazier so well. The only potential witness left on the list was his supervisor, Major Joe Davis.

Before Jack had even met Davis, he knew something had gone wrong in Davis's career. Majors in the infantry, especially those with the Distinguished Service Cross, didn't end up managing the Post Engineers, Drug Testing, and Driver Testing Center unless they'd pissed off someone along the line. Until he found out why Davis was in this dead-end job, he wasn't even sure they could use him.

Davis's office was located in the same building as Frazier's, on the third floor. Jack pushed open the double, frosted-glass doors and was struck by how much the corridor resembled a normal office building. Short-napped gray carpet ran the length of the hall. The high ceiling had been lowered and gentle track lighting installed. The crumbling plaster was covered with new drywall and painted light beige. The only touch the German engineers had missed was Muzak.

Jack went to an office halfway down the hall where the lettering on the door read:

MAJOR JOSEPH R. DAVIS
DEPUTY INSTALLATION COORDINATOR

Major Davis's civilian secretary turned from the filing cabinet as he walked in. "What's happening?" she said.

Jack looked at the leg hair under her stocking and smiled at the incongruity of American slang coming from a German.

"I'm Captain Hayes. I've got a two o'clock appointment to see the major."

Davis must have heard him, because he was already out of his chair, motioning Jack into his office.

Jack started into the office and was met at the doorway by Davis, wearing running shorts and a sweatshirt with the arms cut out. Davis still carried the muscled bulk of a fullback. His ropey legs were the size of dock pilings, his chest like a power lifter's. As they shook hands, Jack had trouble keeping his eyes off the splash of cherry-colored scar tissue running from Davis's jaw to his right wrist. "Tried to stop a rocket with his bare hands," was how Frazier described Davis's winning the Distinguished Service Cross.

Davis had a mop of salt-and-pepper hair that, though off

his ears, was outrageously long for a field-grade officer. The last thing Frazier could afford was to have his sole character witness looking like a middle-aged hippie. Especially when Babcock was claiming that NCOs who worked for this man were fixing driving and drug tests. He'd have to subtly suggest a haircut or forget about using him.

"I've been talking to Judge Beckman. I knew him when he was a prosecutor at Bragg. He says you're the best defense lawyer he's seen," Davis said, indicating with his good arm to have a seat on the couch, while he returned to his desk.

"I've gotten lucky in front of him," Jack said.

He glanced around the room and spotted a framed photo of Davis in a West Point program picture, stiff-arming an invisible tackler. His hair was clipped short and he had a perfect photogenic smile.

"Sir, before we get started, I was wondering if you knew a good place to get a haircut around here?" From the freshly shaved lines around Jack's ears, it was obvious that he'd recently had a haircut.

Davis grinned. "Don't worry, I get your drift, Captain Hayes. I'll have it trimmed before court."

He liked Davis already. Dresman would have his hands full.

"Okay, sir, I'd like to go over the questions I'll ask you on the stand."

Davis reached back to the radiator, grabbed a towel, and began wiping off his neck and hair. "Shoot," he said.

"One thing to keep in mind is don't be shy about praise. We tend to inflate efficiency reports—everybody's performance is *good*—so it's important to tell them how *outstanding* Sergeant Frazier has been."

"No problem," said Davis. He finished toweling off his arms, then draped the towel around his neck.

"How long have you known Sergeant Frazier?"

"Let's see," he said, looking at the ceiling and squinting. "Three years at Bragg, plus he's been working for me here two and a half years."

"Duty performance?"

"Extremely *outstanding*," Davis said, winking at Jack.

"Truthfulness, honesty?"

"I'd trust him with my life." Davis rocked back in his chair, while holding the ends of the towel in each hand. "In fact, he saved my life in Grenada. I don't know if he told you that? I think that's something you ought to talk about."

Jack nodded. "Don't worry, sir, we'll go into it in depth when you testify." Jack paused a moment trying to figure out how to ask his next question so it wasn't offensive. There wasn't any easy way, just do it.

"So you don't get caught off guard, sir, you ought to know that one of the government witnesses, Sergeant Babcock, claims that Sergeant Frazier used cocaine with him."

Davis sighed derisively. "I heard that. Not possible. I check the people who work under me once a month. It's never scheduled. If he were using I would have caught him."

"Well, sir, you better know that Babcock claims that he paid off NCOs who worked for you to switch urine samples."

"Did he give you a name?"

"No, sir."

Davis scowled. "People can say anything, that doesn't make it true. I go out and supervise *every* time we test. I make sure the procedure is set up so we watch when the soldier gives the urine sample. It's labeled there on the spot. The samples are kept locked up until they're sent to the lab. My guess is that Babcock got lucky, that he wasn't using when we tested his unit."

Jack wasn't so sure the system was as flawless as Davis claimed. But given the choice of thinking the Army's drug-testing program didn't work or believing Davis, Jack suspected the jury would side with Davis.

"Is there *anything* else I might need to know about Sergeant Frazier?" Jack asked.

Davis used his thumb and index finger to pinch the sweat off his nose, then snorted. "I don't know if this is what you mean, but about six months before they caught this Sergeant Babcock, CID came and asked if I knew about Frazier going to Amsterdam. I told Billy he was being watched and that he better have his shit squared away."

Jack tried to run through both sides of the argument. Yes,

it meant the CID was suspicious of Frazier, but he would have to concede that anyway. On the positive side, if Frazier was as smart as the government claimed, there was no way he would have continued dealing.

"What'd Frazier say?"

"Said there was nothing to worry about. He wasn't going again and hadn't done anything wrong."

The more he thought about it, the more this was just the kind of trap he needed for Dresman.

Jack asked, "Is this one of the reasons you think he's truthful?"

"You bet," said Davis.

"Sir, when I ask about Sergeant Frazier's truthfulness, I can only ask for a general opinion—is he truthful or not. But the prosecutor can ask you if you have any specific examples. Have that one ready, okay?"

Davis gave Jack his touchdown smile.

"Sir, there's one more thing I need to ask," Jack said hesitantly.

"Sure, anything."

"Is there something in your own file that I might need to know about?"

Davis's smile dissolved. "What do you mean, Captain Hayes?"

They were no longer just two guys shooting the breeze in the locker room. Davis straightened up in his chair and was frowning.

"Any disciplinary actions—letters of reprimand, Article 15's, bad OER's—that sort of thing, sir?"

"Can the prosecutor bring that up?"

"Possibly, depending what it's for. I don't mean to pry, but I need to know if it's something that might hurt our case."

Davis shifted in his chair and rubbed the scar on his neck. "I have an Article 15 for aggravated assault."

Jack waited for him to continue, but Davis stopped. "Could you give me some details, sir?"

"Sure," Davis said, his voice flat and emotionless. "When I got back from Grenada, I found out that my wife was being drilled by half of Fort Bragg. I finally caught one of them and put him in the hospital."

"Was he hurt badly?"

"Broken ribs, concussion, cuts." Davis was looking out his office door, not focusing on anything but the unpleasant memories.

Jack would have preferred a spotless record, yet of all the things Davis might have done, this was something a military jury could understand.

Without being asked a question, Davis began explaining, "I thought about getting out. Then they sent me to the ROTC detachment at the University of Texas. I picked up a masters in Industrial Engineering. Got passed over for major twice, then finally picked up . . ."

Jack tried to interrupt by clearing his throat.

Davis continued talking, staring blankly out the door. "By that time, I had too much time in toward retirement. Plus," he said, holding up his bad arm, "it's not like I had the pro scouts banging on the door anymore." Davis smiled faintly, then looked directly at Jack. "Did you know I was taken by the Vikings in the fourth round? They were even willing to wait for me to finish my obligation."

"No, I didn't know that," Jack said. "Sir, I don't think your record will cause us any problems."

He felt like a heel for having put Davis through this, even if he did need to know. Some things in people's lives deserved to be left alone. Jack wanted nothing more than to sneak out of the room without going through the formalities of saying good-bye.

"Good," Davis finally said. "It's not something I like thinking about."

Jack put away his notepad and stood up to leave. The room was full of an uneasy sadness. The last thing he could afford before trial was to catch this feeling of gloom.

At the door, Davis put his hand on Jack's shoulder. "What do you think his chances are?" It sounded as if Frazier were on the operating table.

"We get the right jury," Jack said, holding up his palms and shrugging, "anything is possible."

PART III

NINE

"I wish to advise you that counsel and I are about to conduct a process known as *voir dire*," said Judge DiMarco.

All ten of the potential jurors concentrated on the Whopper. DiMarco, center stage, was eating it up.

"It's a French term," he continued, "meaning 'to see, to say.' We lawyers, as you've probably figured out, like coming up with these fancy names for things to make ourselves sound smarter than we are. This one simply means you'll be asked some questions to see whether you should be a court member."

Several of the senior officers nodded in appreciation at the Whopper's no-nonsense approach.

"Now our purpose is to assure that Sergeant Frazier—" DiMarco turned and pointed at the defense table. Jack felt Frazier stiffen as the jurors tried to get a better look at him. "—is brought to trial before an impartial court. Questions you will be asked are not designed to embarrass you, but to discover such factors as whether you have any knowledge of this case or any preconceived opinions which you cannot lay aside, or if you have had any experience in your personal life that might cause you to be biased in favor of either party in this case . . ."

Jack knew before he'd asked a single question that all the jurors would say they could be fair. He also knew that some of them weren't being truthful. Jurors didn't intentionally set out to lie; they just found it difficult to admit they couldn't give another person a fair shake, especially in front of a room full of people.

As the Whopper continued reading preliminary instructions, Jack wrote the jurors' names into the ten boxes he had drawn on his legal pad. He told Frazier to do the same, and had told him earlier to watch for any hostile attitudes or frowns Jack might miss while he was individually questioning someone.

The jury was composed of four enlisted men—two first sergeants and two sergeant majors; and six officers—a female first lieutenant, two captains, a major, and two full-bird colonels.

Jack had checked with other lawyers in the division and had come up with useful information on two of the ten—Colonel Everett Ball and Command Sergeant Major James Hass.

Colonel Ball had been the president of a panel that had given one of Sanderford's clients ten years for stealing a $75 radio from a barracks room. When Sanderford saw his name on the convening order, he went nuts: "No matter who else you kick, get rid of this guy. He's a real flamer."

The other juror, Sergeant Major Hass, was someone Jack normally would have been reluctant about having serve on a panel. Senior enlisted men were usually death on drugs. But Hass's son had been in trouble recently—kicked out of school for beating up another student who called him a "nigger." According to the legal assistance officer in Gelnhausen, Hass was furious because the other kid was only suspended for a week. This in itself didn't make him a defense juror, but Jack figured he would at least be sympathetic to the idea that the system wasn't always fair.

Judge DiMarco summed up: "Unless I indicate that a question need not be answered, it will be your duty to cooperate fully in this procedure by answering each question individually and responsively. Can all of you follow these instructions?"

Each juror nodded yes.

"Mr. Prosecutor, do you have any questions for the jury?" the Whopper asked.

"Just a few, your Honor."

Dresman moved the podium so that it faced the jury. "I know all of you are very busy and want to get back to your units. I'll try to keep this short.

"Do any of you know the defendant?

"Sergeant Babcock?

"Lieutenant McCormick?"

The jurors shook their heads no.

"Do any of you know myself or Captain Hayes?"

Once again, no.

"Is there anyone here who couldn't give a significant period of confinement if the defendant is convicted?"

Murmured no's.

"Would any of you have trouble giving a long jail sentence, even if you knew that the defendant was a highly decorated combat veteran?"

The jurors shook their heads no.

"That's all the questions the prosecution has, your Honor."

Dresman sat down and smugly folded his hands in his lap. He didn't need to do any more. Soldiers weren't trained to think in terms of reasonable doubt. They were told to take the hill, drop the bomb. The mission didn't allow room for hesitation, doubt—factors that a good defense juror needed.

The only technique Jack knew to circumvent this bias was to wrap himself in the American flag and make it seem patriotic to acquit.

The Whopper turned to Jack. "Any questions, Mr. Defense Counsel?"

"Yes, your Honor."

Jack moved the podium behind him and set his legal pad on it. He reminded himself again that the best *voir dire* was supposed to be like talking to someone in his living room.

"Good afternoon. My name is Captain Hayes, Sergeant Frazier's defense lawyer. I will tell you right up front that I'm going to take a bit longer than Major Dresman."

Colonel Ball looked at his wristwatch and grimaced.

"My questions are not meant to insult you," Jack continued, "to question your integrity, or in any way to question your intelligence. If you were seated in Sergeant Frazier's seat—and it's possible for any of us to be there—you'd want the same sort of protection. That's the American way, as opposed, say, to the kind of justice they have in places like Iran or Iraq. There, if the government says you did something, it doesn't matter what you say. In our military system, a trial means something. We believe that if the government wants to take a soldier's liberty away, it's going to have to prove its case with decent evidence from credible people."

Blank faces.

"So bear with me," Jack continued. "I don't mean to pry or harass but I'd like you to be honest with me. In turn, I'll try to be straightforward with you."

Jack moved quickly to the end of the box, sensing that the jury was getting bored. He faced First Sergeant Beringer, a small wiry man with thinning brown hair and a nose like a scythe.

"First Sergeant Beringer, does the fact that these charges are at trial make you think Sergeant Frazier must have done *something*, or he wouldn't be here?"

"For it to get this far, I'd lean that way, sir."

Jack nodded along with the answer, empathetic. "I can see that," he said. "Human nature says, 'If he were completely innocent, he wouldn't be here.' Right?"

"Yes, sir."

"Let's analyze it for a minute. I assume you want Sergeant Frazier to get a fair trial, not just a railroad job like some systems give?"

"Right, sir."

"Okay, let's assume for a minute that you're leaving the NCO club, and you're stopped by the MPs. It has been snowing and the roads are icy and you're weaving a little bit. You've had one beer, but when the MPs pull you over they charge you with drunk driving. You say to yourself, 'Hold it, I'm not drunk. I'm innocent.' Do you follow me?"

Beringer cleared his throat. "I believe so, sir."

"And the colonel gets the blotter report the next morning and says, 'We can't have NCOs driving drunk. Get an Article 15 ready for DWI.' But you know you're innocent. So you say,

'I've got to turn this down and go to court. There's no other way, because the colonel says it's my word against the MPs.' So how do you end up here?" Jack paused a moment, but not long enough for an answer. "By saying 'I'm innocent. I want a trial.' Do you think you're guilty?"

Beringer drew in his bottom lip and thought a moment. "No, sir."

"But you're seated there." Jack pointed to the defense table. "You've gotten to trial, right?"

"Yes, sir."

"And there's a trial counsel just like Major Dresman trying to put you in jail?"

Beringer frowned. "I guess there would be, sir."

Be careful, thought Jack, don't let them think you like seeing him sweat.

"Okay, now let's take it a step further. If you're going to have a trial, and you want to have a fair trial, what sorts of safeguards do you want?"

"Well . . ."

"You'd probably want a defense lawyer like Sergeant Frazier's, right?"

"No, sir." Beringer grinned a little. "I'd get someone older than you, probably a civilian."

The other jurors chuckled. Good. The more sympathy he could get for Frazier, even at his own expense, the better.

"That's right," Jack said. "If you could afford one. But you might be strapped paying alimony and child support like Sergeant Frazier and not be able to afford anyone but me."

This thought erased most of the smiles.

"I suppose so, sir," Beringer said.

"Now you'd want some rules, too. They're saying you were drunk, they've got to prove it with some hard evidence. Where's the blood alcohol test?"

"I'd want that."

"And let's just pretend that the prosecutor finds an NCO and an officer who don't like you. Maybe they're facing disciplinary problems themselves." Jack looked at his legal pad to double-check Beringer's unit. "My memory is that they have a consolidated club at Kirch Goens, NCOs and officers together?"

"Yes, sir."

"So this officer and NCO say they saw you pounding down the drinks that night. They're lying, trying to save their own skins. You'd want your lawyer to bring that out?"

"I hope he would, sir."

Jack glanced at Dresman, who was checking his watch.

"But during the first part of your trial, the MPs say you were drunk. It sounds bad for you because you haven't put on any evidence. You're sitting where Sergeant Frazier is. Do you think you're guilty the whole time?"

Beringer made a clicking sound with his mouth, then sighed loudly. "No, not at all."

"How would it make you feel if one of your jurors said, 'Well, if he didn't do anything, he wouldn't be here'?"

"I see where you're coming from, sir," Beringer said, shaking his head in acknowledgment.

A couple of other jurors were also nodding their heads in agreement.

"I apologize for grilling you, First Sergeant. It's just important to see that what human nature tells us at first may not be right."

"No problem, sir."

Jack moved to the other end of the jury box to face Lieutenant Tuttle, a young quartermaster officer with white-blond hair and a toothy grin. Lieutenants, especially young female officers, were generally a throwaway on panels. They did what the senior officers wanted, unless they were very strong-willed. Judging from Tuttle's nervous smile, Jack guessed she would follow the pack.

"Lieutenant Tuttle."

"Yes, sir?"

"The government's two key witnesses, Sergeant Babcock and Lieutenant McCormick, are what we call in the law, accomplices. In plain English, they're convicted felons who were charged with some of the same offenses as Sergeant Frazier. Judge DiMarco will instruct you—"

The Whopper immediately interrupted. "Members of the

jury. I want to caution you that I will *only* give this instruction after there has been evidence presented to support these facts." He stared wide-eyed at Dresman.

Dresman appeared unconcerned. Evidently, he was convinced that the Whopper would protect his interests.

"Thank you, your Honor," Jack said. "If there is evidence to this fact, the judge will instruct you that being an accomplice affects Sergeant Babcock's and Lieutenant McCormick's credibility. That is, it provides a motive to falsify their testimony in whole or in part."

Colonel Hodgini and Sergeant Major Trainor raised their eyebrows.

Jack kept reading from the instruction. "Even though the testimony is apparently credible, it is of questionable integrity and should be considered with great caution. Lieutenant Tuttle, do you promise to consider Sergeant Babcock's and Lieutenant McCormick's testimony with great caution?"

"If the judge gives the instruction, I'll follow it."

Jack looked down the line of jurors. "Can everyone follow this instruction?"

They all droned yes.

"Also, the government's two key witnesses, both convicted felons, have been given immunity. They aren't testifying voluntarily—they have been ordered to testify. The law says—"

"Objection, your Honor!" shouted Dresman.

He had finally gotten the Whopper's nudge.

"Captain Hayes, I don't see what that has to do with these jurors' ability to be fair and impartial," DiMarco said. "Objection sustained."

Damn it, Jack thought, I got greedy. I should have left out the convicted felons part. Move on.

"I'm sure you all have drug problems in your units."

Each juror nodded agreement.

"Who here is concerned about it? Raise your hand."

Jack raised his hand along with the jury. He wanted to make sure he had his anti-drug credentials established from the beginning.

"I'm concerned too," Jack said. "I fly to Graf to do Article

15 counseling sometimes, and I don't want a doper working on my helicopter. We're all concerned. What our system asks us to do, though, is to judge a case on its own merits and not allow our outside feelings to color our judgment. Can you all do that?"

The jurors nodded.

"Has anyone here had an overdose in their unit?"

Captain Munera, an engineer officer from Hanau, tentatively raised his hand. "I had a heroin OD in my unit."

"I'm sure it bothered you."

"Very much," said Munera, glancing down.

"Would that be in your mind during this case?"

"In the back of my mind, I suppose."

"And is it possible it could influence—"

The Whopper cut in. "Captain Munera."

"Yes, your Honor." Munera sat up rigid in his chair.

"If I gave you an instruction to disregard this event and judge Sergeant Frazier on nothing but what is in this case, you'd follow that order, wouldn't you?"

"I'd try, sir."

DiMarco pushed the sleeves of his robe up. "What I'm asking, Captain, is *can* you follow my orders?"

"Yes, sir. I'll follow your orders."

"Fine," said the Whopper. "Anything you'd like to follow up on, Captain Hayes?"

Sanderford had been right. The real obstacle to an acquittal wasn't Dresman or the evidence. The Whopper could crush the defense's hopes any time he pleased, and there wasn't much Jack could do about it.

"No, your Honor," Jack said.

"Any more questions?"

"Just one, your Honor."

What he wanted was for each juror to have said "not guilty" at least once before he deliberated, so that it wasn't an alien phrase.

Jack asked, "At the end of this trial if there has been some evidence of guilt, but not proof beyond a reasonable doubt, what will your verdict be?

"Colonel Ball?"

"Not guilty."

"Colonel Hodgini?"

"Not guilty."

"Major Daniels?"

"I'll follow the judge's instructions."

This was a very bad sign. "Sir, what I'm asking is, if the government doesn't prove its case beyond a reasonable doubt, what would your verdict be?"

Major Daniels's face puckered, as if a horrible-tasting pill was stuck in his throat.

"Would it be guilty or not guilty, sir?"

"Not guilty," Daniels finally said.

"Captain May . . ."

The rest of the jury agreed that they could acquit Frazier. "That's all the defense questions, your Honor."

"Follow-up, Captain Dresman?"

"No, your Honor."

"Very well, if the panel will step into the hall for a minute, I'll hear challenges."

Dresman had nabbed Frazier's escort to act as his bailiff. Sergeant Chambers popped to his feet and shouted "All rise" like he was calling a formation to attention.

The jury wasn't even out the door before the Whopper began. "Challenges for cause, Major Dresman?"

"None, your Honor."

"Captain Hayes?"

"Captain Munera."

"What are your grounds?"

"Your Honor, Captain Munera was obviously bothered by the overdose in his unit. He said it would be difficult to keep it out of his mind during this case. Even under your leading questions, he said he could only guarantee he'd try not to think about it. It was only under continued pressure—"

"All right," said the Whopper. He leaned back and stared at the jury box.

If the Whopper denied this challenge, Jack would keep loading the record with a description of the pressure and Munera's reaction.

DiMarco rocked in his chair for several minutes before

addressing Frazier, and ignoring Jack. "Though I do not believe that I'm legally required to do so, out of an abundance of caution and fairness to you, Sergeant Frazier, I will grant your defense counsel's challenge."

What he meant was, no reason to risk a reversal on jury selection.

Frazier gave Jack a puzzled look, then said, "Thank you, your Honor."

"Peremptory challenges, Mr. Prosecutor?"

"One moment, sir." Dresman took out a chart and was studying it.

"What's he doing?" Frazier whispered.

"Trying to decide how many he needs to convict you," Jack said.

There were no hung juries in the military; a two-thirds majority was all that was required for conviction. If the government didn't get it, the defendant was acquitted. This had its pros and cons for a defendant. In a civilian trial a defendant only needed one diehard holding out for acquittal to prevent his conviction. On the other hand, he also had to convince every juror to vote not guilty to keep from being retried.

If Dresman decided to bump the jury down to eight, it would take six to convict. If he left it at nine, it would still only need six.

"First Sergeant Beringer, your Honor," Dresman finally said.

"Captain Hayes?"

"Could I have a minute to talk to my client?"

The Whopper nodded.

"Any of them you don't feel good about?"

"All of them," said Frazier.

"Look, we only get one free kick. I already know Ball is a nightmare. You saw how Daniels acted. The problem is if we leave Ball, he'll have more influence over them."

Frazier sucked on his teeth a while, then shrugged. "Whatever you think, I trust your judgment, sir."

"Colonel Ball, your Honor."

"Very well, that puts us at seven. We still have our one-third enlisted. Sergeant Chambers, recall the jury."

The members filed back in and Jack noticed that Colonel Ball and Major Daniels were laughing about something. He'd done as much damage control as he could.

"I'd like to thank the following jurors," the Whopper said, looking over the tops of his glasses. "Colonel Ball, Captain Munera, and First Sergeant Beringer. You have been excused and may return to duty. Colonel Hodgini, that means you will be the president of the panel." The Whopper glanced at his watch, "Due to the late hour, I would suggest that we reconvene tomorrow. There are several guilty pleas in the morning, so I suggest we meet at 1500 hours if that is suitable?"

Colonel Hodgini polled the other members and they all nodded their heads in agreement. "That's fine, your Honor."

The bailiff called "All rise" again, and to Jack's surprise, the Whopper remained on the bench while the jury left. Once they were completely out of the room, he leaned over the top of the bench and told the court reporter that this would be off the record.

"Major Dresman, let me give you some advice," said DiMarco. "Almost all those questions during *voir dire* were improper. I would have sustained an objection to any of them."

Dresman's face flushed hot pink.

The Whopper didn't let up. "What the defense was doing wasn't *voir dire*, it was an opening statement about their theory of the case. I'd suggest you get your head out of wherever it is and start paying attention, because contrary to what you may have heard, I don't plan on trying this case for you."

And the check's in the mail, Jack thought.

TEN

"This man," Major Dresman said, moving back from the podium and pointing at Frazier, "is the mastermind behind the largest drug operation in Germany."

Though the jury had had plenty of opportunity to look at Frazier before Dresman's opening, the prosecutor's action seemed to pique their interest. They turned, almost as one, and stared.

To his credit, Frazier followed the advice Jack had given him earlier that afternoon: "Just sit there and look straight ahead with your hands folded on the table. Don't show any emotion—no shaking your head or groaning at his accusations."

When Dresman couldn't provoke a reaction, he returned to his notes at the podium and took several minutes explaining the law of conspiracy—Frazier was guilty of selling drugs, even if he didn't personally do it, if one of the co-conspirators (Babcock, McCormick or any of their men) did so as part of the plan or scheme.

The law in this area was complicated and boring, but two of the jurors that Jack worried about, Major Daniels and Colonel Hodgini, were taking copious notes. He knew that if a question arose during deliberations, the other members would defer to these two. And from the way they'd responded during *voir dire*, Jack suspected they wouldn't be explaining things with Frazier's best interests in mind.

Dresman finished reviewing the law and built toward his conclusion. "The United States," he intoned, making it sound as if he were reading the Constitution, "is not asking this panel to convict on circumstantial evidence or mere speculation. You will hear directly from witnesses who dealt with the defendant, who received drugs from the defendant and then sold drugs for the defendant. Once you've heard this evidence, the prosecution is confident that you will return and look the defendant straight in the eyes and tell him, 'Guilty of all charges and specifications.' "

It was a solid opening. Dresman had covered the elements of the offenses the government must prove, then summarized his witnesses' testimony, even diffusing some of Jack's potential cross-examination by reminding the jury that his two star witnesses had immunity and that Sergeant Babcock would receive a three-year deal if he testified against Frazier. Any lingering doubts about reserving his opening until after the government's case were gone; Jack needed to gain back the momentum.

The spectator section was completely full and started buzzing before Dresman reached his seat. Most of the staff judge advocate's enlisted clerks who could sneak away from their jobs were present, along with many of the lawyers. Their conversations had a festive tone, as if they were talking to friends before a movie.

Jack managed to block out the noise and took a few seconds to look at the outline of his opening again. Halfway through his review, DiMarco slammed his gavel.

"Quiet!"

DiMarco scanned the gallery with his intense brown eyes, daring anyone to mumble even one more word.

"This is a courtroom, not the snack bar," he said. "We have an NCO with fifteen years' service facing extremely serious charges, charges that, if proven, could cost him his career, his freedom. As long as this is my courtroom, I'll not have it turned into a gabfest. If you cannot conduct yourselves properly, I suggest you leave right now."

When he finished, the only sound was the stenographer's machine as she typed the last sentence onto the tape.

They'd gotten a lucky break. In a matter of seconds, the

Whopper had created the kind of atmosphere the defense needed.

"Do you desire to make an opening statement, Mr. Defense Counsel?"

Jack rose. "Yes, we do, your Honor."

There were two theories on how the defense should approach an opening. One was to remain vague about the defendant's story and play up the presumption of innocence. That was fine if your client wasn't taking the stand, or he if he was still trying to figure out what his story should be and needed to hear the government's witnesses.

But when the defense could put their man on, and he had a version of the facts consistent with innocence, spending time on legal theories was a waste. The jury needed to have Frazier's version of the facts in mind, so that every time Dresman tried proving a point, he would have to distract himself with disproving what the defense had said.

Jack crossed off all the introductory remarks from his outline. After the Whopper's lecture, anything he could have said about paying close attention or the importance of the proceedings would have sounded hollow. He stood at a modified parade rest, with one hand free to gesture, and began.

"This is a case of one man betraying his friend. This is a case of two convicted felons attempting to shorten the time they have to spend in prison. Even if it means lying. Even if it means framing an innocent man. To understand why these prosecution witnesses thought they could pull this off, it's necessary to return to January 1990.

"Sergeant Frazier had just arrived in Germany to take over the driver testing center. Prior to this, he had spent twelve years in Special Forces. You may wonder why an NCO would change jobs so quickly? It was not because of any discipline problems. Sergeant Frazier took part in the Grenada rescue mission and received the Silver Star for his actions in saving another man's life. During the invasion of Panama, he was wounded and received the Bronze Star for valor. The switch in MOS took place because of Sergeant Frazier's wife, Sherri. After he was wounded, she demanded that he take a less dangerous job or she was taking their two boys and leaving. So in an attempt to save his marriage, Sergeant Frazier became an administrative specialist."

Several members of the jury nodded their heads in understanding.

"But even after Sergeant Frazier changed jobs, Mrs. Frazier wasn't happy. He was still spending too much time in the field, she said. It was after one of these arguments that Sergeant Frazier met Sergeant Babcock at the NCO Club at *Fliegerhorst Kaserne*. They had a few drinks and found out they had a lot in common. They were both Texans, Dallas Cowboys fans, and they liked to bowl.

"About a month after they met, Babcock showed up at Sergeant Frazier's off-post quarters, terrified. He had been caught smoking hash on CQ duty by the officer of the day— Lieutenant McCormick."

Dresman raised his eyebrows quizzically, and made some quick notes. Good, thought Jack, you should be sweating. There's lots more they haven't told you.

"Babcock will testify that Lieutenant McCormick gave him two choices—to find him a major drug supplier, or he would turn Babcock in.

"This may sound like odd behavior coming from an officer, but there are several things Major Dresman failed to mention about his supposed *credible* witnesses. The evidence will show that McCormick thought nothing of blowing up the Frankfurt MP station so he could rob the Finance Center. He gave no concern to the fact that two MPs were maimed, this man whom the prosecution wants you to believe . . ."

Jack picked up his pad so he could read back McCormick's words. "He did all this because 'I needed to approximate the experience of war so I would be ready to fight the Soviets.' "

Jack glanced at Dresman with disbelief.

"I make this digression because it seems only fitting that you have the full picture of the prosecution's witnesses, especially when a career soldier's reputation and liberty are at stake.

"Anyway," Jack continued, "when Babcock told Sergeant Frazier what happened and asked for his help, Sergeant Frazier told him that he was sorry, but nobody was worth going to jail for. Babcock never mentioned the problem again, and Sergeant Frazier never asked. With twenty-twenty hindsight, Sergeant Frazier realizes he should have been more cautious after that. But he will tell you that he was having his own marital problems at the time and wasn't thinking things through.

"About two months after Babcock came to his house, Sergeant Frazier was reading *Euro-Car News* and saw the car of his dreams—a sixty-nine Mercedes SL for two thousand dollars—advertised for sale in Amsterdam. He made a trip to Holland to look at it and thought it was a steal. The only drawback was that it would take several more trips to complete the customs and sales paperwork.

"On the second trip Babcock asked if he could come along. He said his wife was bugging him, and that he wanted out of the house. At the time Sergeant Frazier thought nothing of it. Babcock went with Sergeant Frazier on three trips and said he was shopping while Sergeant Frazier was busy at the *rathaus*.

"Bad judgment?" Jack nodded his head yes. "That's something that we've all been guilty of from time to time. But bad judgment does not mean that Sergeant Frazier is guilty of a crime. Does it look bad?" Jack nodded in concession. "Certainly. But how else would McCormick and Babcock be able to frame him?"

Weak, Jack told himself. It was the best he could do with the facts. Now that he had Frazier's story out of the way, he could concentrate on attacking Babcock and McCormick again.

"When you listen to Babcock's testimony," Jack continued, "it is important to consider the circumstances around his implicating Sergeant Frazier.

"He will tell you that at the time he was arrested for drug dealing, he and his wife had just had a child. His wife told him in no uncertain terms that if he went to jail for a long time, she was divorcing him and he would never see his children.

"What you need to ask yourselves while you listen to his

testimony is—What would a man faced with that kind of pressure be willing to say? What would he be willing to do if he was offered a three-year deal, so he could save his family?"

Jack paused and gave the idea a moment to germinate.

"Since we are talking about how the government's witnesses came up with their stories, it is worth keeping in mind when Lieutenant McCormick mentioned Sergeant Frazier's name for the first time.

"McCormick will tell you that on the night he was trying to 'approximate war with the Soviets,' he was caught by the German *polizei*. He will tell you how the *polizei* had a three hundred-pound officer sit on his chest until he passed out. Two of his ribs were broken. McCormick will testify that he thought he might be killed if the American authorities didn't show up. And he will tell you that Agents Black and Maxfield of the CID came to the KRIPO Station in Maintal, saw what was happening, and said that maybe they should leave him, unless he was willing to make a statement.

"So that night McCormick gave a full confession, naming Sergeant Babcock, and Sergeant Babcock alone, as his source for drugs.

"Six months later, after McCormick has been convicted, received ninety-nine years at hard labor, and would like the general to look favorably on his clemency petition, he implicates Sergeant Frazier.

"What I would ask you to think about as he testifies is this. When would he have been more likely to tell the truth— on the night he thought he might be killed if he didn't come clean with CID, or six months later when there is clemency at stake?"

Lieutenant Tuttle and Colonel Hodgini were frowning. They seemed displeased that Dresman was asking them to convict on this kind of testimony. Jack decided to push on with what the government had failed to reveal.

"Major Dresman took great pains to detail the evidence against Sergeant Frazier, but he did not tell you the things Sergeant Frazier has done to try to prove his innocence.

"On November 15, 1991, Sergeant Frazier's company commander read him these charges, and offered him a deal if he would name the other people who were involved. Sergeant Frazier didn't take the easy way out—he refused to name another innocent person. Instead, he told his commander he was innocent and that it would be a lie if he claimed someone else was involved.

"That same day, even though he didn't have to, he went back to his commander and offered to have his off-post quarters searched. The CID, along with a drug detection dog, searched the apartment and found nothing—no drugs, no drug paraphernalia, no records indicating he was dealing drugs.

"When this didn't end the nightmare, he gave CID a power of attorney to review his banking records. You will have those records and see the same thing CID saw—an NCO who after fifteen years of service had only five hundred dollars in savings.

"Finally, no one, least of all Babcock and McCormick, thought Sergeant Frazier and I would go to Amsterdam to confirm their story about the supposed drug connection— Franz Kooij. But Sergeant Frazier and I did just that. We went to this address they'd come up with and found Mr. Kooij. He will be a witness in this courtroom and tell you that he had never met Sergeant Frazier before our visit, that he doesn't know Babcock and McCormick, and that it is a lie that he sells drugs.

"This case," Jack said, trying to make his voice sound matter-of-fact, "comes down to credibility.

"You will have to ask yourselves whether you believe the word of two convicted felons—a dope peddler and a crazy man—who are trying to save their skins, or the word of a fifteen-year Army veteran with the Silver and Bronze Stars. You will have to ask yourselves, Where is the hard reliable evidence against Sergeant Frazier?

"When you do that, I believe the government will win this case."

The note takers, Daniels and Hodgini, looked up.

"The reason the government will win this case is found in the hallway of the oldest courtroom in England. Above the door are these words: 'In this hallowed place of justice the

Crown never loses because when the liberty of an Englishman is preserved against false witness, the Crown wins.' "

The second Jack turned to go back to his chair, DiMarco began instructing. "Members of the jury, what you've just heard is not evidence, but what counsel *believe* the evidence will be. Inferences were drawn that may or may not be proven. I'd ask that you wait until you have heard all the testimony before you make any decisions."

The Whopper checked his watch. "Due to the late hour, I suggest we reconvene in the morning, if that suits you, Colonel Hodgini?"

Hodgini conferred with the other jurors. They were all shaking their heads no.

"Judge, we'd like to hear from Babcock and McCormick."

Dresman stood up. "Your Honor, we didn't make any arrangements to house the prisoners here. We have to take them back to Mannheim so they don't miss count."

"Very well," said the Whopper. "Colonel Hodgini, it will have to be in the morning. We are in recess until 0900 hours tomorrow."

Before he left that evening, Jack went to use the upstairs latrine. As he washed his hands at the sink near the door, he heard angry whispering. It was Frazier's voice. He could only make out "bastard" and "two hundred grand."

Jack stuck his head around the corner and saw Frazier and his escort, Sergeant Chambers, standing halfway down the hall, near where the prosecution witnesses were sequestered. Frazier looked at the ceiling a moment, then began whispering angrily, while he poked Chambers's stomach. None of which seemed to have any effect on Chambers.

Jack waited until the conversation ended and Chambers stepped inside the witness room.

"Sergeant Frazier." Jack motioned for Frazier to come see him. "What the hell was that all about?"

Frazier closed his eyes and breathed deeply, trying to calm himself. "That crazy son of a bitch McCormick wants me to pay him two hundred grand to say I wasn't involved."

He snorted in disgust. "Like I should have to pay him to tell the truth. Like I got that kind of money."

"Look, I don't want you up here around the prosecution witnesses. The last thing we can afford is Dresman claiming witness tampering. You read me loud and clear?"

"Yes, sir."

ELEVEN

When Jack arrived for court the next morning, the division appeared to be on alert. A line of cars a block long was backed up outside the front gate, while MPs checked IDs. As he slowly drove forward, Jack could see that something more serious than an alert was taking place. The bomb disposal van was parked just inside the front gate. Teams of MPs wearing thick body armor searched the interiors of cars with a German shepherd. Another group of *polizei* ran a large mirror on wheels under each vehicle before allowing it to pass.

"What's the deal?" Jack asked the MP as he got out of his car and showed his ID.

"There's been some sort of terrorist attack, sir."

Anne would be worried sick. Just another thing to reproach him about for bringing her to this country.

As he neared the staff judge advocate's building, Jack realized that the incident must have involved someone in the legal office. MPs in full battle dress, carrying M-16s, completely ringed the building. Sharpshooters lay prone on the roof, their silhouettes dark against the bright sun.

They've assassinated Colonel Basham, thought Jack. Why in the world a lawyer?

Jack hurried to the building, only to be denied entry by two MPs, who crossed their rifles in front of him. "Sorry, sir. No unauthorized personnel."

"I'm in a trial here today."

"We'll need to see orders and ID, sir."

Jack dug through his briefcase and came up with the

convening order. The MP double-checked the ID against his face several times, then looked at the order for confirmation.

"Sergeant, what's happened?"

"Sir, we've been instructed to direct any questions to Colonel Basham."

Thank God, it hadn't been the SJA.

Inside the building there were more MPs stationed outside the courtroom. Legal clerks rushed between the chief of justice and Colonel Basham's offices. Phones seemed to be ringing everywhere at once in the building. The front-desk receptionist was continually telling callers that Colonel Basham would hold a news conference in an hour to discuss what had occurred.

Jack glanced in the courtroom and was relieved to see Frazier seated at the counsel table. His head was bowed, and he was rubbing his eyes.

"Sergeant Frazier, what's going on?" Jack asked as he sat his briefcase down beside him.

Frazier looked up, his face ashen. He appeared to have been crying. "That crazy son of a bitch McCormick killed Jimmy."

"What are you talking about? He's in custody."

Frazier scowled incredulously. "McCormick had lots of people who worked for him. They only caught a couple of them."

There was a horrible odor in the room. Jack tried to figure out what it was, why it seemed familiar. *Rotten eggs.* The same odor his capital murder clients reeked of as they stood to have the jury decide if they should be given a death sentence.

"He's going to do me next," Frazier said, his eyes darting wildly around the room. "At least if we were out in the bush, I'd have a chance. I'd just cap his ass."

"Calm down. Nothing's going to happen."

Just then Dresman stuck his head in the courtroom. "Could I see you, Captain Hayes."

Jack stepped into the hallway.

"I don't know if you've heard, but Babcock's been killed.

We're going to use his testimony from the Article 32 investigation."

"Like hell you are."

Dresman straightened himself, jutted his chest. "Watch your mouth, Captain. I'm in no mood for any of your disrespect."

Field-grade asshole. This was just how he'd bullied the defense counsel during Desert Storm.

"We're moving for a mistrial, *sir*. There's no way my man can get a fair trial now. This place is like—"

"Here's how the proceedings will be conducted," Dresman said, barging on as if what Jack had to say were irrelevant. "I've informed Judge DiMarco that we'll need a motion session this morning. Because of security precautions, the jurors will be late anyway. It will give us time to settle what forms of Babcock's testimony are admissible. I suppose the judge will want to *voir dire* the jury again. And just so there's no cry of foul play, I want to let you know that we've struck a deal with McCormick for his testimony."

Jack shook his head in disbelief. "How much?"

"Thirty years."

"Jesus, you guys amaze me. McCormick's a stone killer. You want him walking the streets in ten years?"

A legal clerk approached Dresman and handed him a piece of paper. He scanned it quickly, then handed it back. "Good, tell Colonel Basham I'll be right in." He turned back to Jack, his face flushed with excitement. "I've got a mission to complete. The colonel thinks it's worth it if we can take your man off the street. I agree."

Save me from the self-righteous with a mission, thought Jack. There was no use arguing with Dresman anymore. He had to calm down and think of some way to keep out Babcock's testimony. "I need to see McCormick."

Dresman motioned one of the MPs over. "Sergeant, take Captain Hayes upstairs and tell the guards I've authorized him to see Lieutenant McCormick."

The witness room was located in what had once been the hayloft of the barn. The rooms had very low ceilings, and the two large MPs sent as McCormick's escorts were having trouble not bumping their helmets on the ceiling.

"The captain has been authorized to see the scum," said the MP accompanying Jack.

"You his lawyer?" asked the larger of the two MPs.

"No." *Odd.* The bunch from Mannheim were usually pros, never getting involved with the cases of the inmates they transported.

Jack walked in and found McCormick with his feet up on the couch, drinking a 7-Up. He was holding an ice pack against the right side of his face.

McCormick turned and put his feet down, and Jack saw the reason for the ice. His left eye was almost swollen shut. He was going to have some shiner.

"What happened to you?"

"One of my escorts did it. He apparently didn't care for the comment I made about his buddy who was killed in Babcock's jeep. He's been relieved," McCormick said imperiously.

McCormick took the ice pack away from his face to show Jack the results. There was a golf-ball size knot below his eye. When he blinked, the pupil looked like a pool of blood. "Not very professional beating someone in shackles, wouldn't you say? I gave him your name as a good defense lawyer." McCormick laughed to himself, then put his feet up on the coffee table. "Would you like something to drink?"

Jack shook his head.

"Major Dresman has told them to get me anything I want. I'm thinking of having pizza for lunch. Since Babcock is no longer here, you'd be surprised how valuable I've become."

Frazier was right. He wasn't safe.

Jack pulled up a chair and sat down across from McCormick. His pallor was cadaverous from being in an isolation cell so long. Jack could see his spindly, hairless leg above his sock and it revolted him.

"Did you see what happened?"

"It was incredible." McCormick's one good eye sparkled. "My jeep was four hundred yards behind Babcock's. As we got off the autobahn coming from Mannheim, it would appear—

I'm only giving you an after-action report, so better intelligence will be required—but it appears that Babcock's jeep was hit by a hand-held, antitank round as it stopped at the end of the exit ramp. My guess would be a LAW from the nature of the explosion and fire. The fire is what eliminated Babcock. I never knew Babcock had such strength. Somehow he managed to get out of the back of the vehicle, but he was engulfed in flames. He couldn't really do much about the flames, though, because his hands were cuffed." McCormick took a long, satisfying drink. "Have you ever smelled burning flesh, Captain Hayes?"

"No."

"One of my guards vomited when he saw Babcock," McCormick said calmly. "I thought his friend who burned in the jeep was a much more gruesome sight. Burned his face off down to the bone. Secondary explosion of the gas tank."

It didn't matter what Frazier had done. Nothing was worth cutting this sick bastard any kind of break. Jack must have allowed his disgust to show because McCormick's tone turned hard. "Babcock is much better off. He never would have made it in prison."

"You had this done, didn't you?"

McCormick eyed Jack suspiciously, then smiled. "Me? I'm sure you would never try and help the prosecution, Captain Hayes, but just in case someone is listening, I did not have Babcock killed. If I were looking for the perpetrator, I think I might focus more on your client. Did you ever ask Sergeant Frazier what he did in El Salvador with Special Forces?" McCormick raised his brow, causing him to wince in pain. "No? Talk with him about his nighttime missions with the *El Blanco*. I think you'll find them very enlightening."

"I understand that we have a tragic development that must be taken up this morning," said Judge DiMarco as he scaled the bench and sat down. "Major Dresman, is there any group claiming responsibility yet for this act?"

"To the best of my knowledge, no, your Honor."

"It goes without saying, gentlemen, that we should all

take extra precautions for our safety now. Don't drive the same routes we normally do. Captain Hayes—"

"Judge." To Jack's surprise, Frazier was standing, addressing DiMarco. Jack expected an eruption, but the Whopper merely peered calmly over his reading glasses at Frazier.

"Yes, what is it, Sergeant Frazier?"

"I know I'm only supposed to talk through my lawyer. But I'm worried about my safety, too. There's all this great security around the courtroom, but if someone's going to take us out it will be on the road. Is there any way you could have them take me back tonight in a different vehicle, so we're not already known? I suspect if you don't say something, it won't get done."

The Whopper nodded his head in appreciation. "That's a good point. Major Dresman, see to it that witnesses go out of here in different vehicles. Now, I understand we have a defense motion for a mistrial and that the prosecution has moved for the use of Babcock's Article 32 testimony?"

Jack stood. "Yes, your Honor."

The Whopper turned his hand up, indicating Jack should proceed.

"I'm moving for a mistrial. There is the danger that the jury will think that Sergeant Frazier is responsible for Sergeant Babcock's death."

The Whopper listened with his hands steepled in front of his face. "Captain Hayes, I've thought about that problem, but"—he raised his chin for emphasis—"at this point do you really think you'll find a new panel who isn't aware of this incident? I heard about it on the way over on the radio. It will certainly be front page news tomorrow in *Stars and Stripes*. I can't very well tell them not to print."

The Whopper was fishing to see whether Jack might withdraw the motion so it would be lost on appeal.

"How do we even know your client will be prejudiced against until we speak to the jury?"

"Your Honor, the problem is that I've made an opening where we've told the jury that Mr. Kooij did not know Sergeant Babcock. I intended to have Mr. Kooij, in court, look at Babcock and confirm this fact."

The Whopper rocked back in his chair and thought awhile. "That wasn't done at the Article 32 investigation?"

"No, your Honor. We requested Mr. Kooij be brought, but it was denied."

Dresman jumped to his feet. "There had been no showing at that point that he was relevant, your Honor."

"Sit down, Mr. Prosecutor," said the Whopper, without even bothering to look at him. "I suppose that will be part of your objection to the use of Babcock's Article 32 testimony?"

"Part of it, your Honor. I did not conduct a thorough cross-examination of Sergeant Babcock."

"You weren't allowed to?" The Whopper drew in his chin.

"We didn't, as a matter of strategy. We didn't want to reveal the government's weak points."

"Well," said the Whopper, shaking his head, "that's not the government's fault. I'm sure Major Dresman would much rather have his live witness here than merely his statement.

"Do you have the testimony you plan to read to the jury, Mr. Prosecutor?"

Dresman took a thick stack of papers to the reporter, had them marked as his first exhibit, then handed them to DiMarco. He came back and tossed another copy on the defense table.

Jack looked through the exhibit. Babcock's testimony was very short. No mention of paying off NCOs to fix the drug tests, no description of Kooij, no address where Kooij lived. The truly damaging material was in the original statement given to CID. If he could limit Babcock's testimony to what he said at Article 32, he would be in good shape.

"Your Honor, if you're going to allow his testimony, it should only be the sworn testimony from the Article 32. We certainly never had a chance to cross-examine Babcock on the other statements."

"But, your Honor,"—Dresman's face grew red—"If Babcock were alive we'd be able to use those statements. The jury won't get the whole truth."

The Whopper jutted out his bottom lip. "It works both ways, Mr. Prosecutor. If you wanted that information in, you should have spent more time doing it at your Article 32. The defense didn't plan for Babcock to die, either. Besides, you'd only get to use Babcock's prior statements to impeach or rebut recent fabrication. So my ruling is this—You may not use Babcock's statement to CID. I will, however, allow you to read Babcock's testimony from the Article 32. But I also plan to give a cautionary instruction that the defense was not permitted to have Babcock identify Mr. Kooij and that they should take that into account in considering the weight to give the testimony."

Dresman began to argue and the Whopper stopped him. "That's all, Mr. Prosecutor. Nothing you're going to say will change my mind. Please be seated." He turned toward Jack. "Captain Hayes, I'm denying your motion for mistrial for now. If I find there is prejudice when I *voir dire* the jury, I'll reconsider. All right, Mr. Prosecutor, let's not keep the jury waiting any longer."

By the time the Whopper finished questioning the jury about their reactions to Babcock's death, there was nothing left for Jack to ask. Yes, they knew about it. Probably a terrorist attack they said. No, they wouldn't let it influence their judgment. No, they didn't think the defendant had anything to do with it. Yes, thought Jack, you say this, but in deliberations you'll be asking whether Frazier had someone knock him off.

Dresman started his case-in-chief by reading Babcock's testimony to the jury. As he did, Jack thought about the show Babcock would have put on. Smiling like a jackass with a mouth full of briars as he told of Frazier's escapade on the train with the customs police; his big ears turning red as he blushed over Frazier selling him the answers to the driver's test; his head thrown back in anger as he told how McCormick blackmailed him over smoking hash. All lost. When Dresman finished, the jury seemed unmoved. The information had come off as dead as Babcock. Jack knew the jury would be reluctant to convict on a piece of paper when they couldn't judge the credibility of the witness.

TWELVE

"The prosecution calls Lieutenant Robert McCormick," Dresman said.

There was a loud commotion in the hall, and at last four beefy MPs carrying M-16s marched in surrounding McCormick. They had barely made it through the door, when DiMarco exploded.

"Are those weapons loaded?"

"Yes, your Honor," said the black sergeant in charge of the detail.

"Good God, you have a room full of people here. Take the clips out of those weapons immediately."

"Judge, this man is an escape risk. We've been told—"

"I don't care what you've been told," shouted the Whopper. "I'll not have someone shot in my courtroom." He studied McCormick's bruised face a moment, then closed his eyes and sighed bitterly. The Whopper obviously took the beating of a witness in his trial as a personal insult, a reproof to the dignity he wanted a court-martial to have. And at least for now, Dresman was going to pay the price for that.

"I will tell you another thing, Mr. Prosecutor."

Dresman finished instructing the guards to take their weapons outside and wait.

"Yes, your Honor."

"I'm not having a mistrial here because of government misconduct." The Whopper turned to the jury. "As you can plainly see, Lieutenant McCormick was injured in an assault. Why it took place has nothing to do with this trial. Sergeant

Frazier had nothing to do with it, and you are to draw no improper inferences from that fact. Do you understand?"

The jurors all indicated they did.

McCormick watched his guards trudge out, amused by this latest fiasco. He walked to the witness stand—a chair placed on a raised dais—and was sworn in. The swelling had gone down enough in his eye so that he could squint and see. Jack had been concerned that the jury might misjudge McCormick, feel sorry for him. But they had evidently heard enough during the opening statement to keep that from happening. They were studying him with an equal mixture of curiosity and hostility.

Dresman quickly took McCormick through the trouble spots he knew Jack would raise: the reduction of his ninety-nine-year sentence to thirty years for testifying; the shooting incident at the border that caused him to be relieved; the escape from Mannheim. With leading questions, Dresman was able to control how much McCormick could say. Finally, though, to describe Frazier's part in the conspiracy, it was necessary to ask open-ended questions.

"Please tell the jury how you became involved with the accused," Dresman said.

"He sold me his drug connection in Amsterdam."

"I mean before that."

"Oh, that," he said nonchalantly. "I caught Sergeant Babcock getting high while he was CQ. I was officer of the day. I told him he had to find me a drug connection."

"And did he?"

"Yes, sir."

"Tell us about it."

"After I was relieved, I could see that our company's training was totally inadequate—we just weren't doing the kind of guerilla training that will be necessary once the Russians invade Germany again . . ."

One of the sergeant majors on the jury turned to the first sergeant seated next to him and mouthed, "What?"

"I found that many of the men who were disciplinary problems weren't being motivated properly." McCormick straightened himself in his chair and continued. "With the right leadership and incentives, I found that even the worst men in my battalion could become fine soldiers.

"I had organized a small drug ring, using a source in Gelnhausen. But in order to get the explosives for the Finance mission, I needed more money.

"So," McCormick said, smiling to himself, "when I caught Sergeant Babcock, I gave him an incentive to come through, and he was back in a few days with the drug connection in Amsterdam."

"Did you know who that person was?"

"No, not until I met Franz Kooij and Sergeant Frazier when I bought the connection."

"How did your operation work before this?"

"Sergeant Babcock's source would purchase the drugs in Amsterdam, and we would supply the logistics for getting them back and selling them. Babcock acted as a conduit. He would drop the drugs off to one of my men in Amsterdam and then return the profits to his source once we'd made the sales."

"How did you get the hash and cocaine back?"

"My unit had gone up to Nijmegen for a *volksmarch* with our German sister unit. It was a complete waste of time, in my opinion . . ."

Dresman held up his hand, indicating enough, but Mc-Cormick kept right on talking.

". . . so I used our free time to take my men and reconnoiter the border. We found a suitable place—" McCormick stopped and looked around the room. "I wish we had a blackboard or map, so I could diagram the small-unit tactics I employed. I believe it would be helpful for future exercises."

Dresman shook his head.

"Well, we found a place to cross—optimal overhead cover, but free movement along the ground. Once the operation started, I would drop a team of men off about five Ks from the border and they would cross, while I drove the car through customs."

"Did Sergeant Frazier know about this?"

McCormick paused and looked at the floor a few seconds. "I'm not sure if he knew the specifics, but Babcock said the source wanted a safe way to bring drugs back. Babcock said he wanted a secure means of transport."

"And did you sell the drugs?"

"I didn't personally, my men did."

"Did your source know this?"

"Of course," McCormick said, looking at Dresman as if he were stupid. "That's how he made his return. He fronted the money for each mission and got half the profits."

"How much was that?"

"One hundred thousand dollars a mission."

"And how many missions are we talking about?"

"Five."

"Now, you indicated earlier that the accused sold you his drug connection. Could you describe how that happened?"

"In the fall of 1990 the division knew it would be sent to the Persian Gulf. Babcock said his source was with a unit that was going and wanted to sell the rights to his connection. I told him I was interested, so Babcock arranged a meeting. I was to show up at the Amsterdam *bahnhof* and would be taken to meet the source and his connection."

"Did that occur?"

"Yes, Babcock picked me up and drove to a place on Marnixstraat."

"Do you remember the address?"

"Not now, but I had a map of where the building was. One of my men destroyed it, though, the night we were caught."

Dresman had been busy since the Article 32. All the flaws in McCormick's story suddenly had answers.

"Go on," Dresman said.

"Babcock took the money upstairs and came and got me. I went up and Sergeant Frazier and Franz Kooij were there. Sergeant Frazier introduced me and said that I would be taking over his operation."

"Did you ever make any buys from Mr. Kooij?"

"No."

"Why not?" asked Dresman. His trial aide was standing at the bar, motioning him over. He moved back and took the note.

"We were caught after the Finance mission."

"What do you mean by the Finance mission?" Dresman said as he read the message.

"I decided that as a reward to my men, we would perform a true tactical operation. I planned to rob the Finance Center the day before end-of-month pay to demonstrate how unsecured our facilities are here in Germany. I had planted an explosive device—C-4 with an electrical detonator—in the main Frankfurt MP Station. I planned to blow up the station as a diversion, so we could get in and out of the Finance Center. Everything worked perfectly, except that two MPs did not leave the building when I phoned in the bomb threat. If they had reacted in the proper manner, there wouldn't have been any injuries. I want to make it clear that I had no intention of harming any U.S. personnel."

Several of the jurors looked as if they wanted to climb out of the jury box and beat McCormick's other eye closed.

"When we eliminated the building, there was pure chaos. In the phone threat I had said that we were Red Army Faction, so they thought there had been a terrorist attack. Every MP unit in Frankfurt showed up. I would recommend this as an excellent diversion tactic against any enemy force . . ."

Every one of the jurors glared with pure hate at McCormick.

"We were able to gain access to the Finance Center's vault with C-4.

"Everything worked as planned until we reached Maintal. The *polizei* had set up a roadblock and were checking cars.

"I was prepared to shoot them, but one of my men panicked and got out of the car. The next thing I knew, a KRIPO agent had a nine millimeter at my head."

"Did you give a statement after that?"

"Yes, to CID."

"Did you mention Sergeant Frazier's name?"

"No. I didn't see any reason to involve any more people than necessary."

Dresman was whispering to his clerk again, then sent him out of the courtroom.

"Your Honor, at this time we would like to conduct a

show-up ID. Mr. Kooij has arrived from Amsterdam, and we would like to have this witness identify him."

Dresman was making a shrewd move. Even if Kooij denied knowing Babcock and McCormick later, the effect wouldn't be the same. Jack tried to think of a way to prevent Dresman from doing it, but finally decided that objecting would just help him more by indicating how damaging it was.

"I presume Major Dresman will stipulate that this is Mr. Franz Kooij who lives at 25 Marnixstraat?" Jack said.

"Certainly."

"Fine," said the Whopper. "Ask Mr. Kooij to step in."

Jack had intended to take Kooij aside and make sure he looked presentable before he testified. He could only hope his trial aide had caught wind of what Dresman was up to and had checked him over.

The bailiff stepped out into the hall and asked Kooij to come in.

Kooij walked like a gangly athlete, swinging his arms freely, looking around at all the people staring at him. He appeared much younger than Jack remembered. Maybe it was the Army fatigue jacket and jeans that did it, or more likely, the fact that he didn't have his hand stuck between the couch cushions, holding a gun. His hair was washed and looked almost blond in the courtroom light. It hung down to his shoulders, and he threw his head back to get it out of his eyes as he came and stood between the two counsel tables.

Dresman motioned for him to come and stand beside him at the podium.

"Now, Lieutenant McCormick, you stated that you've met Mr. Franz Kooij."

"Yes, sir."

"Do you recognize the man standing beside me?"

McCormick looked at Kooij a few seconds. "Could you have him turn around?"

Dresman attempted to grab Kooij to turn him around, but Kooij pulled his arm away. Finally Dresman motioned for Kooij to turn around.

"Were you about this close to Mr. Kooij?"

"A little closer," said McCormick, indicating for Kooij to move about two yards forward.

Stop showboating, thought Jack, just get it over with.

"Take your time," said Dresman. "I want you to be sure."

McCormick wet his lips and stared intently at Kooij. He allowed thirty seconds to pass, all for effect. "I've never seen him before."

It took a moment before the answer registered on Dresman. Jack could see the follow-up question form on his lips, then stop.

The spectator section buzzed, despite the Whopper's earlier warning. All the slurs about lawyers being sharks seemed apt at this moment. The prosecution case was hurt—blood in the water—and everyone was excited about the kill to come.

"Quiet!" DiMarco slammed his gavel several times.

Dresman's eyes pleaded with McCormick, seeming to say, "Tell them it's a joke, please." But McCormick sat expressionless. The question was answered, now he was bored. Dresman mumbled that he had no more questions and sat down, every bit of the morning's cockiness drained from his face.

Explanations of how this happened raced through Jack's head. Frazier had paid someone else to show up that day they were in Amsterdam. Possible, but why had Kooij had the gun between the cushions? Why had Frazier been so frightened? Or maybe just this once a client was telling the truth and they'd caught McCormick and Babcock in their own lie? He didn't care. Dresman had just gone a long way toward losing his own case.

Jack's initial reaction was to ask no questions. There seemed nothing else he could ask that would hurt the prosecution any more. But in the back of his mind, he continued to worry that the other details of McCormick's and Babcock's stories made too much sense. Dresman would be smart enough to argue that identifying the drug source wasn't an element of the crime he was required to prove. No, he'd need to show McCormick was a liar, too. And if he could hint that McCormick was so loony that he had Babcock killed and nothing he said was reliable, well, that would be an added bonus. Jack motioned for Kooij to sit in a chair beside the defense table so the jury had a clear view of him. He had no plans of going back to the identification, but Kooij's presence would keep reminding the jury what had occurred.

"Lieutenant McCormick, when I interviewed you at Mannheim, you didn't know Mr. Kooij's address, did you?"

"I didn't need to know the address, I had a map."

"But you didn't mention this destroyed map when I interviewed you before, did you?"

"You didn't ask about it."

Jack smiled politely. *Serve him up a nice slow one first so he thinks I'm stupid.*

"Lieutenant McCormick, you're a Mormon, correct?"

"I was."

"Objection," Dresman said. "That's totally irrelevant, your Honor. I don't know why he's wasting the jury's time—"

"Your Honor, if I can have just a few more questions, I can tie it in directly with this witness's truthfulness."

DiMarco took in a deep breath and thought awhile. "I'll give you a couple more questions, but if you don't pull this together, you won't like the instruction I'm going to give."

"Lieutenant McCormick, after you were convicted, the Mormon church sent an Elder from the Stake in Hanau to talk to you, didn't it?"

The Whopper stopped McCormick from answering. "What is a Stake?"

"Sorry, your Honor. It's the Mormon equivalent of an archdiocese," Jack said.

Judge DiMarco motioned him to continue.

"Yes," said McCormick.

"In the Mormon religion, you are obligated to be truthful with the Elder, aren't you?"

"Yes."

"And yet you told him you were totally innocent, didn't you?"

"They didn't have any reason to know."

"They excommunicated you for not being truthful, didn't they?"

McCormick narrowed his gaze. Jack was glad he didn't have a weapon.

"They were going to do that anyway."

"When you made your statement to CID the night you were caught, the German *polizei* had one of their officers sit on your chest until you passed out, then would revive you and do it again. Two of your ribs were broken. You thought they would kill you, didn't you?"

"I thought it was possible."

"So you made a statement to Mr. Black and Mr. Maxfield that night because they took you out of there?"

"Right."

"But you weren't totally truthful with them, because you didn't tell them about Sergeant Frazier, did you?"

McCormick smirked. "I suppose you *lawyers* could look at it that way."

Good boy, thought Jack. Let them know it's all just a game—you choose when it's convenient to tell the truth.

"Now Lieutenant, you keep referring to your men. How many people are we talking about?"

"Fifteen."

In summation, Jack would point out that only four had been caught. There were plenty of them left running around who could have killed Babcock.

"And so if I understand you correctly, these drug-running *missions* were your way of training your men to fight the Russians. Did you plan to sell the Russians drugs?"

Lieutenant Tuttle and Major Daniels lowered their heads and smiled.

"Of course not," McCormick said bitterly.

"Well what did they learn?"

"They were learning unorthodox warfare techniques."

"And what would those be?" Jack asked sarcastically.

McCormick turned to the jury, ready for more instructions at Jack's expense. "Escape and evasion, use of explosives, means of disrupting command and control—"

"Assassination?"

"If need be," McCormick said quickly. Then a sly smile of recognition crept over his face.

"That would include blowing up jeeps?"

Dresman was red-faced and bellowing. "Your Honor, that's totally improper."

"Captain Hayes, Major Dresman, get up here." The Whopper leaned over the bench, his knuckles white where he was grabbing the rail of the bench. "You pull one more stunt like that, Captain Hayes, and I'll have you jailed for contempt. You understand?"

"Yes, your Honor."

"You're done with this area. Do you have any other questions?"

"Yes, your Honor."

"Well hurry up and finish. Step back."

Before Jack reached his seat, McCormick spoke up. "I told you this morning who CID should be looking for."

"Yes, you did" Jack said, raising his eyebrows for the jury's benefit. "Yes, you've told us."

Just as Jack came out of a conference in Dresman's office, he was met by McCormick and his guards walking out for the trip back to Mannheim. He was shackled just as he had been the first time Jack had met him.

"Captain Hayes, can I talk to you?" McCormick was grinning smugly.

Jack had intended to avoid any further dealings with him, but now there was no choice but to acknowledge him. "What is it?"

"Tell Sergeant Frazier that I'm a man of my word."

With that his guards shoved him forward and out the door.

Even on his way to Leavenworth, McCormick was still trying to mess with people's minds. Jack would spare Frazier this last threat.

THIRTEEN

Jack took Frazier into a spare office next to the jury delibera-
tion room to discuss the offer Dresman had just made. Frazier
was still beaming over the government's debacle with Franz
Kooij. He continued grinning until he saw Jack's expression.

"What's the problem, sir?"

"Nothing bad," Jack said, leaning back on the edge of the
desk. He motioned for Frazier to have a seat in one of the
chairs. "The prosecutor talked to me a few minutes ago about
a deal we need to think about."

"No deals," Frazier said, shaking his head wildly. "I'm
not pleading guilty after we've just shown what liars those
bastards are."

"Just hear me out," Jack said. "They're not talking about
jail. The government is willing to give you a Chapter 10
discharge."

Frazier took off his gloves and unbuttoned his topcoat.
He looked blankly at the chair opposite him and began folding
his gloves into neat halves. "So what does that mean?"

"It means a discharge in lieu of court-martial. You'd be
administratively discharged with an other-than-honorable
discharge. The advantage is that there's no chance of going to
jail. You walk out of here, right now, a free man."

"And the alternatives?" Frazier asked, putting his gloves
down and finally looking at Jack.

"We go back in, put on our case, and let the jury decide."

Frazier rubbed his eyes with his thumb and forefinger a

moment. When he looked at Jack again, he seemed to have aged ten years.

"We've got two choices if you want to go for broke," Jack said.

"One approach is to rest now. Don't put on any evidence, rely on McCormick's inability to identify the supposed drug connection, Babcock's motives to lie to save his family. We argue that Babcock and McCormick thought they could frame you because they didn't think anyone would go to Amsterdam and check out their bogus story.

"My only hesitation with that strategy is that the jury will compromise. We've already told them you were going to testify. If we don't put you on, they may think you were lying or knew for a fact that Babcock was buying drugs. Some of them might think you're guilty even though McCormick can't make an ID on Kooij."

Frazier shook his head and looked at the floor. "The other approach?"

"Put on our case. I'll probably just call you and Major Davis. It seems to me that we don't gain anything now by putting on Kooij. The government's stipulated to his identity. All having him testify does is give Dresman a chance to attack him. After hearing his knowledge of art history, I'm not sure the jury will believe he's an art student."

Frazier bobbed his head in agreement. "You're right, I wouldn't have him testify."

"So, I put you two on and rest our case," Jack continued. "The one drawback is that Dresman has the right to call rebuttal witnesses to anything you say. If we don't put on any evidence, he's stuck with what's come out so far.

"I already know he'll call your CO to say you aren't truthful. I can handle that. But once you take the stand, we open up the door for him to attack your credibility. So you ought to consider that. You know better than I do if you've got any skeletons we need to worry about."

Frazier took out his cigarettes and asked if he could smoke. The legal assistance officer who used this office once a week had a *No Smoking* sign on his desk, but Jack told Frazier to light up anyway.

"If I took the Chapter 10 would I still get my retirement?"

"No," Jack said. "But you ought to keep in mind that it means no federal conviction and no chance of going to jail. And, believe me, if they come back with a guilty verdict on any of these charges, you can expect to get tagged with plenty of jail time."

Frazier looked around for an ashtray and was finally forced to flick the ash in the waste can.

"What would you say my chances are right now?"

Frazier looked at Jack with an expression that was probably the front he used before patrols in Central America: scared shitless underneath, yet acting as if this were business as usual.

For all the times Jack had been asked this question, he'd never come up with a satisfactory answer. He'd seen too many cases turn out differently than he expected because of things the jury had noticed that weren't even part of the evidence: a client skating on a rape charge because his wife sat through the victim's testimony and still held her husband's hand during the breaks; a sodomy client convicted because a juror noticed that Jack sat too far away from him at the counsel table. Who knew what the jury may have noticed that had already swayed them.

"Anything I tell you is just a guess," Jack said. "If we don't put on a case, I'd say your chances are at least sixty-forty. If you take the stand and do all right, and we don't get killed on rebuttal—a little better than that. We're definitely in the game, and I couldn't have said that at the beginning of the trial."

Jack fastened his collar and tightened his tie. "Look, you don't have to make the decision this second. Use the lunch break to think it over."

Frazier took one more quick puff, then threw the cigarette away. He stood up and buttoned his coat.

"I don't need any more time, sir. This may sound crazy, but the only way I can ever get my reputation back is for that jury to say 'not guilty.' I'm too old to start over and find a new career. I'm a soldier. I don't have any choice except to go for broke."

At that moment, Jack realized that he would never understand how Frazier's mind worked. He had been certain that Frazier would go to lunch, come back, and take the graceful way out: never admit his guilt and instead claim that he didn't want to risk going to jail. A Chapter 10 was almost as good as an acquittal when the stakes were this high. Jack felt he owed him one more shot by laying out the worst-case scenario.

"I just want you to understand that if you get convicted, you may get sixty or seventy years, at least."

Frazier put on his gloves and smoothed out the fingers. "Don't worry, sir. I understand the downside to what I'm doing."

"What do you want to do about taking the stand?"

Jack could hear the disappointment in his voice and tried to check it. The Chapter 10 would have allowed him to count this case as a big win. All his defense-lawyer buddies would have been calling on Monday, congratulating him for getting a good hit on the government. He could have taken Anne to dinner and celebrated tonight, instead of spending the evening worrying over his closing argument.

"It's like you said, they want to hear me say I didn't do it," said Frazier. "I guess we better give 'em the chance."

Jack waited until the jury was seated, then rose to call his first witness.

Dresman interrupted before he could speak. "Your Honor, the prosecution would like to request a week's delay, so we can have CID travel to Amsterdam and check on the existence of the real Franz Kooij."

Jack began to argue, but the Whopper was already motioning with his reading glasses to sit down. DiMarco tilted his head to the side and openly scowled at Dresman.

"In case you were stricken with convenient amnesia over the lunch break, let me remind you, Mr. Prosecutor, that you've already stipulated to that witness's identity."

"Your Honor, we've only stipulated that the man the defense produced *calls* himself Franz Kooij. That wouldn't preclude the government from finding the real Mr. Kooij and bringing him to court."

The Whopper wasn't buying any part of the request. He shook his head throughout Dresman's argument and thrust his chair forward as if he wanted to reach out and pull Dresman up to the bench by his tie.

"Major Dresman, you've known for several weeks that this man would be called as a witness. The defense saw fit to travel to Amsterdam and investigate, and you didn't.

"You have all the powers of the government behind you—CID agents, MPs, the Dutch authorities—yet you chose to sit on your duff and do nothing."

Whatever mileage Dresman thought he might get by raising this motion in front of the jury had evaporated. The Whopper seemed to get hotter as he recounted each missed government opportunity.

"I set strict deadlines for the defense to complete their investigation in this case. I'm not going to change those now just because you were surprised by what your own witness had to say. If you can locate this *supposed* other Franz Kooij before the end of trial—fine. If not, I'm not granting any further delays. Is that clear?"

Dresman hung his head slightly. "Yes, sir."

The Whopper turned to Jack. "Call your first witness, Mr. Defense Counsel."

The best trial lawyers recommended calling the defendant as the last witness. The reasoning was that you want to start with a strong witness that the jury would remember. Between his two witnesses, Major Davis was without question the impression he desired to leave with the jury. Especially if Frazier started claiming he "only got high on bowling and Budweiser." The unspoken reason was to prevent the defendant from contradicting other witnesses.

"The defense calls Major Joseph Davis," Jack said.

A few minutes later Major Davis walked through the courtroom. He had more of a practiced amble than a walk—the rolling movement of a former jock who had run hundreds of wind sprints and knew never to waste energy during locomotion except for a good reason.

Davis looked impressive in his uniform: the left side of his chest was speckled with colored ribbons and badges—Distinguished Service Cross, Air Medal, Bronze Star with "V" device for valor, Combat Infantryman's Badge, Scuba Badge, Master Parachutist Badge. Yet what all eyes went to—and then tried not to linger on—was the rivulet of scar tissue on his neck. The jurors could look at Davis and know he was one of them, that he had paid the price of being a professional soldier. Jack counted on this fact to carry as much weight as any of Davis's testimony.

Dresman swore in Major Davis, asked his unit and position, then turned him over to Jack.

"Major Davis, how long have you known Sergeant Frazier?"

"Three years in the Green Berets at Fort Bragg. And I've been his supervisor here in Germany for two years."

"Did Sergeant Frazier serve under you in Special Forces?"

"He was in my company. He saved my life when this happened." Davis pointed to the scar on his neck. "He got the Silver Star for it. He deserved more."

"Could you tell us what he did?"

Major Davis closed his eyes briefly, remembering. "It was the Grenada rescue mission. Our teams were supposed to secure the airport. G-2 had told us that there would only be light resistance, so we parachuted in." Davis grimaced. "Let's just say their intelligence was deficient. There were probably two fortified companies of Cubans there. We were sitting ducks on the runway. No cover. We were taking lots of machine-gun fire from a bunker. People dropping everywhere. I decided to try and advance and take out the bunker. We got about ten yards, when I saw this Cuban pop up with an RPG and aim at my platoon sergeant. I tried to pull him down . . ."

Davis swallowed hard, then squeezed his lips together, struggling not to cry. Almost a minute passed before he started again. "I tried to pull him down, but the rocket hit him. He blew up in my hand." He breathed deeply several times and pushed on. "The shrapnel tumbled up my arm to my neck. I was lying out on the tarmac screaming for help. I knew I would bleed to death if I didn't get out of there quick.

Sergeant Frazier's team had managed to find cover under a jeep"—he grinned at Frazier—"but Sergeant Frazier was always short on common sense. He crawled out on his belly with those bastards taking potshots at him. He managed to grab hold of my boots and pull me back to the jeep. I don't know how they didn't hit us. Bad shots, I guess." He smiled. "I think God was looking out for us that day."

The room was quiet. Jack pretended to look at his notes a minute, giving what Davis had said time to sink in. Frazier stared straight ahead, his expression distant, sad. How many other times had he seen these kinds of horrors? *He blew up in my hands.* Maybe this wasn't enough to look the other way for some crimes—murder, rape—but for what Frazier was accused of perhaps it should be. Could medals ever repay a person for this kind of sacrifice?

Just a few more questions to leave them refocused on Frazier.

"How would you characterize Sergeant Frazier's duty performance?"

"If the balloon went up tomorrow," Davis said, making sure he caught every juror's eye, "you'd want one hundred Sergeant Fraziers in your unit. He's a true leader. If he had been an officer, he could have easily been a general."

The jurors busily made notes on everything Davis said.

"Major Davis, do you have an opinion about Sergeant Frazier's truthfulness, or lack thereof?"

"I've trusted him with my life before. I wouldn't hesitate to do it again."

The Whopper looked over his reading glasses at Dresman. "Cross?"

Dresman went to the podium and nodded in deference to Major Davis. After Davis's account of Grenada, Jack doubted whether Dresman would try taking Major Davis head-on. "Just a few, your Honor."

"Major Davis, you'd agree that a soldier's performance has to be judged by his conduct twenty-four hours a day and not just the eight to ten hours he spends at the job, wouldn't you?"

"Yes."

"And you don't socialize with Sergeant Frazier after duty hours or on weekends?"

"No."

Safe, smart. Leave it all to final argument to say that Major Davis only knew about part of Frazier's life.

As politely as possible, Dresman said, "So your opinion about Sergeant Frazier's truthfulness is based on his job performance and on saving your life."

"No, there's more to it than that."

"I'm sorry, but I must have missed something," Dresman said, holding his hands up and shrugging for the jury's benefit. He had begun to sit down, when Major Davis answered.

"About a year before Sergeant Frazier—"

Dresman was instantly back on his feet. "That's fine, Major Davis. Your Honor, there's no question posed to the witness."

The Whopper rocked back in his chair. "No, I don't see it that way. You were inviting an answer. Go ahead, Major Davis."

Major Davis turned to the jury. "Like I said, about a year before Sergeant Frazier had these charges read to him, CID came to me and said they believed Frazier was traveling to Amsterdam to deal drugs. I told them I didn't believe it. I took Sergeant Frazier aside and told him he was being watched and that he sure as hell better have his act together. He told me he had been making trips to buy a car and it was taking longer than he expected. I also tested him for drugs every month. It was never announced. He always came back negative."

"So that's it?" Dresman said.

He was trying to minimize the damage by dwelling on the subject, pretending the information was so inconsequential that he could afford to keep going over it. Judging from the way several of the jurors' heads had shot up from note taking when this information came out, it wasn't working.

"If Sergeant Frazier was the brains behind all these drug deals, do you think there was any way he would have been dumb enough to continue dealing, knowing he was being watched?"

The question hung heavily in the air. The jury looked to

Dresman, who was acting as if no question had been asked. Finally, the Whopper interceded.

"Sorry, Major Davis, witnesses don't get to ask questions. Thank you for testifying."

Major Davis stood, saluted the judge, and walked out.

"Call your next witness, Captain Hayes."

After all the hours he'd spent in preparation, it didn't seem fair that winning or losing this case would come down to the next few hours, much of which would be beyond Jack's control.

Nonlawyers were always trying to compare trial work to other professions—acting, building a house. But it wasn't like those jobs at all. If an actor blew his lines, the worst that happened was the play received bad reviews, maybe closed. The carpenter who made one error in judgment could always compensate later for the wrong measurement. When Jack asked one too many questions, there was no taking it back or patching things up—his client went to jail. There were no rewards for doing an adequate job; everything in this profession came down to an absolute: you either won or lost. The client behind bars in Leavenworth didn't give a damn about his lawyer having tried hard.

Jack felt his heart rate quicken to triple time as he stood and announced Frazier as his next witness. There was a soft murmur from the gallery as Frazier walked to the witness stand.

Billy took his seat in the exact position he and Jack had discussed—hands resting on his thighs, legs spread at shoulder width—all his body language saying: "I'm open and honest. I've got nothing to hide."

Jack moved to the far end of the jury box near the judge's bench so that Frazier could look at him and the jury at the same time while avoiding Dresman's grimace.

He started by laying the foundation to introduce the documents in the case: Frazier's banking records for the previous three years, showing how little money he had; the paperwork involved in buying the Mercedes in Amsterdam, necessitating five trips. Halfway through, Jack made a quick detour to allow Frazier to explain how he had allowed

Babcock to come along because his wife was pregnant and bitchy, not thinking about the consequences.

"You heard Major Dresman read Babcock's statement describing the incident on the train with the customs officials. Is that accurate?"

"No, sir. None of that happened."

Good, Jack thought, just keep it to simple answers like we've discussed.

"Did you ever use drugs or give Sergeant Babcock cocaine?"

"No, sir."

"Did you ever buy drugs in Amsterdam and give them to Sergeant Babcock to deliver to Lieutenant McCormick's men?"

"No way, sir."

"Other than the time you and I met Franz Kooij a month ago, had you ever seen or talked to Mr. Kooij before?"

Frazier looked squarely at the president of the jury. "Sir, he was a complete stranger to me."

"Did you allow CID to search your apartment on the day these charges were read to you?"

"Yes, sir."

"Why?"

"I had nothing to hide. I guess I thought that if I could show that to CID, they'd see what a lie all this was. But they didn't seem interested in anything that proved I was innocent."

This seemed the best place to stop. Frazier was beginning to expand on his answers enough to make Jack uneasy. All the jury really wanted was Frazier's denial. Going any further risked getting Frazier excited and orating on his innocence.

"Your witness," Jack said to Dresman.

The true test of the Frazier "make-over" would come during the cross. He had tried to prepare Frazier for what Dresman would do by staging mock cross-examinations with him, always reminding him to keep cool and never volunteer any information that wasn't asked.

Dresman got up and moved in front of his counsel table. He was holding a two-page, typed statement. Jack figured he would spend the first half of cross impeaching Frazier line by line with Babcock's and McCormick's confessions.

"Sergeant Frazier, you've testified that you allowed your company commander, Captain Olson, and Agent Maxfield to search your apartment?"

"Yes, sir. They also used a drug dog."

"And you weren't worried about them finding anything, were you?"

"No, sir."

"You weren't worried about them finding your hash pipes, hash, or cocaine either, were you?"

"No, sir. That's because there was nothing like that at my apartment."

"And you weren't worried about your green logbook where you kept your drug transactions?"

Billy answered without faltering. "I don't have any idea what you're talking about."

"You didn't worry about any of these items being found because you'd sent someone out there before CID arrived to clean the place out, hadn't you?"

"No, sir."

Still information he could give, McCormick had said at Mannheim. The thought bumped at the edges of Jack's concentration. No, he told himself, if Dresman had another witness, he would have put him on early when his case-in-chief fell apart.

"And you called this person before you went back to your CO to make sure the place was clean and you consented to have your apartment searched, isn't that correct?"

Dresman was firing out the questions fast now, barely waiting for Frazier to finish. His attempt at subtlety having failed with Major Davis, he now gave way to his usual belligerence.

"No, that's not true, sir."

"You told the person to destroy the green logbook and get rid of the drugs, didn't you?" Dresman moved closer and shook the statement at Frazier.

"Sir, that's not true. Whoever told you that must have been on drugs."

Jack mentally cringed. Frazier still appeared calm, but this kind of answer was the creak of the scaffolding starting to collapse on the facade they'd created. A few more answers like that one, and Jack could see the entire thing going, allowing the old Frazier, bullshit and all, to reappear.

Dresman reddened at Frazier's comment and moved even closer. "Sergeant, do you understand that you're under oath?"

"Yes, sir."

"Do you understand you can be prosecuted for perjury for lying on the witness stand?" He thrust the statement forward until it almost jabbed Frazier in the arm.

Jack had to get Frazier a break. "Your Honor, Sergeant Frazier will gladly answer all these questions, but we ask that Major Dresman not attempt to physically harass the witness just because he isn't getting the answers he wants."

DiMarco agreed. "Major Dresman, there's no need to get that close to the witness unless you want him to examine the document in your hand."

Dresman moved back, his contempt snarled on his face. "Just one more question, your Honor.

"You were able to avoid being caught because you had a source of information on the drug team's activity in the MP station, didn't you?"

"No, sir."

Dresman snorted. "No further questions at this time."

If this was all Dresman had, they were headed for the homestretch in fine shape. Maybe this was hearsay that Babcock had told Dresman that he thought he could rattle Frazier with. Frazier had done fine. Jack could feel the end in sight, the chance for a win. Stay focused, he told himself, you're not there yet.

"Any redirect?" asked the Whopper.

"No, sir."

"It's 1645 hours. How many more witnesses do you have, Captain Hayes?"

"No more in our case-in-chief, your Honor."

"This might be a good place for us to adjourn for the day and get a fresh start in the morning."

[144]

Dresman was instantly up. "Your Honor, we have one rebuttal witness we believe is critical for the jury to hear so they can evaluate the defendant's testimony."

DiMarco looked at his watch again. "If you have given immunity to one of McCormick's men, I suspect we'll be here awhile."

"No, your Honor. This is new information. This witness's testimony will call into question the entire truthfulness of the defendant. The direct examination shouldn't take more than thirty minutes."

Jack hadn't planned to let Dresman know what was coming with Captain Olson, but he didn't want Frazier's company commander having the last bite of the day, even if he could damage his testimony on cross-examination.

"Your Honor, could I have a minute to speak with Major Dresman?"

The Whopper indicated yes.

Jack took all the awards and letters of commendation that Olson had signed for Frazier and motioned Dresman over to his table.

"If you put him on," Jack whispered, showing him the exhibits, "you'll regret it. He's done nothing but praise my man. You're gonna get hurt a lot worse by this than I am."

Dresman leafed through the exhibits, then handed them back. "That was my way of keeping you busy, my friend. I never planned to call Olson. I've got your boy by the balls and now I'm gonna squeeze."

Dresman turned away. "Your Honor, we'd still like to put on our witness. I promise we are only looking at a twenty- or thirty-minute direct."

The Whopper drummed his fingers a moment. "Mr. President, what would the members like to do?"

Colonel Hodgini looked up and down the row at his fellow jurors, all of whom were nodding their heads. "Your Honor, we've already discussed this. If we're going to have to come back on Saturday, we'd like to get as much as possible done today."

"All right, Major Dresman, I'll let you put on one more witness, but that's it."

Dresman smiled. "Thank you, your Honor."

Jack had tried to warn the bastard. He deserved to eat this one.

Dresman signaled to the bailiff to get the witness. "The prosecution calls Sergeant Cindy King."

FOURTEEN

Her name felt like a baseball bat to the stomach. The bailiff had left the courtroom to get her before Jack could even think to stall.

"Your Honor, the defense has had no notice of this witness. How are we supposed to be able to object and prevent improper testimony if we don't know what she's going to say? I'd at least like to have a day or two to check out her story."

Jack had a pretty good idea of what she would say from listening to Dresman's cross-examination. This was all reflex, scrambling for any way possible to prevent the axe from falling, praying that there might be some way to prevent it if he had a few days.

Dresman hadn't bothered to sit down. He knew that the law was on his side, and the Whopper wasn't about to drag this trial out any longer than necessary.

"Your Honor, the defense knows there is absolutely no legal duty to reveal rebuttal witnesses. I believe if Captain Hayes would bother to consult with his client, he would discover that the witness and his client are *intimately* acquainted. The defendant should be able to tell him exactly what the witness will testify to."

"We'd at least like to interview her before she testifies, your Honor," Jack said.

The Whopper looked at his watch again. Jack had seen him talking with Colonel Basham on one of the breaks and figured they had a dinner engagement.

"What *is* the nature of the testimony?" the Whopper asked.

"Sergeant King will testify that she went to Sergeant Frazier's apartment on the day he allowed his company commander to search and that she removed drugs as well as a green logbook containing the records of the defendant's drug dealings. Further, she will testify that she used cocaine or hashish with the accused on a daily basis."

Frazier lost it. Against Jack's advice, he was shaking his head and whispering loudly that it was all a goddamn lie in a voice that was supposed to impress everyone with his innocence.

Jack whispered to him harshly to cool it, then addressed the judge. "Your Honor, we've not had access to any of this witness's records or had any chance to check her truth and veracity."

DiMarco pulled on his earlobe.

"Your Honor," Dresman said.

"Yes."

"I have Sergeant King's chain of command standing by in Giessen. Captain Hayes could interview them over the phone right now. I have her 201 file with me," he said, holding up a pink records jacket. "He could look at it on the break."

"Why wasn't this witness called in your case-in-chief?" the Whopper asked.

"A lot of her testimony wasn't relevant until after the accused testified."

Bullshit, thought Jack. Something was off about her or she would have been called earlier. All this posturing about the accused testifying was a smoke screen. If she was going to testify consistently with Dresman's offer of proof, the testimony would have come in whether Frazier took the stand or not.

"Captain Hayes, I'm going to let him put his witness on. I'll listen closely for any improper questions, and you should do the same. Major Dresman, I expect you to have the witness's chain of command available first thing in the morning for Captain Hayes to interview. He has the right to speak to them in person. I also want all her personnel records made available to him. Is that clear?"

"Yes, your Honor."

Jack motioned his paralegal up to the bar and told him to find out Sergeant King's unit and talk to her chain of command.

"Does that satisfy your objections, Captain Hayes?"

Discovering why Dresman had not put her on earlier might take him weeks. It would mean poking around her unit, talking to friends and people who knew her, hoping someone might slip up and reveal what her problem was. It was also equally possible he'd never find out. He wasn't going to blame himself. Frazier had finished himself off by not telling Jack this information in advance.

"Your Honor, I won't know until I've interviewed the people in her unit."

"Well, do that, and if you come up with something concrete, I'll consider giving you more time. As things stand, I'll expect you to be ready by 1300 hours tomorrow."

Jack leaned over and whispered to Frazier, "What's this all about?"

"I used to date her. I broke it off and she was pretty torn up. I guess this is her way of getting back at me."

Jack began thinking through his "scorned woman" defense—if I can't have him, no woman will, or in this case, jail will. From the way Frazier twisted the ring around and around on his little finger, Jack doubted that it would be this simple.

A few seconds later Sergeant King walked into the courtroom. She was a tall large-boned blonde who looked to be in her late teens. She had a knockout figure that even the drab lines of the women's dress uniform couldn't hide. Her eyes were pale blue and radiated confidence. Wearing makeup—which she wasn't for some reason—she would be beautiful.

Sergeant King's youth would kill Frazier: the men on the jury would think that Frazier was a lech for robbing the cradle. If they weren't disgusted with him, they would be overly protective of her, seeing their daughters in her and viewing a tough cross-examination as unfair. In those who were not bothered by the age difference, Jack would have to fight their unconscious jealousy that an old fart like Frazier could have ever won a beautiful young girl like this legitimately, that he must have had her hooked on drugs to get her to sleep with him. And if Frazier was seeing her while his wife was still around, Lieutenant Tuttle might think he was just using Sergeant King for sex. No matter what, they were in trouble.

Dresman took a Bible out of his briefcase and asked Sergeant King to place her hand on it while he administered the oath. He emphasized the words "so help me God," then had her take the stand.

"Sergeant King, what is your current unit?"

"Fifth to the 59th Air Defense Group at Giessen. I'm part of the security detachment for the Patriot missile batteries."

Frazier certainly knew how to pick them, thought Jack. Not only was he banging a teenager, but a cop to boot.

"How long have you known the defendant?"

"For two years. We were lovers for about a year and a half."

The jurors' late-afternoon drowsiness was gone. They all seemed entertained by this development and were glancing back and forth from Frazier to Sergeant King, checking for reactions. Neither seemed to acknowledge the other's presence.

"Was he married at the time?"

"Yes, but his wife had gone back to the States by the time I started seeing him. He always said he was going to get a divorce."

Any hope of using the divorce for sympathy during sentencing vanished.

"Did you have sexual—"

The Whopper interrupted. "Members of the jury. Evidence that Sergeant Frazier may have committed adultery, an offense under the Code, may be considered by you for the limited purpose of its tendency, if any, to show the defendant's motives for making an admission to the witness. You may not consider this evidence for any other purpose and you may not conclude from this evidence that the accused is a bad person or has criminal tendencies and that he therefore committed the offenses charged. Can you all follow that instruction?"

Yes, the jury said.

Just the opposite was true. Giving this instruction was like saying "You will not see a red barn. The barn is not red. Under no circumstances will you see a red barn." When the jury went back to deliberate, the first thing out of their mouths would be "Let's talk about this red barn."

"Very well. Proceed, Major Dresman."

"Did you have sexual intercourse with the accused?"

Sergeant King looked at Frazier and her face soured, the idea repugnant. "Yes."

"And did you have a nickname for Sergeant Frazier?"

"Yes."

"What?"

She looked down and blushed bright red. "Roadmaster," she said into her hands.

"Why was that?" asked Dresman, the principal getting the whole story before punishment.

"It was stupid—drug talk. The boys I'd been with were so quick, so I called them fire engines. Being with Billy was like riding in a big old Buick."

All the NCOs on the jury were smirking.

"And during the period you were lovers, what was your duty position?"

"I was the desk sergeant at the 504th MP Company in Hanau."

"And were you familiar with the operations of the Drug Suppression Team?"

"Yes."

"Could you tell us how?"

Soberly, looking at the jury now. "I was friends with a couple of the agents. Plus, I would overhear them talking. I saw the informants when they came in and always knew who was working undercover."

"What, if any, information did you give the accused about the activities of the Drug Suppression Team?"

The Whopper frowned, then stopped Sergeant King from answering.

"Major Dresman, I'm concerned about this witness incriminating herself. I've seen no grant of immunity or order to testify. Has she been informed of her rights?"

"Yes, your Honor. She has been read her rights and has waived them. There is no immunity. I plan on having the witness explain her reasons for coming forward with this information."

Jack couldn't wait to hear this lie. Another under-the-table deal like McCormick originally had.

"What information did you give the defendant, Sergeant King?"

"It wasn't like I reported DST's activities. Billy never really came out and asked. That wasn't his way. We'd just make shoptalk—who I worked with, anything interesting that was going on. I finally figured out that he was pumping me for information."

"How long did this go on?"

"The entire time I knew him."

"Were you aware the accused was dealing drugs?"

"I thought—"

Normally, Jack wouldn't have objected, for fear it would appear he was hiding things. He was counting on the Whopper's warning to Dresman to make it seem legitimate.

"Objection, your Honor. She either knows or she doesn't. This jury deserves better than her guesses."

"Sustained. Mr. Prosecutor, if you want to continue with this witness, I want questions that are within this witness's knowledge."

"I apologize, your Honor." He must have known that the defense was being hammered and that a little dressing-down by the Whopper wasn't hurting his case.

"Sergeant King, did you ever use drugs with the accused from February 1990 to November 1991?"

"Yes."

"What were they?"

"Hash, cocaine."

"How often?"

"Almost every day, except when he was gone for Desert

Storm. I'd never been able to afford coke. Billy would give it to me as a present."

Frazier might as well pack for Leavenworth. He could feel his anger growing toward Frazier. Not because he had been lied to—almost all his clients did that constantly—but because Frazier hadn't had enough confidence in him to let him know this was coming. They could have prepared!

"Sergeant King, let me direct your attention to 16 November 1991. Did you receive any information concerning the defendant on that day?"

"I found out that the drug team was trying to search Billy's off-post quarters."

"What, if anything, did you do once you'd received this information?"

"First I tried calling Billy. I was going nuts because I couldn't get him. Finally, he called me. I went to his office and he convinced me to go to his apartment and get rid of the drugs and a green logbook where he kept his drug transactions."

"Why couldn't he have done this?" Dresman saw Jack stand to object, then added, "If you know."

"He said CID might be watching him and that I wouldn't be suspected, since no one knew we were dating."

"Did you go to his apartment?"

"Yes, I went out to his apartment and parked a block away. I used the back entrance, so I wouldn't be seen. I cleaned the apartment out. At least, I believed—"

Jack was out of his chair, but Dresman stopped her himself.

"That's all right, we'll cover that in a minute. What exactly did you remove from the apartment?"

"Hash, cocaine, pipes, mirrors—everything we had used to get high with. I also took the green logbook that Billy told me to get out of the hall closet."

All the points Jack had planned to argue during summation to show reasonable doubt were coming undone like so many slipknots. He kept waiting for some sign of flakiness, some part of the story that didn't make sense. The longer she testified, the less likely it seemed. She wasn't as polished at testifying as most cops, yet she still had that sureness of voice that indicated there was no doubt that the events had occurred exactly as she described them.

"What did you do with these items?"

"I threw them all away in a dumpster down the block."

"Did you speak to the defendant after this?"

"Yes," she said, nodding her head calmly. "He wanted to know if everything was okay. I told him yes and that we needed to talk."

"Why was that?"

"Billy had told me not to look inside the green logbook. But I did anyway. It was filled with people's names and lists of amounts in grams and ounces that he'd sold to them. I had asked him several times before this if he was dealing and he'd always denied it. The book made me see what a daze I'd been in."

Frazier was taking notes on all she said and would periodically glance up and shake his head.

"You mentioned a meeting with the accused later that night. Did it take place?"

"Yes."

"Where?"

"Bruchköble at the *Zum Lowen*. Billy and I ate there all the time."

"What was said?"

"I talked to Margaret, Sergeant Babcock's wife, and she told me—"

Jack knew this was about paying for Babcock's lawyer. They were getting hurt badly enough by what King knew without allowing her to bury them any worse with hearsay.

"Objection, now we're getting hearsay."

"Sustained," said the Whopper. "One more time, Major Dresman, and I'll cut this witness off."

Dresman bowed slightly toward the bench. "I'm sorry, your Honor. It won't happen again." He looked at his legal pad, crossed several things off, and began again. "What did you and the defendant discuss at this meeting?"

"We didn't talk long. I told him that I had looked in the book and knew he was dealing drugs. He denied it as usual.

He claimed he was just hiding the book for Babcock. I told him that I still had the logbook and that if he ever got caught and tried to turn me in and save himself, I'd give it to the MPs."

"Sergeant King, when did you come forward with this information?"

"A week ago."

"Have you been promised any leniency by the government?"

She looked upward. "I know God has forgiven me. That's all that matters."

"I understand that, Sergeant King, but has the government made any deals with you?"

"No."

Frazier leaned over. "If she's a Christian, I'm the Pope."

"Why did you come forward with this information?"

"Shortly after I stopped seeing Sergeant Frazier, I was born again. I've taken Jesus Christ as my personal savior. It's so wonderful knowing I can talk to God and—"

"Thank you, Sergeant King. What we need to know is why you came forward with the information."

Sergeant King smiled, her round face aglow with smug contentment, as if she knew a secret no one else had been let in on.

"I talked to my pastor, and he told me my soul would burn in hell if I didn't come forward with the information. I knew that it was the right thing to do."

"Thank you, Sergeant King. No further questions at this time, your Honor."

"I don't suppose you would like to get your cross over with, Captain Hayes?"

"No, your Honor. We'd like to check into this story."

The Whopper nodded his head. "Very well. Court will be in recess until 1300 hours tomorrow."

None of the jurors appeared very happy at the prospect of spending their Saturday afternoon hearing more of this case. Jack couldn't say he was excited about coming back for the coup de grace, either. He suspected that the jury would tack on some extra time for having their weekend ruined.

Jack led Frazier into the room where they'd spoken earlier that day. He took off his jacket and laid it on the desk. His shoulders and neck ached from keeping up his courtroom front—never showing that he was surprised by anything, never permitting his gestures or voice to telegraph his true feelings. He knew he wasn't going to be able to control his anger any longer, and frankly, he didn't really give a damn.

"You just never fucking got it, did you? The whole idea was to always admit the bad things and then minimize them. We're supposed to be the ones with nothing to hide. Tell me how I'm going to keep a straight face putting on that defense now."

Frazier wouldn't look at him.

"If you'd just been straight with me we could have dealt with her. I could have played the 'hell-hath-no-fury' defense on them. If I'd known she was coming, I could have dug up dirt on her."

Frazier raised his head, his eyes watery. "I was afraid to tell you. The Babcock thing looked bad enough, I thought—"

Someone rapped sharply on the door three times. Jack had told his paralegal not to disturb them. He was in for an ass chewing, whatever the reason.

Jack yanked open the door. Dresman stood there, trying to suppress a smile. "I realize this is a bad time, but I just got out of a meeting with the colonel. Considering what's come out, he wants to put your man in pretrial confinement. I think I've talked him out of it, though."

Jack hated Dresman's patronizing tone. The bastard was a new man.

"I know you probably need to talk to your client tonight, so I suggested barracks arrest as an alternative. We'll need to get Sergeant Frazier's civilian passport and ID card."

Jack wanted this over with as quickly as possible. He stepped back into the room and shut the door.

"I need your ID and civilian passport."

"Who wants them?" Frazier looked panicked.

"The prosecutor. Look, you either give them up or they're taking you to Mannheim tonight for pretrial. It's up to you.

And don't even think of booking on me. They can try and sentence you in your absence now. And take my word, eventually they'll find you."

From Frazier's reaction, the government had been smart to take this precaution. Going AWOL was definitely one of the options he was considering. Billy took out his ID, then reluctantly fished his passport out of his jacket.

When Jack came back from dealing with Dresman, Frazier reminded him of the dogs he'd seen at the pound next in line for the needle. Dark bags showed under his eyes, and he looked forlornly at the floor.

The sight gave him a second wind. This was the part of his job Anne would never understand. Someone depending on him to save them, against all the odds. It was the most powerful narcotic in the world.

"Is there any chance of still putting in the Chapter 10?"

"No," Jack said absently.

He sat down again and began rubbing the back of his neck. He'd indulged himself with enough self-pity.

"What can you tell me about this girl?" Jack asked.

"None of the drug stuff is true. I just want—"

Jack cut him off. "That won't do us any good at this point. We've got to have dirt on her. Anything I can use to show that she's so mad at you she would say anything. We're probably not going to be able to rattle her on that story. I've got to find a way to destroy her credibility."

Billy thought a moment. He seemed to have regained some interest in saving himself. "For starters, this stuff she says about being such an upstanding Christian is a crock. One of her girlfriends got her into that Holy-Roller shit when we were going out together. She wouldn't go to bed with me for a while." Billy smiled to himself. "She was back in a week, saying she liked sinning too much. This goody-two-shoes appearance is crap too. That girl is hard as nails. When I knew her she was always wanting expensive presents. If you couldn't provide for her"—Frazier sliced the air with his hand—"you were history."

Jack wrote all this down in his pocket notebook, not having any idea how to use it. There was no way of knowing how many born-agains might be on this jury. Even hinting that she wasn't sincere could be extremely dangerous.

"Anything else?"

"I don't know if this is usable, but I heard from one of her friends that she was a bin case. She told me she looned out after we broke it off—was seeing a shrink. She claims Cindy told him a bunch of lies about me."

"Would this woman come forward and testify to that?"

Frazier stuck out his bottom lip and shook his head. "I doubt it. She's a cop, too. No way she'd risk getting involved."

"Do you know if this was Hanau or Giessen?"

"I'm pretty sure it was the clinic in Giessen."

Jack put away his notebook. The Whopper would never allow him access to someone's psychiatric records unless he could make affirmative allegations that what he would find went to establishing the accused's innocence. And a mystery woman's hearsay statements wouldn't be enough.

"Do you think that will help?" Frazier asked.

"I wouldn't count on it," Jack said. "You don't know anything else we could use against her?"

Frazier stroked his mustache flat. "I don't know if this is true, but she claimed she was pregnant with my kid the last time I saw her. But she doesn't look like she had a kid to me."

Jack put his jacket back on. He had sworn off drinking during the trial, but now he felt like going home and getting drunk. From what he'd just heard, it probably wouldn't make any difference in tomorrow's outcome.

"What's going to happen now, sir?"

"You a beer drinker?"

Frazier seemed puzzled. "Sure."

"If it were me, I'd go home, pack my stuff, and then get good and drunk. It's going to be a long time before you get to have one again."

FIFTEEN

Talking to Frazier had taken longer than Jack expected, so he was an hour late picking Anne up at the 97th General. She had traded shifts for the evening, and they were supposed to have a quiet dinner at home.

"I thought you might have been killed," Anne said as she slid into the car.

"Sorry, I should have called. Things have just fallen apart—Babcock being killed, a surprise witness tonight."

When he said that he needed to go to Giessen on business before they could go home, Anne's expression flattened from mild anger to resentment. He had represented a sergeant who worked at the mental health clinic and it was worth a shot at trying to convince the guy to let him see Sergeant King's records. His paralegal had called ahead and been told that the former client had gone to the Top Hat Club.

"Has there been anything on the news about what happened today?" he asked.

Anne unpinned her tricorn nurse's hat, shook down her hair, and brushed it out with hard strokes. Jack couldn't really blame her for being angry with him.

"They found what the people used to do it. One of the gals at work whose husband is in the infantry tried explaining it to me. Some sort of thing you pull apart and shoot tanks with."

"A LAW."

"Yeah, that's it." She sounded surprised. "Do you think we're in any danger?"

"No. The person who did this already got what he wanted."

Anne looked at him strangely. When he wasn't forthcoming with any other information, she began brushing her hair again, all too familiar with his drifting off into his own world when he tried cases.

McCormick. He had played the government for a fool—having Babcock killed so his testimony would be indispensable, then torpedoing their case by not identifying Kooij. It didn't make sense. McCormick is a sicko, he told himself; why do you keep thinking that he acts logically?

As he drove down Autobahn 5 toward Giessen, McCormick's words as he was being led out to prison gnawed at Jack: *Tell Frazier I'm a man of my word.* Was it a threat to keep Frazier quiet? No, McCormick had his sweet deal and the government couldn't take it away now. Then something came to him as unexpectedly as a bird smashing into his windshield—bribe.

Only three people had ever seen the real Franz Kooij: Babcock, McCormick, and supposedly Frazier. What if Frazier had paid McCormick and Babcock not to identify Kooij? They both could have said Frazier committed the crime, kept their deals, yet ruined the government's case. The night before in the hallway with Frazier whispering angrily about having to pay $200,000. What if he was paying them not to identify Kooij? Then McCormick sees a chance to grab even more out of the situation by having Babcock killed. He would be keeping his word with Frazier. It would have worked, too, if Frazier's old girlfriend hadn't found Jesus. Frazier never would have thought she would risk going to jail to get back at him.

He allowed the idea to sift through his head, settle in. Possible. Then he tore it down in one sweep. No! Don't do this to yourself! This is just the kind of mind game McCormick would want to play on you. You beat him on the witness stand, so he wants the last laugh. Jack could hear McCormick mocking him: "You weren't as smart as you thought you were. One comment and your will to help someone crumbles."

"We'll see, asshole," Jack mumbled, managing his first grin of the night.

"What?" Anne asked.

"Just talking to myself about this case."

"What is it you're doing tonight, anyway?" she asked. Her voice had softened, attempting to have the evening get back on track.

"I need to see some records on Frazier's old girlfriend, Sergeant King."

He drove on and several miles later she asked, "Couldn't you do it during the week?"

"They're psychiatric records. I have to see them tonight."

Jack put on his blinker and got into the lane for the Giessener Ring, the beltway encircling the city that was a shortcut to the Giessen Army Depot. As he glanced to check the lane behind him, he could see Anne's brow wrinkled in concentration.

"I thought you needed a court order to see those. No one has access to those at the hospital without our lawyer's okay."

"I know someone who works at the clinic."

"And?"

"He's going to give me access to the files."

"You can't do that!" Anne was incredulous. "Those records are completely confidential."

"There's stuff in them that may help Frazier. I just can't get the witness I need to testify to it. If I've seen them, I can make a representation to the judge so we can get them."

Anne turned so her entire body was facing him. "Honey, this isn't right."

"I owe it to Frazier. He saved my life in Amsterdam."

She groaned softly. "Please. He put you in that situation."

Jack felt her continuing to stare at him, waiting for more explanation.

"For once I may have a client that might be innocent. Even if he did what they say, nobody should go to jail on the kind of testimony the government is paying for. You asked earlier who killed Babcock? I think McCormick had it done and they just cut him a thirty-year deal."

Still believing she could reach him, Anne said, "That doesn't justify breaking the law."

Anne's disapproval, and the possibility that she was right, ticked him off. "Why don't you let me worry about what's legal." It was not how he wanted to handle this, but it was out before he could stop himself.

Anne turned away.

He knew how close this was to the line, but Anne was misjudging it. This was why great lawyers won the impossible cases. The civilian lawyers had always told him that if you weren't coming up to the line between what was ethical and what wasn't and tap-dancing on the paint, your client wasn't getting his money's worth.

Five minutes later, the unit police checked them through the main gate of the depot. They drove past the barracks that boxed the parade field, then behind five rows of docks and old wooden warehouses until they reached a Quonset hut with a large neon figure of a top hat and cane on the roof.

Jack reached into the backseat and retrieved his briefcase. "I was just thinking," he hesitated, "it might look better if I had a nurse with me."

Anne closed her eyes, then shook her head. "Do you realize if I were ever associated with something like this, I'd be fired? No questions asked. They'd probably try to have my license pulled, too."

"Okay, forget it, I'm sorry I asked." He already felt bad that he had tried to pull her into this. She was right; he had no business getting her involved. If something went wrong, he should be the one to pay.

"Will you at least come sit in the bar. This parking lot is not a safe place for a woman," Jack said.

Anne shook her head.

"Then lock the doors, and promise me you won't talk to anyone."

"Fine," she said blankly, without looking at him.

He would have to worry about patching things up later. Right now he couldn't let Sergeant Dobbs feel any of his frustration or fear. This was a small favor, something that he would have asked for during the week if he had more time.

Jack opened the door to the club and was hit by a loud wave of Madonna blaring from the speakers. It was still early enough that the place was fairly deserted—a few guys watching an NBA game on big-screen TV, a sergeant and his German girlfriend playing eight-ball, the small parquet dance floor in the rear empty except for the blue and orange lights pulsating on it in time to the bass. The Top Hat's main clientele—small-time scag dealers, lower-ranking enlisted men, and narcs—didn't arrive until the clubs shut down in Giessen.

The man Jack was trying to find, Staff Sergeant Henry Dobbs, had been one of his first defense clients. As far as clients went, he wasn't a particularly bad person—he just had trouble getting to work on time, and once he got there, wasn't worth much. His commander had made the mistake of gearing up a reduction board, instead of barring him from reenlistment. At the time, Jack had thought their victory was due to his brilliant job in grilling Dobbs's supervisors. In retrospect, it was a victory that had little to do with his lawyering skills. The board was made up of other NCOs—several of whom, Jack found out later, had drinking problems themselves, and who were sympathetic towards Dobbs because he had started going to AA. Dobbs had wept openly after the board's decision to retain his rank and had told Jack that if he ever needed *anything*, just to ask.

"What can we do for you, sir?" the bartender asked.

"I'm looking for Sergeant Dobbs," Jack said. "Has he been in tonight?"

"Back there," the bartender said, pointing to a heavyset man in the rear booth, still wearing his corpsman's whites.

Dobbs sat with a pitcher of beer and a couple of empty shot glasses on his table. Until Jack saw him, he had almost forgotten how much Dobbs's immediate supervisor had disliked him: "Not only is your client a worthless sack of shit, but somebody hit that boy with the ugly stick, bad." Time hadn't done much to improve things. Dobbs's reddish-blond hair, the consistency of a Brillo pad, was combed forward to cover a receding hairline. What really made people uneasy around Dobbs, though, was his gaze. Bug-eyed to begin with, his large, blue eyes were magnified behind thick glasses and seemed to swim around when he spoke.

Jack walked up and extended his hand. "How's it going, Sergeant Dobbs?"

It took a few seconds for Dobbs to recognize him. "Captain Hayes, what are you doing here?" he asked, offering a limp handshake. "Have a seat. Let me buy you a drink."

Jack slipped into the booth and took off his hat.

Dobbs stood up and steadied himself a minute before shuffling to the bar. He came back with a clean mug and two shots of peppermint schnapps.

"So what's going on, sir?"

"I need a favor," Jack said.

Dobbs kicked the shot back and chased it with a beer. From the pasty look of his skin and the web of broken blood vessels in his cheeks, it was obvious Dobbs was hitting the bottle hard again. It was just a matter of time before Jack or another lawyer would have him as a client.

"Anything you need, sir."

"I want to see some records at the psych clinic."

"Sure, no problem," said Dobbs. "Do it first thing Monday."

Jack leaned forward so he wouldn't have to shout over the music. "No, I need to see them tonight."

Dobbs hesitated a minute before swallowing his beer. "We're not supposed to give those out without the shrink's okay. He's even picky about who handles them in the office."

"I don't want to keep the file, just look at it. It'll only take five minutes at the most."

Jack slid the other shot of schnapps over to Dobbs.

"I don't know, sir. If someone found out, my butt would really be in a sling. They're still tryin' to can me."

This was why you should never try calling in a marker from an old client. Jack hated the feeling that he would have to beg.

"Sergeant Dobbs, I've got an NCO with a wife and two kids, who's depending on me. He's just trying to gut it out and make twenty the same way you are. If I don't see that file *tonight*, he's goin' to jail. It's just that simple."

Dobbs used both thumbs to push the beads of sweat off his mug and then began swirling his beer. He was trying to do everything possible to avoid looking directly at Jack.

"You remember when everyone else at your unit thought you were a fuck-up, and I believed in you and got you to hang in there because sick people were counting on you?"

Dobbs didn't answer.

When they'd gone through the reduction board, it had seemed that the only way to motivate Dobbs was to use this sort of sappy altruism.

"You remember, Sergeant Dobbs?"

Finally Dobbs looked up at Jack. His eyes, the size of half-dollars, were so glassy that Jack couldn't tell if any of this was getting through.

"I haven't forgot what you did for me, sir."

"Good," Jack said, "because you've got people counting on you again tonight."

"Sir, even if I wanted to, they've got a CQ posted in the building with orders that nobody goes to the second floor. The pharmacy is on the same floor as the clinic. They've been having trouble with break-ins."

"I'll handle the CQ," Jack said. He was lying. He had absolutely no idea what he would say to persuade another NCO to let Dobbs go anywhere. He hoped some inspiration would come to him on the way over to the clinic.

There wasn't much else Jack could say. Pressuring Dobbs any more would probably backfire. Jack leaned back in the booth and nursed his beer, trying to give the impression that he was willing to stay all night, if that's what it took to convince Dobbs to go.

After several full minutes, neither of them speaking, Dobbs drank the other shot of schnapps and motioned to the bartender. "Ray, keep my place open. I'll be right back."

Jack had hoped the five-minute walk to the infirmary would help sober up Dobbs a little. But when Dobbs fell while going up the wheelchair ramp, Jack began to have doubts about whether any of it was worth trying.

"You all right?" Jack asked.

"Lost my balance is all," said Dobbs, grunting as he tried to get back on his feet. "Must have been ice."

Jack grabbed an elbow and helped him up. Dobbs had torn the right knee of his pants in the fall. He reeked of beer. This is exactly how the people you represent get caught, thought Jack.

"Well, if you lose your balance *inside*, act like you've got a cramp or something and grab my arm."

Dobbs straightened his field jacket and nodded.

The pneumatic doors shot open, and they walked into a wide corridor that served as the pediatric clinic's waiting room. The place was a bad imitation of a nursery, with baby pink walls and amateurish murals of Bo Peep and Little Miss Muffet. Magazines and coloring books were strewn over the floor and on the row of tangerine and aqua plastic chairs bolted to each wall.

The young black sergeant on Charge of Quarters duty sat at a table with his feet propped up next to a telephone, leafing through a *Penthouse*. He had positioned his station so that it was directly in front of the stairway leading to the second floor.

"You know him?" Jack whispered.

"By name is all," said Dobbs. "He just made E-5 last month."

"All right," Jack said, slowing his pace so that Dobbs didn't have trouble with "ice" again. "Let me do all the talking."

The CQ had glanced up momentarily as they came through the doors. He seemed unconcerned. It was only when Jack and Dobbs got close enough for the CQ to see the captain's bars on Jack's overcoat that he turned the magazine over and acted as if he were noting something in the log.

Jack's strategy was to walk in and act as if there were no question as to whether he would be allowed up to see the records.

"Yes, sir," said the CQ, standing up and coming to attention.

"I'm with the SJA's office. We're going to the clinic to see some records. Sergeant Dobbs here will let me in."

The moment that the CQ saw Jack beginning to walk around the table, he moved to the bottom of the stairs and blocked their way by holding his hands out like a basketball guard.

"Sir, I've got orders that no one goes to the second floor. CO said no exceptions."

Jack tried to remember how the company commanders he'd dealt with handled insubordination—momentarily surprised, then a tone that was perfectly calm, yet one that made it clear that if this person didn't immediately obey, he would regret the mistake of being born. "Sergeant, I have orders from a general court-martial judge to see those records. I'd suggest that if you want to keep those stripes, you get out of my way."

The CQ wasn't budging. Judging from the deep scars running through his eyebrows and the sharp bend in his nose, he was no stranger to scuffles; he was ready to physically stop them from going any farther, if that was what it took. Faced with contradictory orders from two captains, one of whom he didn't know and was accompanied by a drunk, the CQ could protect himself much better by saying no than by letting them in and answering for it later. Jack had one more trick. If this didn't work, they might as well go home.

Jack took out his pocket notebook and removed a blank page. "If that's the way you want it, Sergeant. I'll need your full name, Social Security number, and unit. I want to make sure the judge has it right for the contempt proceedings."

Jack picked the phone off the desk and began dialing to get an off-post number.

"What are you doing, sir?" the CQ asked.

"Calling the judge to let you explain why you're disobeying a full colonel's order."

Jack got a busy signal and tried again. The sergeant sat down and began slowly writing his name on the paper. Jack got an off-post line, then dialed Larry Sanderford's number.

The CQ finished writing his name and then looked over to Dobbs anxiously. "You'd be with him the entire time, Sergeant Dobbs?"

Dobbs nodded.

Cathy Sanderford answered.

"Sorry to disturb you, ma'am. Could I speak to Judge Sanderford, please."

Cathy laughed and said she'd get her husband.

Jack saw that the CQ hadn't written his unit yet, so he covered the receiver. "Get with it, Sergeant, the judge will—"

"Captain Sanderford speaking."

"Sorry to bother you at home, your Honor, but I'm having some difficulty with an NCO who won't comply with your order on those psychiatric records."

"What are you talking about?" Sanderford said. "Jack, are you drunk?"

"Yes, sir. I told him there was an order."

The CQ stared at the cigarette ad on the back of the *Penthouse*. Jack reached down and flipped the magazine over. He sighed and shook his head, acting as if this was just one more thing the sergeant would have to answer for. Jack prayed that the CQ didn't want to hear all this from the judge himself.

"Yes, sir. I told him he could be placed in jail for contempt."

The CQ looked to Dobbs again for reassurance, then waved his hands, signaling Jack to stop, and mouthed the words, "Go ahead."

"Your Honor, I think we've cleared the problem up. Sorry to have had to bother you. Good night." Jack hung up the phone.

"Sorry, sir. It's just that we've been having—"

Jack didn't wait for him to finish. He grunted as if he were still angry, and motioned for Dobbs to follow him up the stairs. He wanted to get this over with quickly before the CQ became suspicious and called somebody to double-check.

At the top of the stairs, Jack peered around the corner to get a feel for where they were going. The light from the exit signs and fire lights reflecting off the white walls allowed him to make out the sign for the Mental Health Clinic. The fewer lights they had to turn on, the better; he didn't want to give any further explanations of what they were doing. When Dobbs caught up, Jack told him not to turn on the hall lights and motioned for him to unlock the door.

Dobbs took a ring of keys out of his pocket and began fingering through them one at a time, hunting for the door key. He tried several similar-looking keys before he found one that seemed to fit. It wouldn't turn.

"What's the matter?" Jack whispered.

"This frigging lock always gives me trouble."

Great, Jack thought, they weren't even going to be smooth enough to get caught while they were inside. He tried to think what he would tell someone if they came upon them, and realized how lame any excuse would sound.

Dobbs jiggled the key several times and finally got the door open. He walked in and flipped the light on as if it were his living room.

Jack surveyed the clinic and felt a bit envious. Whatever spare money was available in the division for furnishings must have been poured into this office—a Scandinavian oatmeal-colored couch and chairs, teak coffee tables, several framed Klee prints on the wall. Even the office help had the same executive desk and chair that Jack had in his office.

Dobbs was already at the filing cabinets behind his desk, taking off the metal security bar.

"What's this person's name, sir?"

"King, Cindy. She's with the 5th to the 59th ADA."

Dobbs began looking through the Ks.

Sanderford must have thought from their phone conversation that he was on drugs. Jack wasn't sure how he would explain it on Monday.

Dobbs had opened another file drawer and still hadn't found the file. Jack walked over to the file cabinet, started back through the first drawer, and found it immediately.

"I got it," Jack said.

Dobbs looked up, surprised. "Guess I missed it, sir."

Jack pulled out a chair and sat down. "Why don't you stand at the door, in case someone comes up."

Jack opened the file and began reading. The first page was personal history: age—nineteen; parents—divorced; worked as waitress for a year before coming in service. He flipped through several pages until he found the first mention of Frazier's name and started reading closely. The interview horrified him. Sergeant King claimed that Frazier had raped her and that she was pregnant with his child. His eyes moved to the next appointment note.

"Yes," Jack said, leaning back in the chair and raising his hands toward the ceiling as if it were heaven. "Somebody's looking after my boy." He took out his notebook and began scribbling furiously.

"Find what you were looking for?"

Jack didn't answer. He traced his finger down the page as quickly as possible, then went to the next sheet. The doctor had wanted King to press charges against Frazier, and she had admitted that she was lying about the rape so she could have an abortion at the Army hospital. It would not be a pleasant cross-examination, but this was the kind of dirt Jack needed to destroy King's credibility.

He kept reading. At the end of the file was a notation saying that Dresman had called and looked at the records. The bastard knew all about them. He had a duty to reveal this information to the defense! Dresman was more than willing to allow Frazier to go to jail, though he knew King hated him and had lied in the past, and might well be lying about the drug charges.

"Is there a copier here?" Jack asked, looking over to the doorway.

Dobbs gave him a chilly stare. "You didn't say nothing about copying. I can't do that."

He probably didn't have to have a copy. What he would need was some way to call Sergeant King's bluff if she tried denying this stuff. Otherwise, he would be stuck with her answers. He was certain the Whopper would strictly limit him on introducing extrinsic evidence to rebut what she said. Jack began opening the desk drawers, looking for a supply of similar file folders.

"What are you doing?" whispered Dobbs. He was looking at Jack as if he were completely out of his mind.

"I need an empty folder that looks like hers, and some blank intake records."

"Bottom drawer on the right."

Jack took the new file folder, put Sergeant King's name

and unit on it, punched holes in it, and put in enough intake sheets so that it was the same size as the original.

"That wasn't the judge you were talking to, was it?" Dobbs looked at him bewilderedly, as if he had just realized something about what was going on, or maybe something about someone he had trusted.

"No," Jack said as he put Sergeant King's file back in the file cabinet and locked it. He took the new file and stuffed it inside of his raincoat. Finding this new dirt had given him an additional lift and it was just as well, because he still had many long hours ahead tonight preparing his cross-examination questions and changing his closing argument.

Dobbs leaned against the doorjamb, staring at the ceiling. If he passed out, Jack knew there would be no way he could get him back on his feet. But as Jack was about to switch off the lights, Dobbs turned and looked at him with those weird eyes. "Sir, I know it's not my place, but if it were me I wouldn't go through with whatever you're planning to do. I think you're looking at some major-league trouble."

Dobbs's stare gave Jack the heebie-jeebies. No wonder they didn't want this guy working in a place where people came in wondering if they might have a screw loose. Even if a person wasn't crazy when he came in, he might think he was after having Dobbs give him the once-over.

Jack smiled weakly. "The guy will probably still be convicted. Then nobody will care what happened here tonight."

Anne jumped as Jack unlocked the car door and tossed the file and his briefcase into the backseat. She was drinking a beer, which meant she had left the car and gone inside the bar.

"I hope no one saw you," she said, slurring her speech slightly.

Jack decided to let it slide. They were both tired. He couldn't afford to get upset and not be able to concentrate on the work he had left to do.

"How am I ever supposed to recommend therapy to patients if it's not confidential?" she asked.

Jack started to put the car into reverse, then stopped. "What's your problem tonight?"

Anne spun toward him, the nylon of her uniform hissing against the seat cover. "My problem!" Her eyes shot wide open. "I'm not the one breaking into offices and stealing files."

Jack told himself the way to defuse this was to remain calm.

"For starters, I didn't break in. Second, this is just a fake file." He had himself under control until he saw her grimace at his explanation. "Before you get so damn self-righteous about all this, you ought to know that she's been lying her ass off about Frazier. She lied about him raping her just so she could get an abortion. My guess is she's lying about these drug charges, too."

Anne pushed a strand of hair off her forehead. He could see tears beginning to cause her mascara to run. "Jack, when you began practicing, you used to say that ethics kept you above the kind of people you represented. Now you're just like them."

Being tipsy was no excuse for the way she was acting, he told himself. Anne was supposed to be on his side. She had seen him through enough trials to know how cornered he was feeling—how at this point in a trial it seemed like everything in the world was against him.

"You think Dresman gives a damn about the truth?" asked Jack. "He knew Sergeant King's commander had sent her to see a shrink. There's a note in the file that Dresman looked at the records. You know I had my paralegal call her chain of command and they said she's been nothing but a model troop, and *they* were the ones who referred her to Mental Health. You think they're concerned with the *truth*?"

"All I know is that it doesn't make what you're doing right." Her voice had gone to a dull monotone. She looked at him strangely. "What's happened to you?"

Her expression made his heart sink. There had been a glint of recognition that a woman gets when she understands that the man she is with has something so different in his values that spending any more time together would be wasted energy. If they had only been dating it would have been easy enough: fewer phone calls and dates, then drifting into seeing someone else. But this was his wife, someone he had invested five years of marriage in, someone he had wanted to start a family with, and now she was acting as if the person she had been living with no longer existed. He felt abandoned, left to defend himself at the first sign of trouble.

Jack started the car and backed out. He had to put the wall up, not think of his crumbling marriage, if Frazier was going to have any chance of an acquittal. He had to be like the best pro athletes: no matter how screwed-up their personal lives were, when it came game time they could always block out the world and concentrate on winning.

When Jack and Anne came through the door of their apartment, the phone was ringing. Jack didn't intend to answer, but the phone kept ringing. He had two equally disturbing thoughts: Frazier had done something and been caught, or else it was Dobbs.

"Captain Hayes speaking."

"Was that a joke or are you high?" asked Sanderford.

Jack watched Anne go into the bedroom and slam the door. He doubted if he'd be welcome in there tonight. It didn't matter. He would be up all night, getting his cross ready.

"I had to get past a CQ to look at some psychiatric records. I know it's a close call, but I think I'm okay."

"Are you out of your mind?" asked Sanderford.

"That bastard Dresman knew about the records and didn't give them to me. We had a right to them under *Brady.*"

"Jesus Christ, Jack. That's a burglary and probably a theft, and you can bet they'll call it conduct unbecoming an officer."

"The files had clearly exculpatory evidence in them. Dresman had a duty to give them to us."

Sanderford moaned derisively. "Get a hold of the reins, buddy. You've seen how the system works. If the shit hits the fan, they'll ignore Dresman's misconduct and focus on you. I know you like skating on the edge, but you're way out of bounds on this one."

Sanderford's concern worried Jack. But now that he had the evidence, how was he supposed to forget about it?

"I'm not letting Frazier go to jail, when there's evidence to show King's lying. Besides, I've already done it."

"Yeah, but no one needs to know. If you don't bring up the records in court, I doubt anyone will ever find out what you did, or care."

"I didn't take the records. I just looked at them. No one needs to know how I came by the information. For all anyone knows, I could have heard about this from one of her friends. Since I have you on the phone, let me run this by you. You think I can bluff Sergeant King with a fake file jacket—just hold it where she can see it, but not say that I have the records?"

There was a long silence.

"Probably," Sanderford said, his voice still exasperated. "But I wouldn't do it. You're just asking for trouble."

Neither one said anything for a long time. Jack was looking for a way to hang up so he could get to work.

"You're going to do it, aren't you," said Sanderford.

"I don't have any choice."

SIXTEEN

Frazier sat in the room where he and Jack had talked the previous night, reading a pocket Bible. His unit, not even pretending there might be a chance for an acquittal, had forced him to pack his personal belongings into duffel bags so they could take him directly to Mannheim. Jack hoped that Frazier hadn't been wandering the halls with the Bible in hand.

"You haven't been outside with that?" Jack said, pointing to the Bible.

"No," Frazier said, defensively. "What's wrong with reading the Bible? I thought we could use the extra help."

"I don't want the jury thinking she converted you, that's why."

Frazier managed a sorrowful grin. Maybe it was the light, but his hair seemed grayer around the temples today. "Didn't even think of that." He stashed the Bible in his gear and stood up to go to the courtroom. His whole body seemed to sag.

"I guess you weren't able to find any dirt on her?"

"Maybe," Jack said, shaking his hand to indicate that it was questionable at best. "I wouldn't get my hopes up." There was no purpose in telling Frazier about the empty file. The fewer people who had to believe in the ruse, the better.

As Jack was about to open the door, Frazier tapped him on the shoulder. His eyes were teared. "Sir, I'd like to tell you something."

No, Jack thought. Don't tell me you did it, not now when I can't even get you a deal. Why couldn't you have done this when they were dangling the Chapter 10 in front of you yesterday?

Frazier swallowed hard. "Sir, I had some big plans in my life. Even thought they were going to come true." He smiled sadly. "No matter what happens, sir, I want you to know that I think you did a great job for me."

"Thanks," Jack said. He doubted that Frazier would be handing out compliments once the jury came back with their sentence. "We might as well get this goat-rope started."

Other than the additional guard Frazier's unit had sent to escort him to Mannheim and the legal clerk who had been forced to come in to type the confinement order, the gallery was empty. Most people, Jack figured, had decided that the excitement had taken place yesterday and it wasn't worth the hassle getting past the MPs out front.

Sergeant King was standing beside the prosecution table, listening intently to something Dresman said. She seemed to lose her concentration as Jack and Frazier walked in, and she continued watching Jack as he took out his files and set up. From his days as a prosecutor, Jack knew the sorts of things that Dresman had told her about him: "Distrust everything Captain Hayes says or does. Don't be fooled by his being nice, it's just a ploy to get you to let down your guard. Every question he asks will have one purpose, and that's to make you look like a liar."

Jack gave her a polite smile. He had purposely not interviewed her, thinking that the less she knew about what he would ask, the more she could build up in her mind how rough the experience would be. At this point he needed to do everything possible to rattle her, keep her thinking a step behind his.

"Court will come to order," the Whopper said, whacking his gavel hard, once. "Have you had time to interview the witness and her chain of command, Captain Hayes?"

"Yes, your Honor."

"Very well. Sergeant King, if you'll please retake the witness stand, I remind you that you are still under oath."

"Yes, your Honor," she said, sitting down and tugging her skirt over her knees.

She looked very prim, almost spinsterish. She wore flat-soled, patent-leather shoes and had her hair pulled back in a bun. Yesterday the born-again sex kitten, today the professional NCO. He would have to be as careful as someone restoring a valuable painting, delicately removing the alterations until the jury saw the street-tough Cindy King, the Cindy King who had falsely cried rape and aborted Frazier's baby.

Jack took the fake file and legal pad and went to the podium. He took a moment and scanned the jury. They seemed tired and in no mood to listen to a protracted cross-examination. Every question would have to have scalpel-like precision; cut her heart out so gently that she didn't know it was happening until she held it in her hands.

"Sergeant King, you told us yesterday that you've become a born-again Christian, correct?"

"Yes, I've made a personal commitment to Jesus Christ," she said, her voice full of syrupy self-satisfaction.

"And this happened shortly after you left Sergeant Frazier?"

Sergeant King listened to Jack's question, then turned and addressed herself to the president of the panel. Dresman had her well prepared. "Sir, I was very lucky. God saw fit to guide me to the other Christians in my unit. They prayed for me and helped me turn my back on sin."

She was being the perfect politician: reshaping the question so she could do the most damage to Frazier.

"Did this happen a few days later or several months later?"

"Very soon afterward."

"So, around the end of November 1991?"

"Yes."

Jack grimaced, pretending that he didn't believe her. "Are you certain of that?"

"Absolutely," she said. "I went to church the Sunday after Thanksgiving and our pastor made a Call. I went forward that evening and let Jesus come into my life."

Jack had what he needed. She had locked herself into changing her life and values before she had seen the psychiatrist and begun lying about Frazier. Jack was ready to change the tenor of his questioning.

"Sergeant King, you were in love with Sergeant Frazier, weren't you?"

"I thought I was."

"You believed he would marry you, didn't you?" He moved away from the podium and stood within arm's length of her on the dais.

"On the day I cleared the drugs out of Sergeant Frazier's apartment, I talked to Sergeant Babcock's wife, Margaret. She told me Billy had been lying about that all along. That he would never remarry."

Jack cradled his legal pad with the mental health file on top so that it was facing her. He tried to draw her attention to the file by extending his arm a little, but she ignored him.

"And you were broken up about this when you discovered Sergeant Frazier wouldn't marry you, weren't you?"

"No," she said, maintaining her cheery smile. "In fact, I look on it as a blessing. It forced me out of the unsanctified life I was leading."

Unless Jack wanted to hear this tape all afternoon, he had to get her to notice the file. If he could just crack the facade, he was confident that the real Cindy King wasn't far below the surface.

"Sergeant King . . ." Jack pretended to lose his train of thought so he would be forced to look at his notes. He lifted the file and turned the page on his legal pad. "Sergeant King, you asked for a transfer from Hanau, didn't you?"

"Yes . . . ," she said hesitantly. Her eyes were trained on the pink records jacket. Jack saw a shadow of panic pass over her face at the moment she must have seen her name on the file.

"And once you arrived at your new unit in Giessen, you began to have trouble, didn't you?"

"I don't know what you mean," she said. Her eyes darted to the prosecution table, a mixture of distress and rage, trying to let Dresman know something had gone horribly wrong.

Jack walked casually back to the defense table and stood behind Frazier. He wanted Sergeant King to have to look at

Frazier every time she answered him. Then, any of the anger she might show toward him would seem to be directed at Frazier.

"You don't?" Jack said, making his voice sound as if she had forgotten something as simple as her birthday. "Isn't it true, Sergeant King, that you had emotional problems after you transferred to your new unit?"

Dresman was instantly out of his chair. "Objection, your Honor. That's privileged information that has nothing to do with this case."

"Captain Hayes." The Whopper seemed to be using only one eye to scrutinize him. "Before you go any further with these questions, I'd like to get some idea of where this might be leading. The fact that the witness has gone to Mental Health isn't a proper matter for impeachment."

"Certainly, your Honor. I can tie it directly to her lying about my client."

The Whopper drew in his chin and seemed to shrug this basis off as being silly. "Just because she may have lied on one occasion in the past doesn't mean you can impeach her with it. The prosecution hasn't put on any character witnesses bolstering her truthfulness." DiMarco paused a moment, jutting his lower lip forward. "If that's the nature of the cross, I'm inclined not to allow it."

Jack's mind raced through the rules of evidence—crimes, felonies punishable by a year or more, crimes that demonstrated a lack of truthfulness. She hadn't signed the statements, so it wasn't a false official statement. His instincts told him this dirt was usable, and now he was squandering it because he hadn't thought through the proper legal basis for getting it admitted as evidence. He'd been so excited about discovering her lies that he had forgotten to plot out the arguments for admissibility.

He should have known this might happen after he'd seen what a stickler the Whopper had been on his motion to go to Amsterdam. Calm down, he told himself. Go through the list: motive, admissions against interest, bias . . .

"Your Honor, what she said to the psychiatrist will show the bias she has against my client."

DiMarco took a deep breath that turned into an exasperated sigh. Jack knew that DiMarco still wanted to prevent the questions and was weighing whether his denial was reversible error. After consulting his judge's desk book, he addressed Jack. "I'll tell you up front, Captain Hayes, I'm *very, very* skeptical of this type of evidence. I'll give you a few more questions. But if you don't tie it directly to what she's saying in this case, I'm going to stop you."

"Thank you, your Honor," Jack said. He tried to settle his nerves so he wouldn't blow the questions themselves. "Sergeant King, you—"

The Whopper interrupted. "Another thing, Captain Hayes. I want you to know that I'm strictly limiting you to her answers. If she denies these matters, I'm not letting you introduce extrinsic evidence, such as the mental health records themselves, to disprove what she said. Do you understand that?"

"Yes, your Honor."

Sergeant King was mouthing "He has my records" to Dresman, who was in turn signaling for her to stop whispering. Even if the prosecution asked for a recess, the Whopper probably wouldn't give it to them during cross. And even if he did, Dresman had to know how bad it would look to the jury that her story was so weak she had to have breaks to be told what to say by the prosecutor.

Jack was terrified that she might have understood the significance of what the Whopper said. If she did, it meant she could deny everything Jack asked and there wouldn't be anything he could do about it. Even if she actually perjured herself on the stand, Jack's experience had been that the government would deny having prior knowledge about what was actually in the records, not prosecute her, and Frazier would spend two or three years in jail waiting for an appeals court to *maybe* order a new trial.

"You began seeing a psychiatrist after you broke things off with Sergeant Frazier, didn't you?" Jack asked.

Sergeant King glared at Dresman as if he should stop all this immediately. Dresman must have promised her that no one would find out about the records.

"Yes," she answered tentatively.

"You were sent by your battery commander several weeks after you arrived, weren't you?"

"I don't remember."

This was exactly what he feared—denials or worse, these "don't remembers" with no way to call her bluff. He had to act confident, as if at any minute he might walk up to her, thrust the records into her hands, and make her read to the jury what she'd told the shrink. Jack opened the bogus records and pretended to read from the sheet. "It was the twentieth of December, wasn't it?"

"Objection, your Honor," Dresman said. "The question has been asked and answered. She says she doesn't remember."

"Sustained," said the Whopper.

All Jack's neat groundwork was crumbling. The Whopper and Dresman were going to gang up on him, and none of this would get in. It wouldn't take long for Sergeant King to catch on to what she needed to say, if she hadn't already figured it out.

"But you remember the exact date you were born again, don't you?"

"That was important," she said, trying to affect the cheesy smile she'd worn earlier.

"And in fact you were pregnant at the time with Sergeant Frazier's child—the twentieth of December, wasn't it?"

"Argumentative and not relevant, your Honor," said Dresman.

"Sustained."

"On what grounds?" Jack shouted. "She's intentionally being obtuse."

DiMarco took off his glasses and looked sternly at Jack. "I'll not have you yelling, Captain Hayes." The calmness in his voice made Jack's outburst seem all the more foolish. "Another temper tantrum like that, and I'll hold you in contempt. The question as you phrased it was argumentative."

"I apologize, your Honor." Craft the question so there's

no way but for her to answer yes or no, Jack told himself. You can't afford to let her and the jury see that you're struggling.

"You were pregnant with Sergeant Frazier's child on the twentieth of December, weren't you?"

"I don't remember," Sergeant King said.

If she wanted to play dumb, he'd widen the snare a little, imply that she was intentionally having a lapse of memory. "All right," he said, calmly, "you were pregnant with his child after you left Hanau, weren't you?"

"It could have been his, I'm not sure."

Good, Jack thought. The more she taunted Frazier with these cheap shots, the better it would fit into his argument that she hated him so much she would say or do anything to hurt him.

Sergeant King turned and looked pleadingly at the Whopper. "Your Honor, I was told that what I said to the doctor was confidential. How can he ask me about this?"

"Your Honor, this is relevant to show the lengths this witness has gone to in order to retaliate against my client since he dumped her."

"That's a lie!" Sergeant King yelled.

"Sergeant King, I'm warning you too," said the Whopper, "that I'll not have any more outbursts in my courtroom. If the question is improper, I'll not require you to answer it. Otherwise, you have a duty to answer."

Sergeant King fixed Jack with a look of revulsion.

"I'll repeat the question, your Honor. You were pregnant with Sergeant Frazier's child, correct, Sergeant King?"

"Maybe, I'm not sure it was his."

She was furious, wanting to hurt Frazier any way she could. She had apparently realized that she was on her own, that all the lawyers in this room were her enemies, in one form or another.

"You got pregnant, thinking this would force Sergeant Frazier to marry you, right?"

She tossed her head back and made a scoffing sound. "You gotta be kidding," she said. "You think I'd want that creep's kid? If I wanted to be barefoot and pregnant, I could have stayed in my hometown. My diaphragm had a hole in it."

The jury was finally seeing the Cindy King that Frazier had lived with. Jack needed to stay calm and goad her into making another outburst.

"But when Sergeant Frazier said it was over, you didn't want the baby because you were afraid your new commander would discharge you?"

"I wasn't about to let that happen."

"That's right, so you started acting nuts so you'd be sent to the mental health clinic. You'd already planned to get an abortion, hadn't you?"

"I don't remember."

Jack flipped over several sheets and glanced at the blank page. "You told Doctor Pangborn on the twenty-eighth of December that you were pregnant and wanted an abortion because your former boyfriend, Sergeant Frazier, had raped you, didn't you?"

"I don't know."

"Doctor Pangborn wanted you to press charges, didn't he?"

"Yes, but I told him I wasn't interested."

"You told Dr. Pangborn this initially because you found out that's what the Army required, that they didn't give abortions by choice, only in the cases of rape and incest, but you never thought they'd want you to press charges. You hated Sergeant Frazier, but you knew that this claim would never hold up in court, didn't you?"

Jack could see her lip buckling, her jaw quivering, as she tried to keep the tears back. There was a long silence as she gazed at the floor. When it became apparent she wasn't going to answer, the Whopper intervened.

"Please answer the question, Sergeant King," said the Whopper.

"All right, I had an abortion from a German doctor. Are you satisfied?" She was clenching her jaw muscles, but tears started down her cheeks.

Jack had to be very careful not to allow this to backfire and to be used to get sympathy from the jury. He was finished pressing. From here on out, the questions were more important than her answers.

[183]

"And when you started thinking about other ways to get back at Sergeant Frazier, you figured since two other people said he was a drug dealer, you could, too?"

She was shaking her head adamantly. "You've twisted everything around to make me look like the bad one, when it's really him," she said, using the back of her hand to wipe away the tears.

Dresman was standing, looking very concerned. "Your Honor, counsel is badgering—"

"You're as bad as him," she said to Dresman between a sniffle. "You told me none of this would come out."

"Your Honor," Jack said as politely as possible. "I'd respectfully ask that she be required to answer the questions."

"Sergeant King, you chose to come forward with this information without exercising your Article 31 rights, so there is no legal basis for not answering the question," said DiMarco.

"Fine," she said. "I'm sick of this whole thing. If I'm gonna be persecuted, I want a lawyer."

Jack tossed the legal pad and file down in mock outrage. "Your Honor, then I'd ask that all her testimony be struck and the jury told to totally disregard all of her testimony in this case."

Before Jack could stop him, Dresman reached over and took the fake file off the defense table and began paging through it.

"It's not her file," Dresman said, his voice raising an octave with each word. "Your Honor, this is completely unethical."

"I resent him making that accusation in front of the jury," Jack said. Dresman was trying the oldest trick in the world: distracting the jury's attention from what had just been said by creating a scene and blaming the defense.

"Approach the bench," the Whopper said. "And, Major Dresman, bring whatever Captain Hayes was reading from with you."

Dresman was still paging through the blank file, mumbling about slimy defense tricks as they huddled at the sidebar.

"So what's going on here, Captain Hayes?"

"Your Honor, I resent the accusation that my cross-examination was in any way unethical. I never said that I had her records. She just thought I did. None of what I asked her wasn't true. If anyone has been unethical, it's been the prosecution. He had a duty to reveal that information for impeachment."

"We never knew anything about it," Dresman said, as hatefully as possible.

Jack began to say that he'd seen the records, then stopped and took the safe approach. He certainly didn't want to explain how he had gained access to the clinic last night. "That's why she said you promised her it wouldn't be brought up."

"I had no idea—"

"That's enough," said the Whopper. "These proceedings aren't the proper place to determine whether what Captain Hayes did was improper or not. Quite frankly, Major Dresman, I can think of several bases off the top of my head to justify it—a witness's recollection can be refreshed with anything. A blank piece of paper will do. The matter before me is whether her testimony should be stricken. Do you have anything to say on it, Major Dresman?"

"Your Honor, anything she hasn't answered is tangential and doesn't justify striking her testimony."

"Captain Hayes?"

The military appellate courts were divided on this issue, and the military's highest court, the Court of Military Appeals, had not ruled on it. Given these facts, Jack knew that what he would say would be for Frazier's appellate lawyer. The Whopper was going to deny the motion.

"Her failure to answer goes to the heart of everything she says. If it's not stricken, the jury gets the impression that everything else she testified about—such as giving Frazier information and going to his house—is true."

The Whopper listened closely and smiled. "Are you saying that you want to cross-examine her about going to Frazier's apartment and removing the drugs?"

"No, your Honor." The Whopper had been through enough trials to know that *this* wasn't the way to discredit her testimony. He also knew that Jack wasn't about to go back over that ground and reinforce it for the jury. DiMarco was guaranteeing there would be no issue for an appeal.

"I realize the case law is divided in this area, Captain Hayes, but I have always been one to let the jury hear as much testimony as possible and let them decide what weight to give it. I'll give a very favorable defense instruction, cautioning the members to be very wary of all that she said. It will also give your client a good issue on appeal."

"Your Honor, he'll sit in Leavenworth three years before it will be ruled on by the appeals court. That's not right."

"I've made my ruling. Step back."

On the way to their tables, Dresman turned to Jack. "He may think that what you did was okay, but I think it was completely unethical."

Jack could care less what Dresman thought. What he was worried about was the jury. None of them seemed pleased with Sergeant King. She was an NCO, albeit a buck sergeant, who hadn't been truthful and who, by crying, hadn't acted like a soldier.

"Any redirect, Major Dresman?"

"No, your Honor."

"Other rebuttal witnesses?"

"The prosecution rests."

Sergeant King stared numbly at the floor. Jack knew he should have been pleased. He had destroyed her credibility, reduced her to a vengeful bitch. But as he sat and watched her, Jack felt hollow, as if he had destroyed something in himself that he would never get back.

SEVENTEEN

"Mr. Prosecutor, are you ready with your closing argument?" asked the Whopper.

"Yes, your Honor."

Dresman walked to the podium carrying his legal pad and calmly laid it down. He was actually allowed two closings: this statement and a rebuttal to what Jack said. Dresman would be short and sweet this first time, then try to bury Jack in rebuttal when the defense couldn't respond.

He gripped the corners of the lectern and put on a stern expression, looking as if he were about to deliver the final sermon on good and evil.

"Sergeant Frazier," Dresman said, glancing back over his shoulder in the direction of the defense table and acting as if even this acknowledgment that Frazier was something more than a thing, *the defendant,* pained him, "has not once made the claim that the prosecution has failed to prove its case. Instead, he has, through his counsel, attempted to confuse you with points that are totally irrelevant to guilt or innocence.

"What must the government prove to establish the defendant's guilt? First, that the substances alleged in the charges were marijuana in the hashish form and cocaine. You don't even need to worry about that element because the defense has stipulated as a *fact* that the drugs seized were hashish and cocaine.

"Second, the government must prove that Sergeant Frazier agreed with another person to carry out a criminal act.

Once again, your decision isn't difficult. In Sergeant Babcock's Article 32 testimony he stated that Lieutenant McCormick recruited him to find a major drug supplier, and that man is sitting right there," he said, pointing to Frazier, "the defendant. Next, McCormick told you about the scheme to bring the drugs back. The defendant bought the hashish and cocaine in Amsterdam, Babcock delivered these illegal substances to one of McCormick's men at the Amsterdam *bahnhof*, then McCormick transported the drugs across the border and his men sold them. Later, Babcock returned the profits to the defendant.

"There is nothing complicated to decide in this trial. Listen to the judge's instructions on what elements the government must prove, trust your common sense, and there is only one verdict that is possible—guilty of all specifications and charges. Thank you."

Dresman was right; the government had made out a case for Frazier's guilt. Luckily for the defense, that wasn't enough. Not only did the government have to prove that Frazier was guilty, but guilty beyond a reasonable doubt. Lay people always thought a not-guilty verdict meant that the accused was innocent. Nothing could be further from the truth. In the military, all the not-guilty verdict means is that the defense had convinced more than one-third of the jurors to have reasonable doubt about guilt. In the space of an hour, Jack would have to make three of the jurors decide that it was easier on their consciences to let Frazier off than to worry about having made the mistake of sending an innocent man to jail.

"Is the defense ready to close?" asked the Whopper.

"Yes, your Honor."

Jack put his notes on the podium, then moved away so that he was standing directly in front of the president of the panel. He tried to take on an expression serious enough that the jury would sense the importance of what they were about to decide, but not so serious that he appeared to be worrying about a hopeless cause.

"Before the prosecution can take a soldier's liberty away," Jack said, "it is not enough to just prove the elements of the offenses. They must prove these extremely serious charges beyond a reasonable doubt. That, as you'll remember from our conversation during *voir dire*, is how our great system of military justice differs from the railroad jobs people get in some countries. In our system of justice, it is not enough to pull a couple of felons in and offer them deals to testify against someone. Our system requires good, decent, and believable evidence—proof beyond a reasonable doubt.

"What do these words mean? I realize that it's not a term that we use in our everyday speech. You don't say to your spouse, 'Honey, I have reasonable doubt whether we should go to the PX today . . .' "

The jurors smiled.

"You will," Jack continued, "have guidance from Judge DiMarco that will help you understand this term. The judge will tell you that reasonable doubt is a doubt that would cause you to hesitate to act in the more weighty affairs of your life. What's an example of that?"

Jack had noticed at the beginning of the trial that all but the lieutenant wore the ice-cream cone and wings above their left breast pocket, indicating they were crazy enough to jump out of a perfectly good airplane. Jack wanted them all thinking about a situation where a doubt took on the importance of life and death.

"I see that most of you are airborne qualified. It seems reasonable to say that whether your parachute is properly packed is one of the weighty affairs of your life. With that as our standard, let's look at the government's parachute packers.

"The first is Lieutenant McCormick. Here is a convicted felon serving ninety-nine years. Here is a man who blew up the MP Station in Frankfurt, nearly killing two MPs, and who was ready to kill German *polizei* merely because they stopped him. Does he mention Sergeant Frazier in his first sworn statement?"

Jack paused and let the answer form in the jurors' minds.

"Does Lieutenant McCormick know the address of the drug connection he supposedly buys from Sergeant Frazier for fifty thousand dollars?" He shook his head, trying to appear exasperated.

"As we go through these points, I remind you that you only need to have one reasonable doubt to vote not-guilty. You will be given many grounds for reasonable doubt, but you only need to be convinced by one of them to acquit Sergeant Frazier."

Jack eyed each of the jurors. He was searching for anyone that might seem the least bit interested, so that he could focus on them. They listened closely, but it was impossible to tell yet what they were thinking.

"When does Lieutenant McCormick make his statement implicating Sergeant Frazier? On the night he tells you he fears that the *polizei* will kill him if he isn't truthful? No. Lieutenant McCormick comes up with this story *six months* after he's received what amounts to a life sentence and wants the convening authority to look favorably on him. And when Babcock is killed, he refuses to testify until his sentence is cut to thirty years." Jack stopped and shook his head.

"And what about the other government parachute packer—Sergeant Babcock. You didn't even see this witness. But the piece of paper you have in front of you tells the story. Here is another convicted felon who is at least forthright enough to admit that he is receiving a cut in his sentence to say that Sergeant Frazier is guilty. Under what circumstances does he make his statement implicating Sergeant Frazier? He was a new father. His wife was threatening divorce if he went to jail for years. Faced with this threat, he had to come up with someone's name who was higher up in the drug organization. It didn't matter whether this person actually existed. The government thought there were others involved and wanted names. So the prosecution threw Babcock a lifeline, a way out. Ask yourself, what *wouldn't* a man be willing to do or say under those circumstances?"

Jack held his hands palms up, and shrugged.

"The judge will instruct you that McCormick and Babcock are what the law calls accomplices—that is, they are involved in an offense with which the accused is charged. His Honor will tell you"—Jack picked up his pad and read the language of the jury instruction—"that 'the testimony of an accomplice, even though apparently credible, is of questionable integrity and should be considered with great caution and given only such weight and credibility as you deem it deserves.' Haven't we seen clear evidence in this courtroom why that should be the case?"

Jack stepped back to the spot where Franz Kooij had stood when McCormick tried to identify him.

"Remember when Mr. Franz Kooij, the supposed Amsterdam drug connection, the man whom the government assured us their witnesses could identify, came face to face with McCormick?" Jack looked at the witness stand and back to where Kooij had stood. "You saw the look on Major Dresman's face when that happened. And yet the prosecutor wants you to take away this soldier's liberty." Jack turned, looked at Dresman, then shook his head in incredulity. "One doubt." He held up his index finger. "One doubt is all any of you need in order to say not-guilty."

Jack took a drink of water to give the idea time to germinate. He started again, in a calm businesslike tone. "It is easy to see why Sergeant Babcock came up with this lie. He had been to Amsterdam with Sergeant Frazier at the time when Sergeant Frazier bought his car. He had been assured that this case would probably never be contested. Why not give Sergeant Frazier's name to the prosecution? But what neither Babcock nor McCormick expected was that Sergeant Frazier and I would go to Amsterdam and find this supposed drug connection. What the government and its two felons underestimated was how hard an innocent man will fight to make sure you know the truth. Every one of us in this room saw the difference between the truth and a lie when McCormick tried to identify Franz Kooij.

"At that moment," Jack turned and pointed at Dresman, "the prosecutor experienced every parachutist's nightmare—a streamer. Major Dresman looked up and there was no canopy, just a long tapeworm spindling above him, and the ground coming up at a hundred and fifty miles per hour. He had made the mistake of trusting the wrong parachute packers.

"So what does the prosecutor do? He panics. He starts

clutching for a reserve chute. Sergeant Cindy King. He thinks she will save him. And when you first heard her testimony, you might have thought the same thing. Sergeant King *appeared* to be the answer to all his problems. She was a born-again Christian and seemed unimpeachable. She explained why there were no drugs in Sergeant Frazier's apartment when CID searched. She explained why there were no records of drug dealing. She explained how Sergeant Frazier supposedly knew who not to sell drugs to. She appeared to be the lifesaver a parachutist wears in case the main chute fails. But her testimony was like a lot of things salesmen will tell us in desperation—an unbelievably good deal until you ask some questions about the product.

"Because under cross-examination, we saw that the reserve chute hadn't been properly packed, either. Sergeant King's story, the government's last hope, wasn't canopying the way it should have. You watched during her cross-examination as she became tangled in the lines and risers of her own lies. Here was a young woman who was bitter about being dumped by Sergeant Frazier. Here was an NCO"—Jack raised his eyebrows to indicate that he was using the term loosely—"who was willing to lie and claim she had been raped by Sergeant Frazier in order to get an abortion. Members of the jury, if during deliberations someone says that Sergeant King is worthy of belief because she is a born-again Christian, remember that here was a person willing to kill an unborn child just because that infant didn't fit into her *career* plans. For the kind of person who calls herself one thing and lives another kind of life, what is one more lie?"

One of the NCOs was shaking his head in agreement. Jack needed to find the right button on two others.

"If you were disturbed by my cross-examination of Sergeant King, hold it against me, not Sergeant Frazier. All I ask is that you keep in mind that it was necessary in order to show you the truth. To show you that this was a woman motivated by hate and anger. That this was a woman who saw a chance to hurt Sergeant Frazier because he had dumped her. That here was an NCO who, when pressed about the truth, hid behind the Fifth Amendment and wanted to play lawyer games with us." Jack pointed to himself, hoping the jury would see his fight with her as just trying to help them.

"The prosecutor believed Sergeant King, and look what happened. Major Dresman pulled for his reserve chute in desperation, and instead of a lifesaver, he found that he'd become tangled up with a liar and had no choice but to ride it down."

Jack paused a moment and then flinched ever so slightly to make the jury think about hitting the ground.

"The prosecutor has already jumped. You don't have to make that same mistake. In a few minutes, Major Dresman will ask you to hook up to his static line and watch for the green light above the bay door. When he does this, you should not only think about who your parachute packers have been, but also about the soldier whose life you will affect forever. You will have to decide whether the lies of two convicted felons and a scorned lover mean more than the word of a soldier with fifteen years of honorable service, a soldier who has bled for his country, a soldier who—as Major Davis told you—'if the balloon went up tomorrow, you'd want a company of Sergeant Fraziers in your unit.' To believe the prosecutor's witnesses, you'll have to conclude that Sergeant Frazier is a millionaire who, when faced with the possibility of going to jail for years, doesn't have the funds to hire the best civilian defense lawyer money can buy. To believe the government's witnesses, you will have to conclude that Sergeant Frazier is smart enough to be the mastermind behind a million-dollar drug ring, but stupid enough to allow his apartment to be searched, to allow his bank records to be audited, and most importantly, to continue traveling to Amsterdam after his supervisor, Major Davis, tells him he is being watched by CID. If you can believe that Sergeant Frazier is as shrewd as the government paints him to be and yet did these things, then you should convict.

"The prosecutor has already stepped past the point of no return and had his chute fail. You seven jurors are in a different position—you've had the opportunity to see who your parachute packers are. Think about them."

Jack tried to call up the look he would have at the funeral

of a close relative. He stood there for thirty seconds, not saying a word.

"If you're hesitating at this moment, you have reasonable doubt. Make a decision that will not haunt you in the weeks to come. When the prosecutor asks you to make a jump that will turn into fifteen seconds of panic and become the biggest mistake of your life, tell him no. Come back to this courtroom and tell him that before the military justice system sends someone to jail, it takes believable evidence from better people than he's scrounged up. Show him that American justice is not like those kangaroo trials we saw in Kuwait. Tell him in the simplest, yet the best way our system allows. Tell him with dignity and pride. Tell him not-guilty.

"Thank you."

Jack had managed to raise goose bumps on his own arms, his personal test of whether the closing had been emotional enough. It was an argument that didn't give the jury much leeway: they either disbelieved the government witnesses and acquitted, or bought the witnesses' stories despite the problems and came back and slam-dunked Frazier.

"Mr. Prosecutor, rebuttal?" asked the Whopper.

"Yes, sir," Dresman said.

Dresman and his paralegal carried from the back of the courtroom an easel with a large art pad resting on it, which they then set up facing the jury. Dresman stood tapping a magic marker nervously against his palm and began.

"The defense's closing can be summed up in this manner." Dresman moved to the easel and wrote in large letters on the art pad: SMOKE. "They've put up a smoke screen to prevent you from seeing the defendant's guilt. They figure that if they make things hazy enough, you will give up. The government has too much confidence in your ability as jurors to think you'd be fooled by this ploy.

"The defense doesn't want you to be satisfied beyond a reasonable doubt, they expect proof beyond any shadow of a doubt. The defendant is like the man who claims that the world is flat. He thinks by making this claim, regardless of the overwhelming evidence to the contrary, his saying the earth is flat should cause you to have doubt. If you followed

Captain Hayes's theory, no criminal would ever be convicted. So long as the defense could raise some spurious issue for you to chase, they would have you let the most heinous criminals go free. This is not the standard the government must meet, nor is it the test you should use in finding the defendant guilty."

Dresman looked back to Jack, presumably to make him embarrassed. Jack continued counting the stars in the American flag behind the Whopper, acting as if what was being said had no relevance to Frazier's guilt or innocence.

"If you analyze what Captain Hayes says, you will soon realize that it does not deal with what the government must prove. Listen to the elements of the offenses. There is nothing in them that requires the government's witnesses to identify the drug source. Think about it. This is the only flaw the defense can find. It's something to divert your attention from what's been proven." Dresman pointed to his easel. "Smoke to hide the defendant's guilt. The defendant wants you to forget about the odd coincidences in this case. For example, that Babcock told the accused he was being pressured by Lieutenant McCormick to find a major drug supplier. He wants you to not think about the *coincidence* that the accused and Sergeant Babcock started making trips to Amsterdam shortly after this conversation. The defendant wants you to forget that he has a civilian passport for travel purposes, when he could have gone to Amsterdam on leave papers and his ID card. All of Captain Hayes's eloquence about parachute packers is nothing more than smoke to make you forget the hard facts that prove the defendant's guilt.

"The defense wants you to disbelieve the testimony of Sergeant King. Once again, listen and think about Captain Hayes's argument. He never once refutes what Sergeant King tells you about her removing the drugs or destroying the defendant's drug records. The defendant claims he wants to be open and honest with you. If so, why didn't he tell you about his relationship with Sergeant King when he was on the witness stand. Why didn't he retake the witness stand in rebuttal and deny using cocaine and hash with her?

"All Captain Hayes wants," Dresman continued, "is for

you to be concerned with whether or not Sergeant King had an abortion. Regardless of where you stand on this emotional issue, it is not relevant to Sergeant King's testimony. That kind of argument is simply more smoke to divert your attention from the defendant's guilt.

"The government is confident that you'll see through this smoke screen. There should never be any fear or doubt when it comes to doing your duty. Convict the defendant of all charges and specifications.

"Thank you."

Dresman's rebuttal had hit every weak link in their case. If any of the jurors wanted to convict, he had given them plenty of justification.

There were parts of every witness's story, including Frazier's, that didn't make sense or seemed less than truthful. Some people might think that this kind of disorder worked to the defendant's benefit—that if the jury couldn't figure out what happened, they would become frustrated and acquit. In Jack's experience, it had just the opposite effect. He had seen plenty of juries get fed up and convict because they figured the defendant was involved in enough dirt that, even if he hadn't committed the crime for which he was being tried, he had done others for which he hadn't been caught and punished.

Jack shifted in his chair, trying to get comfortable for DiMarco's jury instructions. He wished it were possible for him to go home and let the jury write him a letter with its decision. The hours that were to follow would be the worst part of the trial—the long wait for a verdict.

EIGHTEEN

Jack had told Frazier that if the jury was out longer than forty-five minutes, there was little chance for an acquittal. Military juries usually knew before they entered deliberations whether they planned to let the defendant go. If that wasn't in the cards, they started the slow process of discussing, then voting on the charges and specifications, one by one. The Whopper had taken an hour for his instructions, then given everyone an early dinner break. The jury had been deliberating for three hours with no sign that they were close to reaching a verdict. Jack's hunch was that they were working through the lesser included offenses—possession or use as a compromise to sale.

At eight P.M. there was a stir outside the courtroom. The Whopper lumbered in, putting his arms into his robe as he moved to the bench. Dresman was at his heels, looking as worried and exhausted as Jack felt. Jack motioned for his paralegal to go find Frazier.

"Looks like they have a question about something," said DiMarco, as he climbed to the bench. "You know, Captain Hayes, it probably wouldn't be a bad idea to go through the preliminary matters on sentencing with your client, just in case."

"Yes, your Honor." Just in case, my ass, Jack thought. He had never had a case in which it boded well for the defendant if the jury wanted to ask questions. The only thing that ever seemed to get clarified was the defendant's guilt.

As they waited for Frazier, the Whopper said, "Captain Hayes, I've been thinking about your defense. If it had been me, I believe I would have rested after the government's case. Not put on a defense. You could have avoided all of Sergeant King's testimony."

Everyone wanted to be the critic, especially when they'd seen the results. If he were forced to make the decision again, Jack was sure he would have done the same thing. Any lawyer who wanted to survive doing defense work had to learn to go with his instincts and not worry about it later. With what he had known at the time, it had made sense to put Frazier on the stand.

"I kind of locked myself in after the opening, your Honor," Jack said.

The Whopper grinned, full of self-satisfaction. "That's the problem with making an opening argument instead of a brief statement."

Frazier came in and stood at attention. Jack was glad he hadn't heard all this second-guessing, since it was just the sort of talk that made a client think about claiming ineffective assistance of counsel on appeal.

"What's going on, sir?" Frazier asked.

"The jury has a question."

"What does it mean—"

Jack cut him off as the jury filed in and took their seats. Jack tried to read from their faces what this was about. Two of the enlisted men and the lieutenant appeared very unhappy.

"Court will come to order. Let the record reflect that all parties, including the members, are present," said Dresman.

"Colonel Hodgini, the bailiff indicates the members have a question," said the Whopper.

"Yes, your Honor," Colonel Hodgini said. "We'd like to know whether we could consider Sergeant Frazier's adultery as a charge."

Despite everything the Whopper had said, this uncharged misconduct was playing a part in the outcome of the trial. *You will not see a red barn.*

"Mr. President," the Whopper said, his voice full of irritation, "as I previously instructed you, that is uncharged misconduct. It is to be considered *only* for the limited purpose of whether Sergeant Frazier made the alleged admissions to Sergeant King."

Colonel Hodgini listened intently, but still seemed unsatisfied. "Your Honor, we realize that. But we'd like to know if we could prefer it as a separate charge on our own. We've already voted on the drug charges—"

DiMarco's face registered shock, then he immediately stopped Colonel Hodgini. "You've already voted on all the charges and specifications?"

"Yes, your Honor."

Jesus, thought Jack, it wasn't bad enough to hammer him with 120 years' worth of drug charges. Now the bastards wanted to tack on adultery too. As if it would make a difference. Adultery was the antiquated military offense usually reserved for ruining officers' careers. Jack had never seen anything more than an Article 15 given for this "crime." If the jury wished, it was possible to give a year for the offense.

"If you voted, that's it. You can't add charges under any circumstances." The Whopper thought a moment and said, "Unless you want to reconsider your vote on the drug charges, there's nothing left for you to decide on the merits."

Colonel Hodgini looked to Captain May, and they nodded in agreement. The same enlisted men and the lieutenant seemed furious. "Yes, we'd like to reconsider."

The only thing Jack knew to think was that they had believed some of what Sergeant King said and compromised down to a possession and use charge. The higher-ranking officers must have been dissatisfied and wanted to hit Frazier with some more time.

The Whopper dug out his military judge's guide from his salesman's case and began looking for the proper instruction. "All right," he said, finding the exact place he wanted to start, "the court may reconsider any finding before it is formally announced in open court. The court may also reconsider any finding of guilty on its own motion at any time before it has first announced the sentence. A reballot shall be taken of a prior not-guilty finding when a majority of the members vote in favor thereof. A reballot shall be taken on a prior guilty finding if more than one-third of the members favor reballoting. Thus, as there are seven members, five must vote in favor of a reconsideration of a prior not-guilty finding and three must vote in favor of a reconsideration of a prior finding of guilty."

Jack had never heard this instruction given before in a case. The only bright spot he could see was that if there were three jurors who were going for the possession charges as a compromise, they could prevent the others from coming back with a guilty verdict on the remaining charges.

"Any questions?" asked the Whopper.

They all shook their heads.

As the jurors were filing out again, Frazier asked, "What's this mean?"

"My guess is they are fighting over the lesser included offenses," Jack said.

Frazier rubbed the material at the edge of his coat furiously between his fingers. He must have realized that he was in a situation that he couldn't talk himself out of. His last chance to beat the odds had ended the previous night, when the prosecution had taken away his ID card and passport.

The Whopper motioned for everyone to be seated. "Sergeant Frazier, I'm not predicting the outcome, but I'd like to go through the rights you have during sentencing, just in case it comes to that."

"Yes, sir," Frazier said.

The Whopper had on his reading glasses, but he had recited this portion of the boilerplate so many times that he was not even bothering to look at his bench book. "Sergeant Frazier, you have the right to put on extenuation and mitigation evidence. Extenuation evidence is a means of explaining the reasons you committed the crime. Mitigation evidence is your prior record—efficiency, fidelity, courage, bravery, or other traits that characterize a good soldier . . ."

Jack was uncertain whether Frazier was taking anything in, though he was nodding every time the Whopper asked if he understood. If the jury convicted, there wasn't much need to put on additional evidence. They had heard about Frazier's record during the trial, and any apology for committing the

[200]

offenses would just make them angry for having been lied to under oath.

The Whopper was going through the accused's right to make a sworn and unsworn statement, when the bailiff poked his head in the courtroom and said the jury was ready. They had been out less than five minutes.

"We'll finish this after they announce their verdict, if necessary," said the Whopper.

The members filed back in. Jack thought something was different. Then he noticed they were all wearing their jackets and had their hats with them. He had a flash that this meant they had decided to acquit, didn't believe it, and immediately put it out of his mind.

"Have you reached your findings, Colonel Hodgini?" asked the Whopper.

"Yes, your Honor."

"Very well, Mr. Prosecutor, will you please take the findings work sheet from the president and, without looking at it, bring it to me."

Dresman retrieved the folded papers and gave them to the Whopper. The judge looked the sheets over for a long time, examining each page. He handed them back to Dresman and told him to return them to the president of the panel.

"Will the accused and counsel please rise and face the jury."

Jack and Frazier stood at attention and made sharp left faces. He had told Frazier to act like a soldier no matter what happened and not make any outburst. They still had sentencing to go through and any demonstration about the verdict would just make the jury feel more justified in piling on the time. Jack could feel his shirt sticking to his back and sweat running down the backs of his legs.

There was one thing that Jack hadn't told Frazier. The language of the findings signaled in advance whether it was an acquittal or a conviction. It all rested on the words *advise* and *inform*. If the verdict was an acquittal, the defendant was advised; if it was a guilty verdict, he was informed. He had kept this from Frazier because it gave Jack a little time to get ready for his reaction, in case he needed to restrain him.

Colonel Hodgini stood and opened the findings worksheet. He had a look of contempt focused on both of them. Jack knew that if it were possible to find him guilty as well, Hodgini would have done so. "Sergeant First Class William T. Frazier, it is my duty as president of this court to advise you that the court, in closed session and upon secret written ballot, has found you not guilty of all specifications and charges."

It seemed to take a few seconds for the words to connect in Frazier's mind. He looked to Jack for confirmation, appearing not to believe what he heard. Jack whispered under his breath, "You got off."

Frazier grabbed him in a bear hug and started to cry. "Thank God," he said, over and over.

Jack tried to get him to calm down and let the judge get the jury out of there.

"Mr. President, I want to thank you and the other members. This has been a difficult trial. You are dismissed to return to your places of duty."

Jack was afraid to look at the jury. He feared that if he did, they would realize what a mistake they'd made and change their minds.

Dresman appeared stunned and on the verge of tears himself. He quickly gathered up his files without saying anything and tromped out. The chief of military justice, who had been standing at the back of the courtroom waiting to hear the verdict, met him at the door. As they walked off, Jack could see Dresman's boss place his hand at his crotch, then move it to his ear, indicating that Dresman had screwed up.

Jack had kept a smile off his face until Dresman left, but now he couldn't keep his grin from becoming larger and larger as the realization sunk in.

He had beaten them. Not only that, he had done it by himself, without CID agents to investigate his case, and none of the power of the SJA's office to help him.

Frazier stood pumping Jack's hand, telling him what a great job he'd done, at the same time trying to back out of the courtroom with his escort.

Even though Frazier had said he wanted to buy him dinner

next week, Jack knew this was the last time he would see him. He had never heard from anyone who'd been acquitted. It was a strange way of dealing with people. He had gone through something horrible and intimate with another human being, both of them seeing weaknesses and flaws and often learning more about each other than their spouses or parents knew. All these lives and events funneling down to this one room. Then even the relationship with the client evaporating to just a stack of papers in a legal file that was put away and eventually forgotten.

DiMarco had packed his books and robe and had his driver standing by, ready to take him to the *bahnhof*. Jack really didn't want to talk to him, but the Whopper stopped and put his satchel and business case down on the prosecutor's table.

"Congratulations, Captain Hayes."

"Thanks, sir," Jack said.

"Let me give you some advice," the Whopper said, sounding for the first time since they'd met like he had anything but contempt for Jack. "You've got some talent for this. You're also going to make a lot of enemies if you stay in this line of work. You do things in a case that people don't like and they'll come gunning for you after a while, even if it isn't justified. If you want to make a career of the Army, I'd suggest you switch over to prosecution."

They never give up, Jack thought. They were like a cult, always trying to convert you to their persuasion, no matter how many times you said no. Nine more months and he was on that freedom bird back to the States and out of the Army.

The Whopper slapped him hard on the shoulder, gave his driver his bags, and was gone.

Jack looked around and saw the clerk turning the lights off in the rest of the building. The private stuck his head in the courtroom. "Stay as long as you need, sir. I'll let the MPs know you're still in here."

Jack nodded okay. He was in no hurry to leave. Once he left this room, the spell would start to diminish. He would have to think about his problems: the fight with Anne last night; the backlog of cases, all losers, that preparing for this trial had caused; a routine that had him drinking every night just to get through the week.

When he was sure everyone was gone, he did a little touchdown dance, hips swiveling while he fired imaginary six-guns, savoring the moment Colonel Hodgini had said "Not guilty."

PART IV

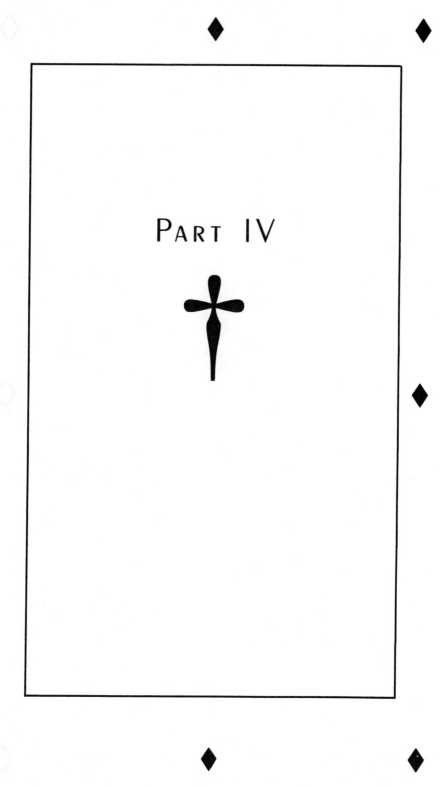

NINETEEN

The following day Jack telephoned his immediate supervisor, Major Harper, pleading to take leave. "I'm burned out," Jack explained. "Annie and I need some time together. She's managed to get us into a ski week at Garmisch." Harper, who usually required two weeks' notice for all leaves, must have heard the desperation in Jack's voice, because he agreed, even offering to cover Article 15 counseling.

By midweek Jack looked healthy again: the dark bruises of fatigue disappeared from under his eyes, and his normally pale face began to tan nicely. At the end of each day's skiing, he and Anne would eat big meals of sauerbraten and dumplings, then gamble in the *spielbank*. Afterward, they would walk the streets of Garmisch, a mountain village filled with rambling chalets and businesses with large frescoes of Madonnas and angels painted on the facades. The luxury of free time and no clients helped exorcise a little more resentment from their marriage every day.

Their final day out was perfect cross-country-skiing weather. The sky was a brilliant blue, and off to the south the ragged peaks of the German Alps and the Zugspitze, Germany's bragging rights to the Matterhorn, poked through the clouds.

During the last two miles of the trail, Jack had trouble keeping his left ski on. The clip was not tight enough to hold the shoe's square toe in the metal prongs on the face of the ski. It had come off again and Jack couldn't make it stay. He watched as Anne and the ten other members of their group glided to a stop for lunch outside a stucco-and-wood chalet and began stacking their skis and poles in the racks. The blue and white diamond banner of Bavaria hung from the eaves of the inn and flapped gently in the wind. Now that he wasn't moving, Jack felt cold. He was ready to walk in when their instructor, Roderich, a tall, dark-haired native of Garmisch, saw that he was having trouble. Roderich took off his day pack and headed back toward Jack, his skis clacking loudly as he kicked his legs back, eating up the quarter mile in twenty effortless glides. He snowplowed to a quick stop beside Jack.

"Problems, yes?" Roderich took off his mirrored sunglasses to have a look.

Jack handed him the ski. "I can't make it stay on the shoe."

Roderich smiled good-naturedly and took the ski. He never seemed flustered by the day's problems, happy to take the out-of-shape Americans skiing five days a week, making more money from tips and working for the military than most young Germans his age in the village.

Roderich examined the pressure clip on Jack's ski a few seconds, then used the tip of his pole to snap off his left ski.

"Use mine. I have tools to fix it in my bag. I can make it stay on till we get back."

With that, Roderich put Jack's ski down, clipped it on, and skated off.

By the time Jack reached the restaurant, everyone was seated and beginning lunch. The inn was cozy and immaculately clean; the walls and tables, highly polished white pine. The smell of cinnamon lightly scented the air. A huge fireplace blazed in the middle of the room, and the two large picture windows offered a spectacular view of the mountains and cable cars taking skiers to the slopes. Roderich had pushed two large tables together so everyone could eat as a group. Jack spotted Anne seated at the end, across from Mrs. Bellin. He cringed, because she was the one woman in the party Anne could not stand.

Jack liked most of the group. Everyone was either in the Army or a dependent, yet the Army or duty was never brought up. Though several of the older men were officers, none of them seemed concerned about rank. Mrs. Bellin was the only exception. On the first day, when everyone else introduced themselves by their first names, she insisted on being called Mrs. Bellin. Her tone made it clear that she considered herself the equivalent of her husband's rank—Mrs. *Colonel* Bellin. She was a handsome woman in her late forties with frosted bleached-blond hair, long false eyelashes, and a slight Southern accent. At lunch she would go on interminably about what wonderful Hummels she had found on this tour, or how as president of the Officers' Wives' Club she had organized such "delightful" trips to castles in the wine country. Jack found her annoying, but Anne, who rarely had a negative comment about anyone, truly despised her. On the second day back from skiing she said, "How pretentious! That woman wouldn't know real class if it came up and accosted her in broad daylight."

Jack walked to the table and sat down next to Anne. She gave him a forced smile and patted his leg. "I ordered you a bratwurst and beer," she said.

Their waitress, a plump older woman wearing a low-cut dirndl, served Mrs. Bellin her soup and returned to the kitchen. Colonel Bellin had gone downhill skiing this day, so Mrs. Bellin looked around for someone to talk with. Finding everyone else occupied, she fixed her attention on Jack.

"It must be a real treat for you to get out of the barracks and take a trip like this," she said, touching Jack's hand lightly.

She thought he was an enlisted man. Good. He had no intention of letting her know any differently and extending the conversation.

"It's a super deal," Jack said.

"My husband says so many of the boys just stay in the barracks and get in trouble with drugs. It seems so senseless, when the Army runs these facilities and will allow a young soldier to bring along a friend, too."

Mrs. Bellin batted her eyelashes at Jack.

Anne put down her knife and fork. "I'm his wife."

Their waitress arrived and served Jack his sausage. As she

was walking off, Mrs. Bellin stopped her and ordered coffee and Black Forest cake in horrible German.

Anne leaned over and whispered to Jack, "That witch touches you again and I'm going to rip those false eyelashes off her face."

"So where are you kids stationed?"

"Butzbach," Jack said, trying to cut it short.

"That's Third Armored Division, isn't it? We were stationed in Gelnhausen after Charles graduated from West Point."

Jack nodded and drank his beer. He thought of excusing himself and standing by the fire to warm up, but was afraid Anne would say something insulting.

"What unit are you with?" Mrs. Bellin asked.

Jack knew Mrs. Bellin had no intention of asking Anne what she did. Her generation of Army wives had been taught that working was below a "lady's" dignity or of no importance.

"I'm at the legal center," Jack said.

"How nice," Mrs. Bellin said, her voice filled with honeyed interest. "So you're a legal clerk?"

"He's a lawyer," Anne said. She looked at Mrs. Bellin as if she wanted to slap her senseless. "And I'm a nurse."

Mrs. Bellin smiled condescendingly at Anne, while touching up her hair. "I'm surprised. *He* looks so young."

She turned back to Jack, not missing a beat. "What kind of law do you practice?"

No law on this trip, he told himself. Jack could think of nothing to defuse the situation other than finishing the discussion and leaving.

"Trial work," Jack said.

"With all the crime we have, my husband tells me we need a lot of lawyers. If you ask me," she leaned forward and whispered, "it's because of the coloreds."

Jack winced. He glanced at Anne, motioning with his eyes that they should leave. Anne remained seated, glaring at Mrs. Bellin.

"I don't understand how a lawyer could defend some of these animals and live with himself afterward."

Anne shifted in her chair, and Jack thought she was about

to stand up. Instead she moved closer to the table so that she was within arm's reach of Mrs. Bellin.

"Jack's a defense lawyer. I'm very proud of him." Anne had her fist clenched.

The colonel's wife had no choice but to acknowledge Anne. They looked at each other with undisguised hatred.

"Oh my, it must be very depressing to have a husband in that line of work."

Anne batted her eyes in imitation of the woman and mimicked her accent. "I suppose it's no tougher than living with someone who is paid to be a professional killer."

Mrs. Bellin blanched. "I think we should just drop this matter."

Anne ignored her. "You know what kills me, Lucy . . ."

Jack had no idea how Anne knew her first name, but was happy that she did.

". . . People like your husband get in trouble, and the first thing they want Jack to do is pull out all the stops. All of a sudden they're not dirtbags and the Constitution isn't just a technicality. They want every one of their rights. All they care about is having someone save them. And don't think it doesn't happen. He's had plenty of officer clients, including colonels and West Pointers."

The others at their table turned to see what the raised voices were about. Roderich must have sensed trouble, because he sprang up and hurried down to Mrs. Bellin. Angry customers weren't in the mood to tip.

"Mrs. Bellin," Roderich said, putting his arm playfully around her shoulder, "come out to the front shop with me. I want you to see the Hummel plates." He motioned to the waitress to take Mrs. Bellin's cake and coffee out front.

Mrs. Bellin feigned a smile and stood up. She walked off, chattering about the exquisite brushwork on this year's edition. Roderich said something to her as they reached the gift shop and she laughed coquettishly, then clutched his arm.

Jack leaned over and hugged Anne. She was trembling.

"Promise that you'll shoot me if I ever become like that woman." Anne leaned her head on his shoulder. "I should've just kept my mouth shut."

"No way, she had it coming." He kissed her lightly. "Why don't we take the afternoon off from skiing? Have a few more beers, then go back to the room?"

"I like that idea."

After motioning Roderich away from Mrs. Bellin, Jack informed him that he and Anne would walk back to the lifts and catch a bus to the hotel.

"Your wife, everything is okay?" Roderich asked.

Jack pressed twenty dollars into his hand. "It's fine now. Thanks for all of your help this week."

Roderich smiled broadly and slipped the money into his pocket. "*Auf wiedersehen,*" he said, bowing his head slightly.

When Jack returned, Anne had ordered two large steins of beer and moved next to the fireplace. They sat with their backs to the fire not saying anything, watching the skiers wind down the slopes.

As they finished their second beer, Jack finally ventured, "After what I pulled in Giessen, I'm surprised you still support what I do."

Anne continued holding his hand; he'd not misread her change of heart.

"I've thought a lot about it." Anne shrugged. "Things aren't as black and white as I'd want them sometimes."

He was happy to leave it at that—not forgiven, yet still accepted. He kissed her. "I'm very lucky to have you as my wife. There's nothing I wouldn't do for you."

She pulled away. "You mean that?"

"Yes," he said, already regretting his answer.

"Join my father's firm." She was not smiling. "Try it. That's all I'm asking."

He sighed heavily. It was not as if she hadn't had to compromise, too. He was fortunate she hadn't left him. A year or two, he told himself, no more. Just enough to build up a group of clients of his own. And he would force the firm to do some *pro bono* work.

"All right," he said dully, "I'll give it a try."

Anne pulled him over and kissed him hard. "I love you, Jack."

TWENTY

Even at Garmisch, Jack could not stop thinking about whether Frazier was guilty or not. To put it to rest, he needed some answers. And the only person who knew what had happened was McCormick. So on Monday he drove to the Confinement Facility and received permission to see the lieutenant.

"I was afraid they might have shipped you to the States." Jack sat down at the small field table across from McCormick, who was completely shackled.

McCormick appeared to have been roused from a nap; his hair was uncombed, his uniform wrinkled. His breath smelled stale.

"Someone forgot to take the hold off my records. I suspect it is more 'special treatment' from my guards."

"You want me to speak to the IG?"

McCormick rotated his head in order to stretch. "I'll repay the favor in my own way. Now, Captain Hayes, I know you didn't come to check on my health. What is it that you want?"

"I need to know whether Frazier was really guilty."

"Why?" McCormick eyed Jack incredulously.

"It's important to me."

"A conscience?" McCormick was greatly amused. "I didn't know you lawyers had those. That could be very dangerous." He stopped smiling. "What would be in it for me?"

Everything had a price. Jack's mind raced to find a carrot. "You're still looking at thirty years—ten years before you're eligible for parole. I'm friends with the best lawyer at defense appellate. She might be able to find a way to bust your conviction, get a new trial."

"I doubt this person could do anything for me."

Enough cat and mouse games, Jack thought. It was stupid to think McCormick would help. He picked up his briefcase and walked to the door.

Just as he was about to summon the guards, McCormick called over his shoulder, "I take it that she's smarter than you."

Prick, Jack said to himself. He turned back toward McCormick. "Editor of the law review at Yale. The smartest lawyer I've ever met."

Finally McCormick said, "You're so sensitive, Captain Hayes. Sit down. I suppose there are a few things I might be willing to fill you in on."

Jack returned to his seat, but left his briefcase on his lap. No more bullshit, or he was gone. "Where was all the money, if Frazier was dealing?"

"I'll give you a hint. *The French Connection*."

Jack frowned, trying to piece the clue to what he already knew.

"The movie," McCormick said impatiently. "Where were the drugs in that movie?"

"The car he sent home? But I thought his wife got it in the divorce settlement."

"Billy gave one of my men a power of attorney to get the car. He took the money out before he drove the car to Billy's wife, then my man wired the money to a numbered safety deposit box in Switzerland. Billy sent him to get it when his trial started."

"What happened to the money?"

McCormick smiled broadly. "Let's just say Billy had some witness expenses."

Jack had guessed right about the bribe. Frazier had paid Babcock and McCormick not to identify the real Kooij. Chambers outside the witness room arguing with Frazier—$200,000 apiece.

"So Frazier's escort arranged with you and Babcock not to identify Kooij the night before you were to testify. But you decided it was better to have Babcock killed to make your testimony more valuable. How did you get word to your men to do it?"

"Captain Hay-e-s, you don't really think I'd admit to a murder, do you?" McCormick frowned in disbelief. "Maybe Chambers telephoned someone with an innocuous-sounding message that was a code. I wouldn't know. Let's just leave it at this, for a *mere* four hundred grand Billy produced some convenient amnesia about Kooij. Babcock's was a little more permanent than mine. Billy didn't expect that added bonus, but I doubt if he minded."

"Where's the money now?"

McCormick clucked his tongue. "Safe. Drawing interest. Invested properly, someone could be a millionaire, say in ten years." He laughed to himself. "If they could keep him in prison."

The thought of what had happened sickened Jack. Frazier and McCormick had used him like a pawn. He had put on perjured testimony. Unknowingly he had cost Babcock his life. And now nothing would ever be done about it. Frazier was acquitted and Jack couldn't violate his oath by turning over evidence that implicated his own client. He closed his eyes and put his hand over his face.

"Don't take it so hard," McCormick said cheerily. "If you hadn't been brave enough to find Kooij, none of this would have been possible. And I understand that you were brilliant in destroying Billy's cop girlfriend. No amount of money would have bought her off. Her testimony . . ."

Suddenly the air felt too close. Jack could not stand another second of McCormick crowing over how they had manipulated him. He stood up to leave.

"I hope you're not backing out of your part of the bargain," McCormick said. "Give my best to—Anne? Right? At the 97th General?"

Jack looked stonily at McCormick. "Don't worry. I'm a man of my word."

TWENTY-ONE

The following day the waiting room of the legal center overflowed with Article 15 clients. Jack had forgotten that Sanderford rescheduled counseling, since they both had Article 32 investigations on Wednesday. The thought of spending the morning persuading people to accept Article 15's in lieu of trial depressed him. Jack had wanted to read through his new case files, hoping they would put the memory of Frazier's trial out of his mind.

Jack's paralegal, Specialist Bortman, caught up with him as he was heading into the office. "Sir, two things. Major Dresman's here to see you. And Colonel Fagan's on line three."

"Tell Major Dresman it will be a while," Jack said. He was in no mood for another lecture about ethics.

Fagan probably had individual defense counsel requests. Any time a defense lawyer won a difficult case, everyone thought he could work the same miracle for them too. Colonel Fagan, the chief defense lawyer in Europe, was the person who sorted out the requests.

Jack turned the toggle switch on the wall to his line. "Captain Hayes speaking, sir."

"Jack," said Colonel Fagan, "that was a big one the government lost. I suspect people will be using that fake records trick of yours for years to come."

"Thanks, sir."

"Did you and Anne have a good time on your leave?"

"Yes, sir." Cut the glad-handing, thought Jack, get to the point.

"I'm looking forward to visiting with you at the dining-in next month," Fagan said.

Jack didn't answer. There was a nervous edge to Fagan's voice he didn't like.

After a moment of silence, Colonel Fagan said, "Jack, I don't want you to worry, but the SJA is conducting an investigation into Mental Health leaking records to you. Colonel Basham wants to keep it all very low-key right now. I've told him—"

"Mental Health didn't leak records," Jack interrupted.

"I told them we were one hundred percent behind you, and that I'm certain you'd not done anything wrong. I called Judge DiMarco this morning and he agreed. He said he'd even give a statement on your behalf . . ."

Jack knew all this "support" would last only so long as there were no problems. The minute it appeared there might be any wrongdoing, Fagan would do everything he could to distance himself.

"Well, anyway," Fagan continued, "I thought I ought to call and let you know this was coming. Keep up the good work."

"Thanks, sir." He hung up.

Jack sat down heavily in his chair. The thought scared him. Depending on how the investigation was conducted, things could get very hot. He'd better have Sanderford as his lawyer, so they couldn't question him about the phone call. And he should call Dobbs and tell him to take the Fifth if they questioned him.

Jack had been off the phone only a few minutes, when he heard a loud voice arguing with Bortman. Then someone pounded on his door.

"Just a second," Jack yelled.

Before he could move to open it, Major Dresman burst in and slammed the door.

"I know what you did," Dresman said. His eyes were wild, glassy.

"What are you talking about?"

"You're going to jail." Dresman spat the words at him. "I found the CQ you tricked. Pretending you had the judge on the line." Dresman shook his head in disgust.

Stay calm, Jack told himself, you'll only get this one shot to scare him off. Jack got up and poured himself a cup of coffee, then went back to his chair and put his feet up on his desk.

"You may take me out," Jack said, "but I'm not going down alone. You read those records before me. *You* had a duty to reveal that information. I plan to make sure every defendant you put in Leavenworth knows that you withheld information in this case. They'll all be claiming you did the same thing in their cases. Defense appellate will have a field day. You might even get a rule named after you." Jack raised his eyebrows for emphasis. "Every newspaper that I can get hold of will hear about this case. And you know as well as I do that kind of publicity will not help Colonel Basham get his star." Jack took a long drink of coffee.

"So, *Major*, I suggest that you tell Colonel Basham the investigation failed to turn up any information."

Dresman's thick neck flared; his jaw muscles quivered. "You unethical son of a bitch."

"You want a war? I'm ready."

Jack took his feet off his desk and locked eyes with Dresman. For a full minute they glared at one another. Finally, Dresman turned away. He muttered something Jack could not hear, then stomped out.

Jack collapsed back in his chair and blew out a long stream of air. *You make enemies.* The Whopper was certainly right about that. Jack would have to watch his backside until he finished his nine months.

Bortman popped his head inside the office. "Problem, sir? I heard Major Dresman shouting."

"No problem, Frank. Just exchanging some differing ideas on trial practice."

Bortman looked quizzically at Jack. "Whatever, sir. You want me to send the group back?"

"Yeah, bring 'em back," Jack said.

A few minutes later, the Article 15 clients shuffled into

Jack's office. There were so many this morning that they were crowded up to the front of his desk. Jack recognized a few of them from previous counseling sessions. None of them seemed interested in being there or in what he had to say.

He pulled himself wearily from his chair and started his street law class. "Good morning, my name is Captain Jack Hayes. I'm a defense lawyer . . ."